PRAISE FOR TONI NIESEN'S ALASKAN MYSTERIES

"Toni Niesen has landed a rapid-fire thriller with *Parts Unknown*. Set in remote and urban Alaska, her fictional adventure takes us into the inner workings of general aviation and the personalities who pursue it with passion. Protagonist, Beri Quinn, kept me turning pages late into the night."

—Elizabeth D. Nobmann, PhD, MPH, RDN, and Member, The Ninety-nines, Inc., Alaska Chapter

"Great book! A suspenseful love letter to flying and Alaska!"

—Eric Bergstrom, Radio Personality for Cat Country 95.1

"Toni Niesen has crafted a mystery as compelling as the Alaskan wilderness where it is set. *Parts Unknown* takes the reader on a twisting adventure that kept me guessing until the very end. Fans of Dana Stabenow will enjoy this new series and be asking for more. Well done!"

—Dorothy St. James, Author of the Southern Chocolate Shop Mysteries

"*Eye in the Sky* is a must-read for anyone who loves books about flying, Alaska, or women with a spine of steel. Beri Quinn is such a woman and co-owns a flight instruction company in Anchorage, Alaska. When one of her students is targeted by assassins, she delivers him to a place of safety, but he keeps inserting himself into her life. Meanwhile, because of her photo mapping skills, she is enlisted by a government agency to investigate possible foreign interference in the Aleutians. This story will have you on the edge of your seat as Beri navigates this tangled web of murder and deceit."

—Patricia Curren, Author of *Wrongful Death* and the Kendra Morgan Mystery Series

"An adventure-thriller set against the lush Alaskan landscape, Niesen has effectively mastered the ability to craft an enthralling mystery through the beauty of evocative prose and magnetic suspense."

—Callie J. Trautmiller, Award-winning Author of *Under the Dirt Sky*

EYE IN THE SKY

AN ALASKAN MYSTERY

Toni Niesen

Green Bay, WI

Eye in the Sky: An Alaskan Mystery by Toni Niesen, © 2024 by Toni Niesen. Author photo courtesy of the Niesen family.

This book is a work of fiction. All names, characters, places and events are products of the author's imagination or are used fictitiously, and any resemblance to actual persons, living or dead, or to actual places or businesses, is entirely coincidental.

All rights reserved. In accordance with the U.S. Copyright Act of 1976, no part of this publication may be reproduced, distributed, or transmitted in any form or by any means, or stored in a database or retrieval system, without prior written permission of the publisher, Written Dreams Publishing, Green Bay, Wisconsin 54311. Please be aware that if you've received this book with a "stripped" off cover, please know that the publisher and the author may not have received payment for this book, and that it has been reported as stolen property. Please visit www.writtendreams.com to see more of the unique books published by Written Dreams Publishing.

Publisher/Executive Editor: Brittiany Koren
Copy-editor: Maria Connor
Cover Art Designer: Ed Vincent/Amit Dey
Interior Layout Designer: Amit Dey
Ebook Interior Layout Designer: Amit Dey

Category: Mystery/Alaskan Thriller

Description: *An Alaskan flight instructor struggles to keep her glider student hidden from would-be assassins while finding herself entangled in an international crime scheme.*

Hard Cover ISBN: 978-1-951375-73-7
Paperback ISBN: 978-1-951375-89-8
Ebook ISBN: 978-1-951375-75-1
LOC Catalogue Data: Applied for.

First Edition published by Written Dreams Publishing in March, 2024.
Ebook Edition published by Written Dreams Publishing in March, 2024.

Green Bay, WI

*In memory of my beloved husband and favorite pilot.
May you always fly high.*

PROLOGUE

The floatplane circled twice over sunlit snowfields high in the Chugach Mountains. Wilderness stretched for miles in every direction. Odds were that no one was watching as the pilot put the plane on autopilot, threw open the door on the passenger side of the Cessna 182 and dumped the body out.

It should have been easy. After all, it was a straight drop into the snowfield—hundreds of feet of deep snow that would not melt for a millennium, but there was an unexpected snafu. A foot, clad in an expensive tennis shoe, managed to wedge itself inside the strut supporting the float, and the woman attached to the foot hung upside down from the wing. She looked like an old-fashioned barnstorming wing walker performing in mid-air. He noticed her other foot was bare. Just his luck this shoe had to cause trouble.

"Why does this shit happen to me?" the pilot muttered. He sat sideways on the passenger seat, his feet dangling out the open door. He slammed his fist into the seat back. "I can't screw up now."

He paused briefly before thrusting his head outside.

A rush of cold air took his breath away. His hair lashed into his face with a thousand tiny whips as he clung with his left hand to the edge of the door. Slowly, he extended his body out into open space until his right hand could reach the problematic shoe. He pulled until his arm ached and despaired it would never work.

Just as he decided to give up, the shoe and the foot inside it came loose in his hand. He barely managed to clamp his feet hard enough around the seat's steel frame to stay inside. The plane lurched upward with the sudden loss of cargo weight as the woman fell, and the jolt nearly caused the pilot to plunge in tandem alongside the body.

Exhausted, he pulled himself back inside the cockpit, closed the door, and disengaged the autopilot. He exhaled audibly, releasing the lungful of air he'd unconsciously been holding.

Eventually, his breathing slowed to normal. The floral scent of her perfume lingered inside the cabin of the plane. Resolutely, he pushed thoughts of her from his mind and focused on a step-by-step review of his original plan.

Damn! The gym bag. He'd forgotten it. He'd already overflown the snow field, but the glacier now below would serve just as well. He again threw open the door of the plane and dropped this last complication.

There. He'd done it. He was finished.

The sun continued to shine, its bright rays filtering through the light drizzle that had begun to fall. To an observer, the light refracting from millions of tiny droplets of water coalesced to create a circular rainbow around the image of the floatplane shadowed against the clouds. To the sweat-drenched pilot, it appeared to be a giant technicolor bull's-eye targeting the acres of snow and ice below. The pilot set a course for home.

Chapter One

It was a perfect July day for soaring. The sun shone through scattered cumulus clouds, highlighting glistening leaves of aspen clumped along the ridges above Birchwood airstrip. The location, a favorite of glider pilots in the Anchorage area, served as my base of operations for the soaring lessons recently added to my flight instruction program. My name is Beri Quinn and teaching others to fly has been a lifelong passion.

I'd enjoyed a peaceful thirty minutes catching lift and rising high above the terrain with my student, Charlie Greer. He was a nondescript guy in his forties, about my height with shaggy dirt-colored hair and tan-gone-sallow skin, but what he lacked in appearance, he made up for in mental acuity and ability.

We'd had a great session, but it was time to end the lesson. Charlie first overflew the airstrip to visualize any activity before preparing to land. He picked up his mic and called the advisory frequency. "This is glider November 2937. Any traffic in pattern at Birchwood airstrip?"

Hearing no response, he made another pass to be certain a plane was not about to take off, then began flying in ever lower arcs over the strip. His third lesson almost complete, he prepared to glide in for a landing, his confidence in his ability evident in the smile on his face. I leaned forward from my rear seat to compliment his performance when he jerked to attention, staring at the runway below.

"What's the problem?" I straightened in my seat, surprised by his sudden change in demeanor.

"Don't you see, Beri? Look down at the taxiway by the white van. Two men just shot Skip point-blank. I'm certain they're waiting for us to land so they can get me next."

I stared down to the side, and sure enough, our tow pilot lay sprawled beside the plane that had hauled us into the air less than an hour ago. I shuddered and tried to clear my head from the horror. "Look, we don't have much altitude, and the nearest alternative landing strip is too far away. If we're not going to land here, we'll have to improvise and fast."

"Uh, where else can we land?" Charlie, wild-eyed, searched the ground below him.

"Head for the beach. The tide was out when we arrived. Let's hope it still is, and we can find a dry stretch of ground outside the mud flats. Plan to make your landing to the south. The wind coming up the inlet will give you a little ridge lift."

"No. You do it. Take over. Please!" He lifted his hands and feet from the controls, all his former confidence gone. "I've got to think."

"Okay, I've got it. Take my phone. Call the police while I bring us down."

Charlie grabbed the phone and stared at it as though he didn't recognize what it was. "No police. I can't get involved."

"Look, Skip may be dead, but if by some miracle he's alive, he'll need immediate medical assistance. We have to call 9-1-1, and now! He's a new father, an all-around good guy, and he didn't deserve this."

"He's not alive. You didn't see it happen like I did. And there's no way I can let the police hold me for questioning. I've got to get away before they find me." His voice grew louder. "You're my instructor. It's your job to keep me safe. From killers, too. Just get us down and fast."

"I'll call 9-1-1 the minute we land and report a shooting at Birchwood airstrip so they can send help for Skip. I won't mention we witnessed it from the air. I'll wait until you're gone to call them back and report the details. That will give you a head start."

"Thanks. You may have just saved my life."

"Tell me what's going on. I need to know so I can protect us both. The shooters may come after me to find you."

Charlie turned away from me and entered a number into the phone with rapid taps of his thumbs. "Damn, no answer."

He dialed again and spoke into the phone, "Gina, baby. Grab my go-bag and meet me near the beach south of Birchwood. I'll be watching for you beside the road. Leave as soon as you get this. It's life or death."

He turned to me. "She's not answering. Hope she gets my message, or we're both toast."

I brought the glider down in an uneventful short-field landing near the waters of Knik Arm, relieved I'd managed to avoid the treacherous mud flats edging the beach. As soon as we came to a stop, I lifted the canopy and breathed in the salty tang of the ocean.

Charlie immediately hopped out.

I grabbed his arm and retrieved my phone. "Okay, now give. I'm calling 9-1-1. Tell me what's going on before you start hiking."

"They're pros," Charlie said. "They think I have information that belongs to some very dangerous people. I came to Alaska to get away and didn't think they'd find me here. No time to explain it all. I need to find Gina. She's in danger, too."

He took one last look at me. "Sorry I have to leave you like this, Beri." He turned and sprinted off in the direction of the road, crashing through dense alders as he went.

I made the 9-1-1 call and sat for a moment, pondering the situation. If only Charlie was wrong about Skip. Surgeons could work wonders these days at the local hospitals in Anchorage.

I prayed this would be one of those times.

After catching my breath, I climbed out and surveyed my makeshift landing strip. Not enough space for a plane to land and give me a tow. How to get out of this predicament? I couldn't risk a high tide taking my bird.

Ross, my partner in our fledgling flight instruction business, would not be pleased. He'd stressed only yesterday how we needed to cut expenses as our bottom line didn't look good. I'd recently added glider instruction in an attempt to build our clientele.

I called Dean George, our mechanic, and asked him to arrange for a Merrill Field helicopter service to lift the glider out. I had to hope they'd arrive before the tide came in. Dean, ever efficient, promised to get them here post-haste.

While I waited, I removed the spar pins attaching the wings to the fuselage and bundled the wings with care. We'd need to make two trips in the copter. One for the wings and one for the fuselage. Good thing Birchwood airstrip was close to Anchorage. It wouldn't take long to make the two-way trip twice.

Not only did I want to beat the tide, I wanted to have the glider back where it belonged before the police knew it was involved. They might consider it an accessory to the crime scene and impound it. I couldn't afford to have the glider taken out of service.

Chapter Two

Detective Diaz looked up from the paperwork on his desk. He frowned and pinched the bridge of his nose. "Ms. Beri Quinn. Haven't heard from you in months. Should have known my luck couldn't last." He shoved the pages he'd been reading into his desk drawer.

The officer who had led me to the detective's desk pulled out a chair and indicated I should take a seat.

I sat and smiled at Diaz. "Hello, Detective."

"Guess you know why you're here. I read the officer on the scene at Birchwood's report and wanted to hear the story directly from you."

"I already told him everything I knew. I didn't actually witness the shooting."

"So you said." He steepled his hands. "What I don't understand is what happened to your student who *did* witness it."

Uh oh. Here it comes. "He panicked and left as soon as the glider came to a stop on the beach."

Diaz unfolded his lanky frame and stood looking down at me. "And you didn't question that?"

"Of course I did." I let my breath out slowly. "That's why I called back to report to the police what he'd told me he witnessed."

"And why didn't you tell us that the first time you called? Besides, I don't understand why you didn't see the shooting yourself."

"To the first question, I was too busy trying to stay aloft long enough to find an alternate landing spot to carry on much of a conversation. I didn't see the murder because I was in the back seat and my attention was directed to my student's landing preparations. He, on the other hand, was looking directly down at the runway. I heard the shots, but by the time Charlie spoke and I looked down, all I saw was the body and doors slamming on their van." I paused and looked down at the table. "I also knew there was a shooting range nearby and thought at first that was where the shots I heard came from."

"Okay, so what did Charlie say to you afterward?"

"Not much. He was in a rush, but he did say he knew the killers were after him. Apparently, Charlie's former associates thought he had something valuable they wanted, and they would go to any lengths to get it. He said he didn't have anything that didn't belong to him, but he and his girlfriend were in extreme danger. They'd thought no one would look for them in Alaska."

Diaz glanced at his notes. "Where did they run from?"

"Sorry. I don't know."

"Tell me what you do know about your student. Did he fill out any forms when he signed up for glider lessons?"

"He already had a pilot's license. He was smart and a quick learner. The only information he gave us when he signed up was his name, address, and phone number. I think you already have that. No credit cards, he always paid in cash."

"Did you get his license number or a cell number?"

"I'll have to check. I don't know if the phone number was for a cell. He used mine to call his girlfriend. Would that help?"

"It might. Let me have your phone."

I was relieved to be back at Merrill Field. Detective Diaz was nice enough, but my clothes were damp with nervous sweat after our meeting. A slight breeze now chilled my arms as I walked along the road past my old office with the airplanes I'd flown for years parked outside. I'd taken over the aerial mapping and flight instruction business after my father retired. It had been home base since I was a girl, but that changed last year when I sold the company. Now, after spending the last half of the school year in Arizona to be near my eleven-year-old son, Jack, I was back in Alaska. Jack would arrive soon after completing summer golf camp in the Lower 48.

It was good to be home, although I hadn't quite adjusted to my new position as a partner with my significant other in Ross McEvoy's flight school. I'd been back two months, and business was slow, despite summer historically being the busiest time of year for lessons. I realized I had a lot to get used to before I could return to my old comfort zone.

It took five minutes to walk to the helicopter outfit Dean had hired to lift my glider off the beach. I paid the bill out of my personal bank account. No need to give Ross more financial angst over the incident. He'd been lukewarm about my adding gliders to our services from the get-go.

Angie, our office manager, greeted me when I walked into the office. She and Dean were my former staff who were included in the partnership deal. Ross was fortunate to inherit two such stellar employees. *I hope he realizes how great they are.* Angie can take some getting used to as she is bossy and prone to dire financial forecasts, but she's a great organizer and a good friend.

"Beri, I'm glad you're back." Angie ran her fingers through her spiky pink hair. "Since Ross is still in Fairbanks, I scheduled his students for this week with you. Let me know if I need to change anything."

I gave the list a quick scan but didn't see any names I recognized. "Looks good to me. Is there anything I need to know about any of his students?"

Angie gave me a look I couldn't quite read. "Check Ross' files. He keeps good notes."

"Will do." I turned to check the computer but stopped when a striking blonde wearing jeans so tight they appeared to be sculpted to her body strode in through the office door.

"Hello, Megan," Angie said. "Let me introduce you to Beri Quinn. She's Ross' partner and will be your instructor this afternoon. Ross is out of town this week."

"Glad to meet you, Megan." I shook her well-manicured hand. "Let me get your file, and I'll be right back with you."

I walked to Ross' office and found her folder. He'd noted that she'd finished ground school with impressive grades and had completed five lessons with him in a Cessna 172. He'd added that she was slow to get the feel of the plane, and he planned to spend more time on basics during their next lesson. I'd check her logbook for specifics before we got started.

An uproar from Angie's reception desk jolted me from my reading. I dropped the file and headed up front.

"No. I will not have another instructor. I want Ross and only Ross. He understands me."

I rounded the corner and ran into Megan leaning over Angie's desk, her face red and her eyes fierce.

Angie said in an even tone, "I'm sorry, but he's not here. I left a message on your phone to give you advance notice. I can assure you Beri's our very best instructor." She motioned to me to come in.

"I don't care who she is. I want Ross. I'll call him next week." She turned and stormed out the door.

"That went well. Guess she didn't like my looks."

"No, I think the problem is that she likes Ross' looks a little too much." Angie rolled her eyes. "If you ask me, she's much more interested in him than in learning how to fly."

I didn't like the sound of that.

"She works for the Alaska Diabetes Association," Angie said. "Did he tell you he agreed to serve on their board of directors and help with fundraising? He'd assisted them years ago when his wife was still alive. She was a diabetic, you know."

"Yes, I remember. He mentioned his plans to volunteer before I left for Arizona. He's supported it for years."

"It's a good cause, but it's too bad she had to come with it," Angie snickered.

CHAPTER THREE

The next morning, I could hear my father, Frank, belting out his alma mater's fight song in his bedroom across the hall. He seemed happier than before I left, but I didn't think my returning home had much to do with it. In my absence, Dad's longtime friendship with Sarah Barton had apparently blossomed into something more. Not that Dad was forthright about it. He'd evaded the subject every time I'd mentioned it. Nonetheless, I'm all in on the development.

Dad hadn't had a romantic relationship that I knew about since my mother divorced him and left Alaska twenty-seven years ago. I was five years old at the time, and she never returned. Dad gave me a locket with her picture in it. He said it would help keep her close. I've worn it ever since. Seems silly now, but old habits die hard.

I hummed a song of my own as I dressed in my usual uniform of jeans, long sleeved tee, and flannel shirt. Layers are a good thing when living in Alaska. Even in summer, I kept a jacket handy. A few flicks of my hairbrush through my shoulder-length hair, a swipe of lip gloss, and I was ready to face the world.

Downstairs, Dad stood over the stove stirring scrambled eggs. With his bald head, he didn't have much to fuss with in the getting ready department and always managed to make it to the kitchen before I did.

"Good morning, Sunshine." He gave my shoulder a squeeze. "Eggs will be ready in a few. What are you up to today? More police questions?"

"No, thank goodness," I said. "I finished with them yesterday."

"Are they making any progress finding the killers?" The toast popped, and he slathered the slices with butter.

"If they are, they aren't sharing anything with me or with Skip's wife. I called her to express my condolences, and she asked me what I knew. She said the police haven't told her anything. She's so overwhelmed with losing Skip and with the baby that her parents have convinced her to move back to California to be near them. She asked me to keep her informed if I learn anything after she leaves." I wiped my eyes with my sleeve.

Dad placed our two plates on the table while I got out the blueberry jam and poured coffee.

"I think the police believe Charlie could clear things up if they could find him."

"They're probably right," Dad said. "I never quite understood why you covered for that fellow and let him get away."

"I didn't have much choice. He ran for his life the minute we landed on that beach. The only concession I made for him was to wait to give the police the full story until I got back to Birchwood." I shrugged. "You'd have to have been there to see the fear in his eyes. Besides, Charlie is such a great guy, I can't imagine him being a criminal. I didn't want to see him get killed."

"You probably managed to get yourself in hot water protecting him. The police will see it as interfering with their investigation."

I choked down my last bite of toast.

"Maybe," I said a few minutes later while clearing our plates, "but I really didn't have time for a lengthy conversation with them until I got the glider off the beach." I scraped the extra scrambled eggs into Tiger's bowl on the floor.

Dad patted the golden Lab's head. "I'll be glad when my grandson gets home. I can't seem to cut my cooking down to only two portions. Tiger's going to gain weight at this rate."

I laughed. "I don't think he minds, but he'll be happy to see Jack, too. One more week and he'll be back from golf camp."

"Golf," Dad said, shaking his head. "If that isn't the darnedest thing for that boy to get excited about. Didn't give a fig about any other sport he tried." He shook his head again. "Golf in Alaska!"

We left the house together. As Dad held the door to the garage for me, he said, "I won't be home for dinner tonight. Sarah and I plan to catch a movie and maybe pick up some fried chicken at Lucky Wishbone. Don't wait up."

I smiled and raised my eyebrows, but didn't say a word.

It was a relief to be back to my routine. Ground school in the morning and two new students in the afternoon. The time went by quickly. It felt good to settle back into the flying I loved. Realizing I hadn't eaten since breakfast, I stopped after work and picked up a deli sandwich for dinner.

Tiger was glad to see me when I got home. His eyes followed every bite I took of my sandwich. He made it clear without complaining that he'd prefer more people food. Eventually, he gave up and crunched down his own vet-recommended kibble. The doorbell rang. Tiger let out a woof and headed for the front door.

I looked out the window and saw a blue sedan with a Pizza-To-Go sign on the driver's door. Strange. I hadn't ordered a pizza. He must have the wrong house.

I opened the door. "Can I help you?"

A man stood holding a pizza box with the brim of his baseball cap blocking his face. When he looked up, I recognized him instantly. "Charlie! What's this all about?"

"Let me in and I'll tell you. Please."

"Okay, okay." I held the door open for him.

He handed me the pizza. "Peace offering. I brought it so anyone watching you would think you'd ordered this. I have to be quick, or they'll get suspicious anyway."

"Watching me? Who'd be watching me?"

"Possibly the people I'm running from," Charlie explained. "They know I was with you at Birchwood. The police are another possibility. Anyway, I need your help." He shoved a piece of paper in my hand. "This is where I hope you'll pick me up Thursday at three o'clock. I need you to fly me somewhere."

"Look, the police are anxious to talk to you. They don't appreciate my involvement in your escaping without talking to them. I can't get more involved."

"It's my only chance. Please. You won't be in any danger if we do this right. The police don't need to know. If it will make you feel better, I'll write out everything I know and you can give it to them when you get back. Just be careful, Beri. Tear up the address and leave your cell phone at your office." He grinned. "Sounds very clandestine, I know, but it's necessary."

What kind of trouble was Charlie getting me into?

Chapter Four

Ross was back. He said he returned early so he could spend more time with me. His reassurance boosted my flagging confidence in our relationship. All those months in Arizona may have taken a toll. Absence doesn't always make the heart grow fonder.

"Lunch?" Ross held out his hand to pull me out of my desk chair. His curly brown hair, a bit long between haircuts, was nonetheless charming. He grinned wickedly and pulled me out the door toward the parking lot.

"Where to?" I asked as he opened the door of his jeep, and I slid inside.

"How does Simon's sound? We haven't been there in a long time. I have a craving for their Cajun chicken fettuccini."

"A real restaurant then, not a fast-food joint?"

He grinned. "Nothing's too good for my favorite business partner."

I pondered that for a moment, hoping it was true.

The restaurant was busy, but we were shown to a table right away. The hostess called Ross by name and showed us to a window table overlooking the inlet and Mount Susitna.

I gazed out at the cloudless sky. A great day for flying, but why was that DC3 so low over the water? "Ross, look at the vapor trail coming from that plane. I think he's dumping fuel."

"Sure looks like it. Must be over gross weight for landing, or he may be having some kind of problem."

"Let's hope it's nothing too major."

"Looks like the pilot's heading for Ted Stevens International." Ross shrugged. "It's probably okay. If not, we'll hear about it on the news tonight."

I put my menu aside and smiled. "Nice that the hostess gave us this table with such a panoramic view, and we didn't have to wait. She treated us like you were a VIP."

"I am, aren't I?" He laughed. "No, I've come here a lot over the years. She probably recognized me."

I wondered who else he'd been bringing here? I pushed back the pangs of doubt creeping into my mind. Why was I so insecure? I couldn't expect him to stay home while I was gone. "Well, this is the first time you've invited me here in a long time. I'm happy you did because I do love their food."

The server approached and smiled at my last comment before taking our orders.

Once she left, Ross filled me in on his trip to Fairbanks.

"Did you buy the Cessna 170 you saw advertised?" I asked, curious.

Ross took a sip of water before answering. "Afraid not. It wasn't a case of false advertising exactly because the plane did have a low-time engine that looked good, but it appeared to have led a hard life. Probably used as a bush plane. The leading edges of the wings were dented, and the tail was bent. It needed too much expensive framework, so I passed on it."

"Sounds like a good decision."

"We need another plane, but we can't afford to buy one right now." He picked up his water glass again. "How did everything go here while I was gone?"

"I don't know if Angie mentioned my brush with the law, but I met with the police regarding the murder I reported at Birchwood. I was forced to make an emergency landing on the beach after my student witnessed a murder in progress at the Birchwood airstrip."

"Yes, Angie filled me in on that." He shook his head and sighed. "You seem to be a magnet for trouble."

"I hope not. Anyway, the meeting went smoothly enough. Lieutenant Diaz didn't press me as hard about my student leaving the scene as I'd expected." I paused. "I didn't fare as well taking over your flight instruction schedule."

Ross raised his eyebrows. "Really. Why not?"

"Not sure. Megan Duval threw a fit when she learned you weren't available for her lesson. She stormed out of the office and said she'd reschedule with you and *only* you."

"Don't take it personally. Megan tends to be the clingy type. She lacks confidence and relies on me too much. I'm not sure she's going to make it as a pilot. It'll definitely take time if she does." He shrugged. "Anyone else give you grief?"

"No, the rest of the schedule went smoothly. Angie signed up a new teenager, a multi-engine rating student, and a couple of glider students."

"Sounds good. I'm glad we'll get some return on that glider you bought. Any damage from your beach landing?"

I shook my head. "No, the glider's fine."

"How did you get it out of there anyway?"

"Fortunately, we didn't have much trouble."

The server arrived with our pasta, and the conversation shifted to the food.

After we finished eating, Ross looked at me with those big brown eyes of his and sighed. "I don't have much going on this afternoon. Just one student later this evening. How about you? If you're free, we could head over to my place for a couple of hours." He squeezed my hand and gave me a wicked smile.

I sighed. "Don't I wish. Afraid I need to hurry back. I have a student scheduled at two."

"Why don't you have Angie call him and reschedule? I could take him tomorrow."

"No, this guy is special. He's eighteen, and his father is an airline pilot who Angie said specifically requested me. He prefers female instructors because he feels women are more thorough with the basics than men. He said, in his experience, male instructors are often too anxious to build their own flight hours and skimp on the groundwork. Besides, women instructors are more dedicated and nicer." I smiled. "After hearing all that, you can see why I wouldn't want to disappoint him."

"Hmph. Maybe, but I'd question whether instructor effectiveness is a gender thing."

"Probably not, but I have to admit it was refreshing to be appreciated after my experience with Megan."

"Also refreshing that we have another new student. We can use all we can get."

"I intend to ask the kid why he wants to fly. Need to make sure he's the one who wants to take lessons, and it's not just his dad's idea."

"You'll figure that out soon enough, sweetheart." Ross stood. "Better get you back to the office."

Chapter Five

Early Thursday afternoon, I dropped my phone in my desk drawer and headed for the door. "I'm taking the Super Cub, Angie. I'll be back late so will see you tomorrow."

As I flew to meet Charlie at the scheduled time, I continued my internal debate about him. Should I cooperate with Charlie's plan or should I keep my distance? Somehow knowing the probable right answer didn't help.

I donned my safety vest, ran through my checklists, and departed Anchorage to the northwest across Knik Arm to Point McKenzie before heading toward the Chugach Mountains north of Willow. I turned on approach to the subdivision, a small housing development built along a private runway. Each home boasted a private hangar and attached garage. I'd been here before and envied this convenient arrangement for pilots who worked in Anchorage.

It wasn't difficult to locate the cedar-sided, ranch-style house and taxi up to the property. As I shut down the plane's engine, Charlie opened the hangar door and peered out. Today, he wore a different brimmed cap and sunglasses. He glanced around before he hurried out to meet me. He carried one box in his arms, and I saw more boxes stacked inside the hangar.

"Glad you came, Beri. I have a few more boxes of supplies if you can take them."

"Depends on how heavy they are and how many will fit in the plane. It looks like you have quite a stack in there."

"I don't expect to take all of them. This one and three more will be enough for now. I'd estimate together they weigh about 150 pounds."

"Let me check, but I think it should work. You may have to hold a box on your lap as they won't all fit in the baggage area." I pushed the back of the seat forward and lifted a box inside. "What kind of landing strip will we use? Is it gravel?"

"Just dirt." He tipped his hat back. "It's a little rough, but not bad. I have the directions here." He handed me a slip of paper with coordinates. "You may have to gas up in Talkeetna for the return trip."

He finished loading the boxes. Then we climbed into the plane and headed out without filing a flight plan. Not an action I'd ever recommend to my students.

Charlie adjusted his headset and tapped me on the shoulder. "It's a cabin I rented under another name. I'm planning to lie low and live off the grid as long as I can while things calm down. Meanwhile, I'll have lots of time to figure out what comes next. In the meantime, I'll hire a professional to continue the search for Gina."

We flew west, just south of Denali to an intersection of the Susitna and Skwentna Rivers, then north along the Susitna to Trapper Creek. A number of small trapping trails meandered through the brush. We followed the creek to a narrow clearing bordered on both sides by stands of birch and aspen. A small cabin and a cache stood fifty feet off to one side.

"Looks a bit tight," I said and circled, noting no tree movement to indicate wind.

"The owner uses this place all winter, but he has his Cub on skis."

I brought the plane down uneventfully and rolled toward the cabin until I had to swerve to miss a large branch on the runway.

I pulled up near the cabin, and Charlie threw open the door. He dropped the box he'd held onto out the door where it landed on the ground with a solid thud.

"Nothing breakable in there, I hope."

"Nah. Just dried beans, rice, and canned bacon. Basics only. Didn't pack many canned goods. Too heavy, but a little bacon is an essential."

I followed him out of the plane and picked up the branch from the strip, throwing it off to the side. "Okay, let's get everything unloaded. I'd like to get home before anyone wonders where I went."

"Good idea. The fewer people who know about this trip the better."

"Sounds like you might lose some weight if you stay out here very long."

"Maybe. But I have my gun and ammo. I expect to find some game I can store in the cache. Maybe smoke some salmon from the creek behind the cabin, too." He picked up the box and headed for the cabin.

I followed, carrying a second box, and waited for Charlie to unlock the cabin's door before dropping it on a hand-hewn table in the dim interior.

Charlie headed back out the door while I checked out the cabin. The inside smelled musty with an overtone of wood smoke. It contained two chairs, a wood-fueled stove, a cot, and a large stainless steel mixing bowl that served as a sink on a small counter. A shelf over the counter held a cast-iron skillet, a pot, and a couple of plates. A shoebox held some cutlery.

Charlie dropped the third box inside the door. "One more to go," he said and turned back to the door. "I'll get the last box and make us some coffee when I return."

I walked out behind him to explore the skinning table and cache outside when I heard my plane rev up. I ran to the runway in time to see Charlie lift off over the trees.

Stranded.

The last box still rested on the ground beside the runway. What was he thinking? At least he'd left all the supplies.

Exasperated, I carried the box back to the cabin and began to inventory the contents. Who knew how long I'd be here? I assumed Charlie would at least return before trapping season, but would he? Like a fool, I'd told no one where I was going. I couldn't believe Charlie would do this to me.

Chapter Six

Fuming, I stormed around the property. I gathered an armload of the firewood I'd found stacked against an outside wall of the cabin and started a fire in the wood stove. I'd worked up an appetite. In a childish attempt to blow off steam, I found a can opener and fried up a can of Charlie's bacon. It smelled wonderful, but I was forced to consider the wisdom of my menu choice. I'd probably notified any bear in the vicinity that dinner was ready.

To get rid of the evidence, I piled the entire batch of crisp bacon strips between two rounds of Pilot bread smeared with peanut butter and washed my crunchy sandwich down with coffee I'd made with creek water. Luckily, I had water purification tablets in my safety vest.

Before trying to sleep, I scrubbed the skillet in the creek after pouring the bacon grease into a small plastic bowl with a tight-fitting lid. Taking the bowl and the other vulnerable supplies up the ladder into the cache, I stacked them inside. A twelve-gauge shotgun rested against the inside wall. I grabbed it, clambered down the ladder, and went back inside the cabin.

The gun had a shell in the chamber, but I replaced it with a fresh one from a box of shells I'd found in one of Charlie's boxes. Tomorrow, I'd gather stones to make an emergency distress signal that could be seen from the air, but tonight I needed some rest. My fury at Charlie's betrayal and my lack of recourse had drained me of energy.

While the bedding on the cot didn't smell inviting, I shook out the blankets and placed the shotgun on the floor beside the cot. I laid down, pulled the covers over my head to block out the nighttime daylight enjoyed only in Alaska in July when the squeak of the door awakened me. I grabbed the gun, sat up, and yelled, "Stop right there! I'm armed and ready to shoot."

"Hold your fire, Beri. It's me, Charlie." He pushed the door the rest of the way open with a shoulder, both hands in the air.

"I can't think of anyone I'd rather blow away than you about now." I reluctantly lowered the barrel of the gun but kept it trained on his knees.

"Let me explain."

I glared at him. "It better be good."

"I knew you wouldn't let me take the plane, but I had to make some arrangements that I couldn't let you know about for your own protection. And I did leave you the note."

I stood up from my makeshift bed. "What are you talking about? You didn't leave a note."

"Yes, I did. In that last box I left at the airstrip."

"I carried that box inside, but I didn't see any note."

"Did you open it?"

"Of course. I took all the bear bait up into the cache before I went to bed. The rest of the stuff is stacked in the corner behind the door."

"Check the box. You'll find my message. Maybe it fell to the bottom."

I walked to the corner, keeping the gun trained on him as I went. It required a juggling act to keep the gun aimed at him while lifting the top box off the stack. After opening the bottom box, I did find a piece of notebook paper flat against the inside edge of the cardboard.

"Okay, there is a note." I scanned the contents, lowered the gun, and scowled at Charlie. "I still don't forgive you. I'd have felt better if I'd known you'd return this quickly, but you still had no right…"

"Of course, I didn't. I had no choice, either. I'm worried sick about Gina. She didn't get back to me after I called from Birchwood. Our place was deserted, and she'd cleared some stuff out. At least, I assume she did and not my stalkers."

I was still mad. "How did stealing my airplane help you with anything?"

"I had to find someone to hire to look for her and make arrangements to lease a plane. I need my own transportation."

"What will you use to leave here? I can't wait. My family is probably already calling the troopers."

"No, I wouldn't expect you to help me again." He grinned. "I refueled it before I came back, and I arranged to have the plane I leased delivered."

"Good luck finding your girlfriend, but this time when I say good-bye I mean it."

"I'm sorry, Beri. Really I am. Thank you for everything you've done. I owe you a lot, and I hated to take advantage of you." He opened the door and carried in two more boxes he'd stacked outside. "I took advantage of the empty plane and brought a few more supplies."

"Check the cache for the things I stowed there last night. The bowl is full of bacon grease."

"What? You ate my bacon?" He looked shocked.

"Sorry." I handed him the gun and stomped out the door. *Why couldn't I stay mad at him?*

CHAPTER SEVEN

"Next time you decide to stay out all night, at least text me and let me know you're all right." Dad spewed the words at me before turning his back and throwing the lunch dishes in the sink.

"You're right. I'm sorry you were worried. Unfortunately, I didn't have my phone, and I wouldn't have had cell service where I was anyway." I put my arms around his waist and pressed my face against his back. "Believe me, it wasn't something I planned."

"You'd better let Ross know where you've been if you haven't already. I called him and chewed him out last night. Turns out he didn't know where you were, either. I couldn't believe you didn't file a flight plan. He was ready to call the Civil Air Patrol."

"I already stopped in at the office after I landed. Ross was flying, but I explained everything to Angie. I need to get back there now."

He turned to face me and returned the hug. "I'm glad you're okay, Cupcake. Before you go, your son called last night. He'll be on the 6:45 Alaska Airline flight tonight. I told him you were with a student so he wouldn't worry that you weren't home."

I stepped away. "Actually, I was with a student. I just didn't expect to get held up like I was." I pulled out a kitchen chair. "I'm so happy he's on his way back. It's been much too quiet without him."

"You're right about that."

"Did you talk to Dennis? Did he say anything about expecting him to come back for next school year?"

Dad shook his head. "No, he didn't get on the line."

"He'd better not try that again. Thanks, Dad. I'll get home early so we can leave for the airport."

Ross looked up from the laptop on his desk and closed the lid. "You had us worried, you know. What happened? Where did you go, and why didn't you file a flight plan? All we knew was that you told Angie you'd be late." He stood and took a step toward me. "Aside from the fact you almost gave me an anxiety attack, I'm happy to see you alive and well."

He pulled me into an embrace and whispered in my ear, "Please don't *ever* put us through that again."

"Glad you missed me, but sorry for the scare." I sank into his arms and rested my head on his shoulder. "I flew Charlie and some supplies to a remote cabin. He felt he was in danger staying in town, and I agreed to help him. After we arrived, we carried his supplies into the cabin. He went back to the plane for the last box of supplies and took off in my plane. He left me stranded there overnight."

I shrugged out of his embrace. "It wouldn't have been so bad if I could have contacted you. The only good thing to come of it is that it didn't happen a day later. I just found out Jack's plane is coming in tonight."

"That is good news. I've missed him, too." He gave me a stern look. "But you're not getting off that easy, Beri. I don't understand why you've been so hellbent on helping this Charlie character." Ross frowned. "Everyone was worried, especially your dad."

"He's given me an earful. I had no idea what Charlie was up to, and I can't explain why I helped him. Everything he's done has caused me trouble, but I couldn't risk him getting killed."

I stepped away from Ross. "Look, I just can't lose another student. Having one missing in the wilderness and another murdered last year was more than I could bear." I rubbed my head, hoping to ease the throbbing headache I'd developed. "I'm still reeling after seeing Skip dead at Birchwood."

"If you're not careful, you could be the one getting killed," Ross said sternly.

"No. I'm done with Charlie. This stunt was the last straw. And he knows it."

Ross pulled me back toward him. "It's hard for me to stay mad at you, but to say you've tested my patience would be an understatement." He kissed the top of my head.

"I'll try to do better from now on. I have to stay clear of Charlie altogether. After all, Jack's coming home tonight." I gave him a final peck on the cheek and moved toward the door. "The Super Cub needs my attention. I'd better get her cleaned out and gassed up before my next student comes in."

I was back at Simon's. Twice in one week was a record. This time Kaitlin Rimes met me at the entrance for lunch. We'd agreed to meet twice a month to work out details for our annual Ninety-Nines scholarship fundraiser scheduled for this fall. I'd been a member of the women's pilot organization since getting my license as a teenager. I loved working on outreach and scholarship programs to encourage more women to enter the flying profession. This year's fundraiser sounded especially fun. We planned a follow-up to last year's popular Pinch-Hitter class.

Kaitlin wore her usually straight black hair in new flattering shoulder-length curls. It was such a different look, I almost didn't recognize her. She smiled at me as the hostess led us to a table and handed us menus.

"I had you there for a minute, didn't I?" she asked.

"Maybe for a second or two. You look like you stepped out of a magazine photo shoot. Are you thinking about changing to a modeling career?"

She laughed. "No, flying is the only job for me. I just got a permanent. It felt like it was time to do something different after wearing my hair the same way since childhood. Speaking of hair, who's that blonde sitting over by the window with Ross?"

I glanced toward the window. Sure enough, Ross was sitting across from Megan, their heads close together, engrossed in conversation. *What the hell?* That didn't look like a flying lesson.

I tried to keep my ire from showing. "It's Ross all right. He's having lunch with one of his students."

"Uh huh." She raised an eyebrow. "They certainly appear to have something on their minds besides airplanes. Or food, for that matter."

The server arrived, and we both selected seafood salads. After ordering, we mapped out our fund-raising plans. Kaitlin avoided bringing up Ross again, and we finished our business before our food arrived.

I'd just about recovered my wits when Ross rose to leave and spotted me across the room. His face registered surprise, but he casually raised his hand to wave before ushering Megan toward the exit. Was he avoiding a possible scene between Megan and me, or did he really think it was no big deal?

I pretended not to notice as Megan glared at me as she left.

Kaitlyn's eyebrows went up.

"Do you feel up for a post-meal game of racquetball? I could use some exercise," I said.

"Need to burn off a little steam?" Kaitlyn patted my arm.

"Sure. I ate a light-enough lunch. How about we meet at the Racquet Club in about an hour?"

"I'll be there," Kaitlyn agreed.

I called the club to schedule a court and checked in with Angie before leaving. I already had my gear in the back of my SUV and headed out to have time for some warm-up stretches.

The parking lot of the Racquet Club was less than half full when I arrived. After retrieving my racquet and gym bag, I pulled open the door to enter the club. Plastered on the glass surface was a flyer with the word,

"Missing!" and the photo of an attractive woman. She looked vaguely familiar, but I couldn't place her. Maybe I'd seen her at the club.

After checking in, I asked the young fellow behind the desk about the missing person.

"Oh, that's Maxie," he said. "Maxine Stedwell, one of our top-seeded tennis players. She's been missing for a couple of weeks. Very mysterious. Her husband is beside himself worrying about her."

"I thought she looked familiar, but I've probably seen her picture on the news."

"That's a good possibility. Hope she turns up soon. Our state tournament chances won't be the same if she doesn't."

I changed into exercise clothes and started my stretches. It didn't take me long to get bored. To pass the time, I jumped on a treadmill and started running. The more I thought about Ross, the angrier I got and the steeper I ratcheted up the incline on the machine. By the time Kaitlyn arrived, I was soaked in sweat.

"Looks like you're already worn out," she said. "I shouldn't have much trouble beating you for a change."

Chapter Eight

Angie poked her head in the door to my office. "Beri, someone's here to see you. He said it's important. Okay if I show him back?"

"Who is it?" I asked.

"He didn't say. Just said he needed to talk to you about a matter of some importance," she said in a mocking voice.

I stifled a giggle. Thinking it was probably someone interested in lessons, I was surprised when a tall, almost emaciated-looking stranger dressed in a business suit and holding a briefcase walked in. He held out his hand. "Beri Quinn? I'm Jason Heckenlively." He shook my hand with vigor.

"Glad to meet you." I motioned for him to have a seat. "What can I do for you?"

"I wanted to talk about a photogrammetry project. I understand you've done work requiring military security clearances."

"Yes, but I'm not in that field any longer. I sold that business."

"Did the sale include a non-compete clause?"

"That's a bit complicated because the original buyer, Cartos, was recently bought out by another outfit, Northern Mapping. I agreed not to compete with Cartos."

"Good, we shouldn't have a problem then." He picked up his briefcase from the floor and laid it on his lap. "I have a proposition for you. I need an experienced Alaskan pilot to fly a sensitive project over Adak Island for the government. I want someone who knows her stuff and can handle the difficulties of flying in the Aleutians. I'm told you fit the bill."

"Maybe, but I no longer have the equipment."

"The equipment is not a problem. The government can supply you with that, and on completion of the project, it would be considered part of your compensation."

"You mean I could keep it? Digital aerial camera, Lidar, and everything?" I asked, surprised.

"Yes, even the plane you'll use." He fidgeted with the latch of his briefcase.

"If that's the case, why doesn't the government or the military do the job?"

"Good question," he said. "There's a problem with the funding. The bill authorizing the project specifies it has to be done by a private enterprise."

"Did you check with Northern Mapping? They'd have the equipment."

"Yes, we looked into that company. There are problems with security clearances, and they lack experience in the area in question." He looked away from me and stared at the weather map behind me on the wall. "We need this job done immediately. Recognizing the unpredictability of weather in the Aleutians, we want an experienced person who can leave on a moment's notice when conditions are right."

I wasn't thrilled with my options. "Couldn't you do the job with satellite imagery?"

"To an extent, yes." His eyes went back to the map on my wall. "But some aspects require a different approach. This is important, and it's imperative we not waste any time. You're our best choice. We'd need you to start a new business."

"I'd need to get a business license."

"That shouldn't take long. If you run into any snags, we could expedite it for you. I have a contract ready for you to consider. I must emphasize that it is for *your eyes only*."

He removed a sealed folder from his briefcase and placed it on my desk. "I'll return later this week. In the meantime, get that license application rolling." He rose and headed for the door.

"Wait. What agency did you say you were with?"

"I didn't," Jason said. "We can discuss that if you agree to the contract. I'll be in touch."

I sat, shaking my head. What was he asking me to get myself into?

Angie came through the door the minute the man left, a quizzical look on her face. "What was that all about?"

"Can't talk about it right now. I need to find out more about it myself." I stood. "Here's a question for you. If you were going to create a fictional aerial photography and mapping company, what would you name it?"

"Hmm… Let's see. Off the top of my head, how about Above It All?" She sat in the chair Heckenlively had vacated. "You're not really considering starting another business, are you?"

"No. I said a fictional company. I just need a name. How about AIA Surveys?"

"Sounds good to me. You'd be first in the alphabet, not that people use phone books anymore."

Chapter Nine

Angie slammed her pen down on her desk. "Damn! We're broke again. I thought those days were behind us."

"What do you mean, broke?" I asked, looking up from the student schedule I'd been studying.

"What do you think I mean? I can't pay the bills. Your income projections from glider lessons aren't proving accurate. We've only added five students since you returned from Arizona, and expenses have gone up." She scrolled through entries on her spreadsheet. "And I haven't even received the invoice from the helicopter outfit that flew your glider off that beach yet."

"I thought I told you. There won't be an invoice. I already paid it."

"You did? You personally?"

"Yes. It seemed appropriate since I was the one who caused the problem." Angie snorted. "Have you told Ross?"

"He doesn't need to know. I'd appreciate it if you didn't bring it to his attention."

"If you say so." Angie's eyebrows were up again. "But if you ask me, he's bound to notice."

"Notice what?" Ross asked as he walked in from the hallway.

"Busted." Angie muttered under her breath.

"We were talking about the sad state of our finances," I said. "Nothing too mysterious."

Ross dropped into a chair next to Angie's desk. "You said it. I took a look at our bottom-line last night. I'm going to have to ask the bank for a line of credit to make payroll, and I'm not sure they're going to give it to me. Our accounts payable are looking meager, and the bills are stacking up."

"I haven't been pulling my weight yet," I said. "Leave me out of the payroll."

"Don't start that. Either we're partners or we're not." Ross stood to leave. "I'm headed to the bank now. I'll let you know how it goes."

After Ross left, Angie winked at me. "Good save. You bought a little time anyway."

I shrugged and dropped the schedule next to the phone. The partnership had sounded so logical when we planned it after I sold Quinn Aviation. I knew I wanted to continue flying, and I'd grown close to Ross. We obtained an appraisal on his flight instruction business while I was in Arizona with Jack. I invested half the estimated value about six months ago to give Ross time to add office space and pay Angie's and Dean's salaries until I returned. Even with the cash infusion, it had proven difficult for the business to stay profitable with the added overhead.

I'd hoped the new glider lessons would bring in more business, but it hadn't helped so far. It would take time. I just hoped Ross and the bank would be patient.

Angie cleared her throat. "Tough way to handle a relationship. He has his pride."

"Yes, he does." I grabbed my tote. "Looks like I need to get busy and drum up some business. I think I'll give my friend, Hutch, a visit and see if he can help us with some publicity. I should have enough time before I need to head to the airport to pick up Jack."

Hutch sat in his cubicle in the Anchorage Gazette office tapping away on his computer. I stood there for a minute, hating to interrupt his concentration. When clearing my throat didn't work, I tapped him lightly on the shoulder.

He startled. "Oh. Hi, Beri. I lost track of time. Sorry about that."

"Must be quite a story you're writing."

"Yeah, it's about the housing shortage in Juneau. Those politicians and government employees need a place to live." He pulled out a chair for me. "Take a seat. It's good to see you, but I doubt you dropped by to chat. What can I do for you?"

"A favor, really. I'm hoping you or one of your staff will consider doing a feature article on gliding."

"Gliding?"

"Yes, I recently added glider lessons to the flight instruction services we offer, but not many people know it's an option."

"At Merrill Field?" he asked.

"That's where we sign up students, but the actual lessons are held at Birchwood airstrip."

"So, what exactly did you have in mind?"

"Ideally, a photo feature with pictures of the tow plane, takeoff, and soaring lesson. With their long, graceful wings, sailplanes are extremely photogenic." I gave him my best smile.

"Speaking of gliding, wasn't there a murder of a tow pilot at Birchwood recently?" Hutch ruffled through some clippings he'd stapled together and piled on the side of his desk.

"Yes. Not exactly good publicity."

"Noted." Hutch chuckled. "So, you're out for some free publicity and damage control."

I straightened and crossed my arms. "I'm that transparent, huh?"

Hutch cocked his head. "Not that bad a concept, though. We could pair it with a follow-up on the murder story. Have they caught the killer yet?"

"I don't think so." I scooted my chair closer. "It would help the damage control part if you didn't run the two articles together. Readers will be much more interested when you run the murder follow-up in a later issue."

"Ah, I almost forgot the marketing angle. Let me check something." He rose and moved to the opposite side of the room.

As I watched, he leaned into another larger cubicle to talk to someone hidden behind a partition. The rest of the room hummed with activity. Employees moved about in random patterns among the multiple cubicles filling the space. A constant low drone of voices filled the air with simultaneous unintelligible phone conversations.

Hutch returned with a grin on his face. "Do you think you could make arrangements for a shoot the day after tomorrow? Al says he's free in the afternoon, but he's leaving on vacation this weekend. He loves everything to do with flying and would be the perfect choice."

"Sounds wonderful," I said. "I'm sure I can arrange it. How about two o'clock at Birchwood airstrip? I'll call you if I run into any problems or too many clouds develop to interfere with lift."

"What would clouds have to do with anything?" Hutch asked.

"We're getting technical, but it takes heat on the ground for vertical lift to develop and clouds block the heat."

"Ah… So, in Alaska, soaring is a summertime sport?"

"Yep, you've got that right. It's one of the reasons I'm anxious to get things moving. Summer's already half gone." I stood to leave. "I appreciate your help. See you Friday."

Chapter Ten

Jack's plane was late. I wasn't surprised since the weather report indicated they'd encounter head winds enroute. Dad and I waited impatiently outside the security checkpoint. It would be so good to have him home. The past school year had been an adventurous one for Jack, half spent touring Europe with his dad's family and half finishing up at a new school after they returned to Arizona. I'd had severe misgivings about the plan, but Jack had flourished. Now, we'd see if he would pick up where he left off with his Anchorage school and friends.

Passengers were starting to stream toward us in greater numbers. I scanned the crowd, looking for a short blond, almost twelve-year-old boy sporting a backpack. I stood on tiptoes to expand my field of vision. It was not often I wished to be taller than my 5-feet-9-inch frame, but it would have advantages at times.

"There he is." Dad pointed to the far side of the crowd. His extra five inches of height won the day.

I ran ahead to wrap my arms around him. "Jack! Welcome home."

Jack wriggled from my grasp. "You're embarrassing me, Mom. Hi, Gramps."

"Hi there, young man. I think you've grown a foot since I saw you last." He shook Jack's hand. "Here, let me take that backpack. Did you check any luggage?"

"My suitcase and golf clubs," Jack said. "I think we have to go downstairs to get them."

"Golf clubs. Bet that cost you a pretty penny in over-weight charges," Gramps said.

"I don't know." Jack shrugged. "Dad paid for my ticket in advance."

"Well, that was nice of him." Gramps put his free hand on Jack's shoulder. "It's sure good to have you back where you belong."

Twenty minutes later, we had Jack's suitcase, but no golf clubs, and the conveyer belt shut down.

"Mom, did they lose my clubs? I have to find them."

"I've said it before, but I don't know what good golf clubs are going to do you in Alaska," Gramps grumbled.

Jack pulled away from him. "I need them. I'm just getting good. My pro said I've got to keep practicing while I'm home." He heaved an exaggerated sigh. "And besides, there are at least three golf courses here in Anchorage. I googled it."

I grabbed his hand. "Let's check with the attendant. They may have held your clubs back because they were over-sized."

Sure enough, we spotted the clubs leaning against the wall by the luggage information window.

Jack raced to grab them and showed the attendant his claim stub. "Thanks, Mom. I'm so glad you knew where to look." He hoisted the bag over one shoulder. "Which way?"

Relieved, we started toward the exit.

"The parking garage elevator is over there," Gramps said and turned him in the right direction. "I'll bet you're hungry."

"Yeah, I'm starved. A Grizzly burger sure sounds great about now."

I laughed.

Jack woke early the next morning. I found a note on the coffee machine saying he'd taken Tiger for a walk. No doubt Tiger had awakened him.

He had been so excited by Jack's return, he'd covered him in kisses, tail wagging nonstop, and he hadn't left Jack's side since.

Dad was the sleepyhead today, so I mixed some batter and set up the waffle iron on the counter with butter and wild raspberry syrup ready to go.

The door slammed. "Mom! Look what I have." Jack held out his hands to display a tiny kitten, eyes still closed and no bigger than a mouse.

"Where did you get him? He looks too young to be away from his mother."

"I didn't find him. Tiger did. He was at the edge of a culvert over by Rabbit Creek Road. Tiger barked and barked until I followed him. I thought he was upset because a dead cat was on the road, but he wouldn't be quiet until he led me to this kitten."

"Oh, how sad. I'll call the vet and see what we should feed him. I think we have an eye dropper you can use in the medicine cabinet."

Jack cradled the kitten in his hands. "He's so little. I hope he'll be all right."

After getting instructions from the vet, Jack fed our homemade, warmed formula drop by drop into the kitten's mouth, more landing on the towel he'd wrapped the kitten in than made it into his mouth.

"Take it slow," I said. "He won't need much at first. Try to keep him warm and get a few drops in him. The vet said to bring him in when the clinic opens in about an hour."

Jack put the eye dropper down long enough to scratch Tiger's ears. "We'll take good care of him, won't we, Tiger?"

"While you feed the kitten, I'll get a shovel and bury the mother cat. We can't leave her on the road."

"Thanks, Mom. I didn't think about that." Jack nestled the kitten closer to his chest. "Can you bury her by the wild rose bush? I think she would like that."

"Good idea." I was proud of my son's compassion but afraid we'd be burying the kitten next to his mom before long. As I went out the door to the garage, I cast a regretful glance at the waffle iron still sitting on the counter.

The morning air was crisp and clear, the scent of moist earth from last night's showers a pleasant counterpoint to my grim mission. Before climbing the slight incline to the road, I checked the culvert to make sure there weren't more kittens hidden inside. A trickle of water flowed through the pipe, but it was drier on the edges. No sign of any kitten siblings. I should have known Tiger wouldn't miss any.

Fortunately, there was no traffic when I reached the road and spotted the sad remains of the mother cat. She'd been hit more than once, but it was still apparent that she'd been a beautiful long-haired cat. Glad that I brought the snow shovel, I scooped her up with the flat blade and carried her gingerly back to our yard. I laid her beside the wild roses and walked back to the garage to get a spade to dig the hole.

Dad came out of the house, wiping sleep from his eyes. "Need any help?"

"No, I'm about finished. Just trying to decide if I should mark the grave somehow."

"Jack told me what happened. Why not leave that decision to him?"

"Perfect." I kissed his leathery cheek. "He's lucky to have such a wise grandfather."

The kitten proved my fears wrong. As we entered the clinic, he snuggled in the towel Jack had wrapped him in. His eyes remained closed, but he made occasional murmuring cries.

The vet smiled as he probed him gently with one finger. "This little guy has spunk. I'm usually not optimistic about saving babies this young, but this one just might make it."

Jack's eyes shone as he looked at me. "Did you hear that? He's going to be okay. Tiger will be so happy."

"We hope so," the vet said. "We won't know for several weeks, but with your help he has a fighting chance." He pulled the towel back around the kitten. "I can't be sure, but he may be an expensive Persian. What did the mother look like?"

I glanced at Jack. "Long hair, white with black tips. Fluffy tail. I couldn't tell much more."

"You mentioned you buried her. I might have identified her owner if I could have scanned her for a microchip."

"I didn't think of that," I said. "She was in bad shape."

"I don't recall any clients of ours who have pets of that breed, but we'll watch for any missing cat bulletins and let you know if one turns up for her."

"Thanks, Doc. Meanwhile, we'll take good care of this little guy."

Jack settled into his seat in the car and turned to me. "I'm going to think of a good name for him. We can keep him, can't we?"

I smiled. "We'll see what happens. If the owner doesn't turn up, we can. If we do manage to find the mother's owner, I'm sure whoever it is will be very grateful you saved the kitten. For now, let's just call him Kitty. That way, you can wait until you see more of his personality and can come up with the best name."

Jack held the kitten closer, his shoulders hunched. He frowned, his mouth a straight line. "Maybe. If you say so."

The log house with the circular driveway was the second stop on my neighborhood tour that evening. I'd been told by the first neighbor I met that she thought the O'Haras, the owners of this house, had a white cat. She'd seen it outside a few times, although she hadn't met the owners. I rang the doorbell, hoping we wouldn't have to give Jack's kitten back.

Expecting to see someone of Irish descent, I was surprised when a petite Asian woman with a stern expression on her face opened the door.

"Hello." I held out my hand to shake. "I'm Beri Quinn, a neighbor of yours. I live nearby."

"I know who you are." She ignored my attempt to shake hands. "You used to own my business on Merrill Field. What do you want?"

"I wondered if you had lost a Persian cat recently?"

She gave me a piercing direct look. "Yes. Did you find her? I hope you don't expect a reward."

"No, I didn't find her, but my son and his dog did. I'm sorry to report that she'd been run over by a car on Rabbit Creek Road. I buried her and thought you'd want to know, so you wouldn't keep searching for her."

She glared at me. "You're the one who hit her, why don't you admit it?"

"No, it happened like described," I insisted.

"SuSu would never have left her kitten. I found it dead in her kennel. It died because it didn't have a mother. I hope you're happy." She shook her finger in my face. "I should sue you. I paid a lot of money for that cat, and I would have made more if I had bred her kitten."

"I'm sorry for your loss." The words were barely out of my mouth before she slammed the door shut.

I turned and walked back. No way was I going to turn Jack's kitten over to that woman. She hadn't even given me a chance to tell her we had him, and she hadn't even managed to keep the one she did have alive. Guess she would just have to sue me.

Jack jumped up when I walked in the door after returning home. "Did you find the owner, Mom? Please say no."

"You can keep the kitten on one condition, but you have to promise you'll follow my rules."

"Sure. What are they?"

"You'll be responsible for caring for him. That means feeding him, cleaning his litter box regularly, and most important, keep him indoors. You can't let him go outside. It's too dangerous."

"Duh, that's easy. I wouldn't want Piper to go outside anyway. You saw what happened to his mother."

"Piper?" I asked.

"Yeah. I named him that because we found him in a pipe."

"Good one." I rubbed the kitten's tiny ears. "His eyes are starting to open a little."

"Yeah." Jack beamed.

"Looks like he's a keeper. Why don't you introduce our new family member to Grandpa tonight. I think he was hoping we'd have to give him back."

"No problem." Jack laughed. "If I know Grandpa, he'll fall in love with Piper, too. He just doesn't realize it yet." He held the kitten close to his face and gave him air kisses. "Gramps didn't want Tiger at first, either."

Chapter Eleven

I returned from an early morning instrument lesson with a professor who squeezed it in before teaching his first class of the day. I was happy to get an early start since I planned to pick up Jack and drive to Birchwood before lunch.

Angie walked into my office and dropped the mail on my desk where it landed with a clink. "Not sure what's in that envelope, but it's something hard."

I looked up from my computer screen. "Thanks, Angie."

"Aren't you going to open it?" She stood in the doorway waiting.

"What's with all the curiosity? I'm in the middle of something right now, but I'll get to the mail in a few minutes."

With a loud sigh, Angie backed out of my office.

I waited to satisfy my own curiosity until after she left. The first two envelopes contained predictable communications from local businesses, but the third was addressed to me with no return address. No wonder Angie was interested.

I tore open the envelope, and a key dropped into my hand. The short note was signed simply *Charlie*.

No. I'm done with him. My eyes moved over his brief message, and despite my misgivings, I gave his request some thought.

Dear Beri,

I have another favor I didn't want to ask before. I know I've already pushed you beyond your limits, but I have no one else to turn to.

I'm worried sick about Gina. I haven't heard from her since the morning Skip was killed, and I'm afraid to try to contact her directly. Could you PLEASE check on her? I'm enclosing the address and a key to our rental. If all is well, place a notice in "Tundra Drums" on KXCE from Annie to Pete.

Say either "the baby is doing well," or "you're worried about the baby." I'll be listening to my radio every evening for the next two weeks. I hope it won't take longer than that.

Charlie

PS: Thank you for all your help and in advance for doing this.

I stuffed the letter back in the envelope with the key and folded it into my wallet. I had to leave to pick up Jack from home. He'd agreed to help me with the glider photo shoot. It would take us at least an hour once we arrived at Birchwood to get everything ready before Hutch and the photographer arrived.

Jack undid the strap holding his end of the glider's wing to the trailer. "Wow, Mom. How do we put this thing together?"

With so little time to get organized, I'd recruited Jack to stand in for a student in the newspaper photos. He'd been anxious to go for a ride anyway.

"The assembly isn't hard. Hold the tip of the wing off the ground while I attach it to the fuselage. We'll have to wiggle the wing back and forth to align the spar pins to secure the wing in place. I'll tell you which way to move it. See, there it goes." I pumped my fist in the air. "I knew we could do it."

He stood by the wing, waiting for my next set of instructions. I marveled at how grown-up he appeared. He was at least two inches taller, and his shoulders were broader than last summer.

"Let's hustle, Mom. They're going to be here soon."

"You're right. Here goes, move the wing a little to the left and up a smidge." Before I finished talking, he'd done as I asked. "Good work."

I added the fairing to the leading edge and moved to the other side of the glider. Jack could obviously do the job; I needed to show more confidence in him. "One wing done. Let's start on the other side."

Hutch and another fellow drove up in a red Jeep as we finished. "Hi, Beri. Looks like you started without us." He motioned to the other man. "This is our star camera man, Al McGraw."

"Glad to meet you," I said.

His stocky build reminded me of the wrestlers at the matches my dad used to drag me to. Al set a black soft-sided case on the ground and extended his hand.

I shook his hand and introduced Jack. "He's been after me to let him try out the glider, so I've put him to work assembling it. He's helped a lot. We're about to finish the second wing."

"Let's snap a picture while you do that," Al said. "You're a lucky kid, Jack. I've always wanted to fly in one of these things."

"Yeah, I'm pretty excited," Jack said.

"Can one of you guys grab a wing tip and help me push the glider out to the runway behind that tow plane over there?" I asked.

Hutch stepped forward. "I'll do it while Al gets his equipment set up."

Luckily, one of my tow pilots was already at Birchwood when I called. After some razzing about the shooting incident last week and the possible dangers he'd face, he'd agreed to pull us into the air at his usual rate.

"Once we get the glider in place, I'll attach the tow rope. Jack and I will climb in, and it would help a lot if you'd grab the wing that rests on the ground. Hold it level with the other wing."

"Then what?" Al asked.

"As soon as the tow pilot pulls the rope tight from his end, I'll wiggle the rudders. That's the signal for him to apply power and go."

"How far and how high will he take you?" Hutch asked.

"We'll probably fly to a couple thousand feet over by the mountains. I won't drop the tow rope until I find a good thermal."

"I hope I can get decent footage from that distance." Al opened his camera case and rummaged through the contents. "The takeoff part shouldn't be a problem. I'll do my best with my distance lenses for the actual soaring."

"You can also follow closer to the mountains in your Jeep and come back for the landing if it would help. It isn't that far."

"I'll figure it out." Al shrugged. "How long can you stay up there without power?"

"That all depends on the lift. I can stay up all day if the conditions are right, but today we'll keep it short, probably about twenty minutes."

Hutch jotted down notes. "How do you get rid of the tow rope?"

"I pull the handle to release it. When I do, the tow pilot will feel the weight change and our pre-arranged procedure is for him to go left while I go up and to the right. He'll land with the rope still attached."

"Do you ever do any cross-country soaring?" Al asked.

"No. It's complicated. Soaring requires a team effort, and in Alaska, you'd need a truck following you. There aren't many good destinations from here with road access. Also, you'd need to take a radio to contact air traffic control if you fly or land in a controlled area. Cross-country soaring is more common in the Lower 48."

"Sounds tricky all right," Al said.

"Let's get started. While I attach the tow rope, Jack, you can climb in the front and fasten your seat belt. Be careful not to touch any controls up there."

"How are you going to drive, Mom, if you sit in the back?" For the first time, Jack's smile faltered a bit.

"Don't worry. There's a set of controls in the back, too." I attached the rope, climbed in, and pulled the plexiglass canopy closed.

After settling in and fastening my seat belt, I reached forward and tousled Jack's blond head. On signal, the tow pilot began to move. He increased power and headed down the runway, pulling us behind. The glider rose in the air before the plane fully lifted off, and we both went airborne midway down the runway. I could see Al below, camera trained upward.

Once we reached elevation, the tow pilot turned toward the mountains. A few minutes later, wind whistled through the cockpit, and the rate of climb indicator rose. We'd found our thermal.

"I'm ready to drop the rope," I called out to Jack. "We're about to soar!"

"This is really exciting, Mom," Jack said as we began flying in lazy circles over the landscape below. All noise disappeared. We floated above the earth.

"Can you see if the Jeep is still at the airstrip?"

"I think so," Jack said. "I see a red dot down there."

"Good. He must have the lens he needed. How are you doing up there?"

"Great. I could stay up here all day. Do your students beg you to go longer than their lessons?"

I laughed. "No, I think they worry it would be too expensive to pay for another hour."

"Can I take lessons, Mom?"

"It won't be long before you can. When you turn fourteen, you can get a license. We could start your lessons before that."

"Guess I can wait another year and a half, but I wish it was sooner."

I gave his shoulder a quick pat. It was good to know Jack had caught the flying bug. "We'd better head back now. I think Al has had more than enough time to take pictures."

"Hey, look. There's an eagle flying over there! He must have found the same thermal as us."

"Usually, it works the other way," I said. "I watch for hawks, eagles, and seagulls to help me find thermals. They circle in the warm air to gain altitude, too."

Jack grew quiet as we descended and headed back to the airstrip. After we landed, we coasted to a stop and turned off on the taxiway. The tow pilot ran out and grabbed a wing to pull us to where Hutch and Al waited.

"Well, what did you think, Jack?" Hutch asked.

"It was awesome," Jack said. "Did you see the eagle up there with us? I felt like I was a bird, too. I can't wait until I'm old enough to get my license."

"I'm jealous," Al said. "I got great pictures, but it would be wonderful to get some from inside the glider, too. Any chance you could take me up for a short ride?"

"Sure," I said, "if the tow pilot is agreeable. Let me check with him."

We pulled the glider back on the runway, Al climbed in with his camera, and I locked the canopy into place.

The tow pilot took off down the runway after spotting my rudder signal and lifted into the air.

"Hey, this is great. I've got to get a shot of this," Al said. He pulled his camera up to take a photo, but the camera strap snagged on the rope release lever.

The tow rope fell from the glider as the plane lifted higher into the sky.

"What happened? Did I do something?" Al twisted back to look at me.

"We're too low." I tried to keep my voice steady. "Hang on, I'm going to have to land." I maneuvered the glider in a shallow turn, hoping I had enough altitude to make it back to the runway.

Another plane had taxied into place for takeoff at the far end of the field. Would he see our predicament and move? I could only hope.

With the red Jeep visible in my peripheral vision, I turned the glider in a slow arc back to the runway. A stand of birch trees blocked the possibility of landing straight ahead. Instead, with only three hundred feet of altitude, I lowered the nose of the glider to maintain enough air speed to make the turn.

We drew closer to the Maule preparing to depart. I banked parallel to the runway. With no traffic control present, the pilot appeared oblivious to our presence.

I lined up with the taxiway about one hundred feet left of the runway proper, let down short and bounced forward. Our airspeed was so slow by this time, I'd been forced to hold until the last minute and make a stall landing, the opposite of my usual glider procedure. I sighed in relief as the craft slowed to a stop, and one wing dropped to rest on terra firma.

Al turned back to look at me, his face ashen. "What just happened?"

"The camera strap caught on the tow latch and detached the rope prematurely. It was a freak accident. I improvised our landing because we didn't have much altitude and there was another plane preparing to take off."

"You mean we almost crashed?"

"I'd say we managed a tricky situation, but everything turned out alright."

Hutch ran up beside the grounded wing. "Al, get out and grab the other wing. Help me steer this thing back to the tie-down. Hurry, I'm anxious to hear you explain what just happened." He shook his head. "That plane almost took off over the top of you. What a story."

"Let's not get carried away, Hutch," I said. "Remember the point of this effort is to attract customers, not scare them away."

Chapter Twelve

I took Jack home, then drove back to the office. I couldn't stop thinking about the key lying in the bottom of my tote. Try as I might to ignore the damn thing, the image of it wouldn't go away. I found myself driving by the address Charlie had given me. The split-level cedar-sided exterior looked similar to many Anchorage houses. Nothing about it stood out, unless it was the overgrown yard dotted with bright yellow dandelions. The vertical blinds in the upstairs windows were closed as were the curtains on the lower-level windows.

I pulled into the paved driveway, parked, and walked up to the front door, rummaging in my tote for the key.

"Can I help you?" a voice behind me called out. I turned to see a dark-haired, middle-aged woman dressed in jeans and a paint-spattered work shirt. "No one's home. I'm from next door."

"Thanks. Any idea when Gina will be back?"

"No. I think they may be out of town. I haven't seen them for a week or two, and I noticed the mailman had to stuff their mail in the box to make it all fit."

"Charlie is out of town, but he hasn't heard from Gina in a while. He's worried and asked me to check on her and their place."

The woman smiled and held out her hand. "I'm Caroline."

"Beri." I shook her hand. "Glad to meet you."

"I hope everything's alright." Caroline's eyes were bright with interest.

"I hope so, too. I'm going to go inside, water the plants, and check to see if she left a note." I handed her my card. "Meanwhile, if you hear from her, please give me a call." I inserted the key and opened the door. "Nice meeting you," I called.

The house was dark and smelled funky. I clicked on the entry light and climbed the half flight of stairs to the living room, clicking on more lights in the adjacent kitchen. Not much to see. Basic furniture that looked like it could have come from Costco. A sofa, recliner, and coffee table sat before an entertainment center containing a modest-sized television. No magazines, artwork, or personal touches. Lots of dust motes.

The kitchen was tidy, but the odor was stronger here. I checked under the sink and noted the trash can was more than half full. I didn't see anything that would account for the smell. Saving further exploration of it for later, I opened the refrigerator. It reeked of spoiled and moldy food. Ugh. I slammed the door closed and pulled a trash bag over to throw out the contents. *What if this turned out to be a crime scene?* I slammed the door closed again.

Moving on to the two bedrooms on this level, I found only one had been furnished albeit sparsely. Bed and dresser. Nothing else. The dresser drawers contained a few feminine undergarments and some tennis clothes. Another drawer contained men's clothing. I rummaged through the contents, noting one rolled pair of socks had a hard center. When I separated the pair, a key was hidden inside. I slid it into my pocket.

The closet held Charlie's clothes and a few of Gina's. I checked pockets and inside shoes, but found nothing. One suitcase on an upper shelf held a spare blanket. The medicine cabinet in the bathroom had a tube of toothpaste still in the box and a bottle of aspirin. No toothbrushes, no hairbrush or comb. No prescription medications. Did she take them? I'd make sure to ask Charlie if I got the chance.

I glanced around the empty bedroom, then did the same in the two additional bedrooms and bathroom downstairs. The family room was also empty and appeared unused. Why had they chosen such a big house?

No vehicles in the garage, but it did contain a red metal tool chest filled with tools, a generator, a paper shredder, and trash and recycle containers. Thankfully, the garbage can was almost empty. I dumped the recycle container contents out on the garage floor and sifted through paper and plastic, looking for anything informative. No luck. I returned everything to the receptacle and checked the shredder. It was nearly full of confetti-sized bits of paper. Someone didn't want to leave information lying around.

I walked back upstairs to check the kitchen trash. It was filled with used coffee pods, a few pork chop bones, and slimy broccoli stalks. I'd just scooped everything back into the trashcan and stowed it back under the sink when the doorbell rang.

Through the peephole in the front door, I could see a heavy-set dark-haired man.

As I debated whether to open the door, Caroline walked up to him.

"Can I help you?" she asked.

"No. I'm just leaving." He turned back toward the street where a forest-green van was parked.

Caroline stood and watched him go. After he left, I opened the door. "Thanks, Caroline. I wasn't sure whether to open the door to him or not."

"He looked sketchy to me." She giggled. "Did you find any clues?"

"Not a one. No plants to water, either." I closed the door and checked to make sure it was locked.

"Wait. Can you open that back up? I'll put their mail inside to make room for more." She ran to the mailbox on the street and returned with her arms brimming. She handed it all to me.

"Good idea, although probably not legal." I managed to reopen the door and took the mail upstairs. As I piled it on the table, I noticed one envelope with a return address for Forest Lake Storage Units. I remembered Charlie mentioning he wanted Gina to grab his go-bag. Could that be where he kept it?

It didn't take long to drive to the Forest Lake Storage Units after I left Charlie's place. I parked outside beside a chain-link fence and entered the office. A bell jingled when I went through the door, but there were no employees in sight behind the Formica-topped reception counter.

I called out, "Hello, anybody here?"

"Be right there," a voice yelled from the back.

A few moments later, a tall, sandy-haired, college-aged fellow burst through the inner door and gave me a sheepish smile. "Sorry about that. Got tied up with something. How can I help you?"

"I'm hoping you can answer a few questions for me."

"I'll do my best. What do you want to know?"

"A friend of mine is missing. I'm worried about him. He sent me his keys so I could check on things at his house. When he didn't return as expected, I looked around his house for clues about where he went. I found this key on his key ring, and I think it opens his storage unit. Could I be allowed to check it? You could go with me if you'd like to make sure I don't take anything."

A wariness came into his eyes. "What's his name?"

"Charlie Greer."

He shook his head. "The key is one of ours, alright, but I'm afraid I can't help. You're the second person asking about him this week. Have you gone to the police?"

"Not yet. I didn't really want to set off alarms. I'm not sure he'd be happy about that. Since he sent me his keys, I figured he's probably all right."

"Sorry, but our rules won't allow it."

"I understand." My shoulders slumped as I started to turn to leave. "Could you tell me anything about the other person asking about Charlie? Maybe it's someone I know."

"I didn't get his name. He was a middle-aged White dude."

"Did he have a key?"

"No, just a good line of gab. And he wasn't happy when I wouldn't cooperate." The kid was silent a moment. "We also had an attempted break-in a couple of nights after he was here. I wondered if he might be the culprit."

"Attempted?"

"Yeah. Our security system alerted the police, and whoever it was didn't get all the way in. He probably heard their sirens coming and left before they arrived."

"Did you get him on camera?" I asked, curious.

"Not really. Just some blurry pictures of a guy's back. I think he knew where the camera was located."

"Any chance I could take a look at the pictures?"

"Sorry. The police took the tape. All I can say is the guy looked about the same size as the one who came in earlier. I'm glad the owner of this place has decided to invest in a security dog now. I think we needed one." He smiled. "That's where I was when you came in. Trying to get Tiny organized in his kennel."

"Thanks for your help. Good luck," I said, and went out to my vehicle.

Chapter Thirteen

The next morning, I found Angie at her desk with her head buried in the local newspaper. "Wow! Front page of the feature section. Almost a full-page spread." She folded the paper and handed it to me. "Nice publicity, Beri. I'm impressed."

"Thanks. I read it at breakfast and thought they did a good job. Jack got a kick out of both his ride and getting his picture in the paper."

"The part about the photographer almost crashing the glider sounded exciting." Angie raised her eyebrows. "Maybe we need to increase our insurance?"

"Exciting doesn't cover it. *Terrifying* is a better word." I shook my head. "Our insurance is fine, but that's one part I wish they'd played down in the article. I'm not sure it will help attract potential customers."

Ross walked in from the hallway, picked up the newspaper from Angie's desk, and scanned the page. "Nice. You didn't mention you planned to do this."

"It came together so fast I didn't have a chance to fill you in. I had a conversation with a reporter friend of mine and suggested the article. I figured we could use some free publicity. He liked the idea so much he set up the photo shoot right away before his photographer left on vacation."

Ross tossed the paper back to Angie. "Could I talk to you for a minute, Beri?" He turned and headed back toward his office.

Inside his crowded office, Ross pulled a chair out of the corner for me. "Have a seat." He sighed and remained standing for a long moment before moving behind his desk to sit facing me. "It sounds like Jack had a good time."

"Yes, he loved it. I didn't have time to recruit an actual student for the shoot. Jack was happy to volunteer."

Ross smiled. "He's a good kid."

"Yes, I'm so lucky."

Ross cleared his throat. "I think you know what I want to talk to you about." He gave me a direct stare before he continued. "I don't like surprises when it comes to business, Beri." He paused. "You didn't tell me about the article. Consequently, I was embarrassed when the airport manager asked me about it this morning. I didn't know what he was talking about until he showed the paper to me. Also, as long as you were doing it, you could have promoted our overall flight instruction services. The write-up made it sound like all we do is teach people to fly gliders."

"I'm so sorry. I did mention our flying lessons here at Merrill Field to the reporter, but I focused on gliding because I wanted to advertise our new options."

"While we're on the subject, I have another bone to pick with you." Ross folded his arms across his chest and shook his head. "Angie tells me you paid the helicopter outfit that flew our glider off the beach out of your personal checking account. That's a business expense. Were you trying to hide it from me?"

"Of course not. I paid that bill because I felt responsible, that's all."

"Seems to me we've had a variation of this conversation before." He paused, stood up, and loomed over me. "Please remember, we're supposed to have a partnership here."

"I know I need to communicate better." I sighed. "Maybe we need to schedule an hour each day to talk. It's hit-or-miss now with students often scheduled late into the day."

"Good idea. Breakfast or lunch, maybe?" he asked.

"Yes, and on the subject of lunch while we're airing grievances, I have a question for you. Do you take all your female students out for lunch at Simons?"

Ross sat back down in his chair with a thud. "I was afraid you'd misinterpreted that. I was simply soothing her ruffled feathers after I flunked her on her flight maneuvers. She was devastated. And besides, we had some Diabetes Association business to discuss."

"I see. So, is she cancelling future lessons?"

"No. She's anxious to get back in the air and practice. She's more determined than ever to get her license."

"Uh huh." I wrinkled my nose. "I think something smells fishy."

"Why, Beri Quinn." Ross gave me that wicked smile of his. "I'm beginning to think you're jealous."

"Okay, maybe I am—just a little." I felt heat rising in my face and hoped it didn't show. "She's obviously set her sights on you."

Chapter Fourteen

"Glad you're finished," Angie said when I emerged from Ross's office. "That mysterious Mr. Heckenlively called and is anxious to talk to you. When I wouldn't tell him how to reach you, he insisted on scheduling an appointment at his office ASAP. He gave me the address, so I went ahead and made one. Better check to see if you can make it." She handed me a slip of paper with the time and room number written on it.

I scanned the paper. "I see the room number, but don't see an address."

"Oh, it's in the Federal Building."

"My schedule looks clear after lunch. I hope this meeting makes more sense than the last one."

The first student arrived, and before I knew it, I'd finished with both morning lessons. My stomach rumbled, reminding me I was hungry. After munching down a handful of almonds at my desk, I walked out to my SUV and headed to meet Jason Heckenlively.

The Federal Building on C Street had stood the test of time. Built before Alaska became a state, it was a solid, nondescript, light-colored building. Planters filled with vivid red and yellow flowers graced both sides of the main entrance, adding a note of cheer.

The security screener at the door asked me for my destination. I gave them my contact's name, but they didn't recognize Heckenlively's name.

"Yes, I'm sure the name is correct. It's not one I'd be likely to forget. His office number is 1257."

"Step to the side for a moment. I'll get someone to accompany you."

I stood waiting while the screener talked briefly on the phone. An echoey sound filled the high-ceilinged lobby as people headed to their various destinations. A few minutes later, a serious-faced security guard approached.

"Ms. Quinn, please follow me." He led me across the lobby to the last door in a bank of elevators. It bore a sign reading "Lower Level Only."

We stepped off on the lower of two levels and wound through several corridors until we reached an unmarked door with a security panel outside. The guard pressed his thumb against the plate and opened the door. We entered a small room with four plastic stack chairs in various colors and a bare coffee table.

"Here you go. Take a seat, and Mr. Heckenlively will be right with you."

The room was dimly lit. My eyes had barely adjusted to the lack of light when the government agent walked in, dressed as he was before in a gray suit and tie.

"Glad you could make it," he said and shook my hand briskly. "Why don't we go into the conference room? It's a bit more comfortable." He led me through an adjoining door into a larger room with a round table. He pulled out an upholstered chair for me before taking one himself.

Comfortable wasn't the word I'd have chosen to describe the room. Six cushy chairs surrounded the table. The only other feature was a small console with a sink and coffeemaker, a tray of mugs and condiments. Both the floor and the walls were bare.

"This is a strange place," I said. "I didn't realize this building had a lower level, much less two of them. The security team didn't recognize your name until I mentioned the room number."

He straightened the pad of paper and the row of pens on the table in front of him. "That's because I'm here on a temporary basis. They're not used to me yet."

"Okay. Enough with the mystery," I said, "please tell me what this is all about."

"Right." Heckenlively took a deep breath before continuing in a low voice. "Forces in our government have concerns about activities taking place within your former industry. It appears, for example, that proposals for mapping projects can serve as a bellwether for resource and land development of interest to our adversaries. Your former business, now called Northern Mapping, appears to have been using this information to purchase adjacent land under various company names to acquire critical properties. We're interested in you because we could use your expertise to insert valid competition into the bidding process. We need a better understanding of what is going on."

"You're asking me to compete for mapping projects?"

"Exactly. And, in the process, help us evaluate Northern Mapping's tactics." He looked up at me and smiled. "I understand you've succeeded in getting your business license as I asked. Now, we can get started."

I shifted uncomfortably in my chair. "So, what happens if I actually win one of these bids?"

"You'll do the job. Just as you've done in the past. It will further establish your credibility in the business."

"What were you referencing earlier when we talked about my Aleutian experience?"

"One of the key areas we are keeping an eye on, that's all. We want to have the ability to perform in that location if it becomes necessary."

"Let me get this straight. You want me to open a sham operation as a front for the government and act as though I've returned to the business I've practiced in the past."

"Exactly. Although I'd question using the word 'sham'. You *will* actually be in the business, and you'll be well paid for your efforts. We'll supply the infrastructure, and when the operation is complete, you'll retain ownership of any equipment we've supplied you."

"Amazing. Sounds too good to be true, which makes me suspicious. There's got to be a catch somewhere."

"Not really. The only difficulty for you will be keeping our involvement totally confidential. That is non-negotiable."

"You still haven't told me what agency I'd be working for." I paused. "Are we talking about the CIA?"

Heckenlively laughed. "Sorry, but you've got the wrong acronym." He held out his credentials. "You'll be working with the NGA—the National Geospatial Intelligence Agency."

"Never heard of it."

"Most people haven't, and we like it that way. Our job is to supply geospatial intelligence to the government, notably the military and other intelligence agencies. We're instrumental in fighting terrorism, assessing natural disasters, and planning for international events. It's been said we're the eyes of national intelligence. We primarily provide satellite and digital imaging as needed."

I frowned. "Sounds like you're a small offshoot of the CIA."

"Not that small. We have thousands of employees, and NGA is entirely separate from the CIA."

"With all that capability, why do you need me? Couldn't you accomplish more with your own experienced people?"

He leaned forward in his chair. "We could, but you offer some unique advantages. One of the biggest is that you are familiar with the Alaskan market. Plus, businesses in the state are familiar with you. They won't see you as an interloper without a track record here."

"Okay, say I'm convinced. If I work with you, would I have the ability to choose my own employees?"

"Yes, with the caveat that they pass scrutiny. Also, we'd have agency employees involved in the analysis of data. If you can give me a list of the potential employees you have in mind, we can get started on their background checks." He cleared his throat. "All employees will need to be kept out of the loop on our mission, of course."

I nodded. "Of course."

"I have a copy of our contract for your signature." He slid the document across the table to me. "As I've said, we need to move quickly so I hope you're prepared to make a decision now."

I scanned the pages, my eyes stopping cold on the salary line. "Wow! You certainly pay well. How about other staff? The ones I have in mind could start on a part-time basis until we get rolling."

"That's up to you. As long as they pass our security check. As for office space, we've acquired a lease in the name of AIA Mapping for the building adjacent to your current operation."

"The avionics shop? They've been there twenty years. How did you manage that?" I asked, surprised.

"Let's just say the price was right."

I paged through the rest of the contract. "If I sign the contract, will I be able to keep a copy?"

He shook his head. "No. You'll have to trust me on that."

"I'll at least need to have my attorney involved to review it."

"No, we can't allow that, either."

I pushed away from the table. "How do I know you're even who you say you are?"

"I'll be glad to show you my creds again, and if it would make you feel better, I understand an attorney named Gerald Sullivan is an acquaintance of yours."

"Sully? Yes, last year he helped me resolve a conflict with the local FAA office."

"He's within our security network and has worked with us on several projects in the past. I'm sure he'll vouch for us and offer you legal advice if you wish."

I nodded. "Yes, that would be helpful."

"If you want to wait until you meet with him, I'll bring the contract for your signature at that time. I suggest you call him tomorrow. I'd have asked him to attend this meeting, but he's out of town until tonight."

"I'll call him first thing in the morning." I rose from my chair.

"Before you leave, there's another item I need to discuss with you. We'll need you to participate in an equipment training class next week. I realize it will require juggling your current schedule." He smiled. "Don't worry about setting up the office. We'll take care of that. The current occupant has promised to be out by end of business today. If you have any specific requirements for the space, you can fill me in when we meet tomorrow."

"I can do that." I walked toward the door. "Do I need an escort to get out of here?"

He laughed. "No, I think you can find the elevator on your own."

I found the way out easily enough. The door to the elevator had barely closed when my cell phone rang, but when I tried to answer, I lost the connection.

Chapter Fifteen

As soon as I stepped outside the building, I checked the number for the call I'd lost. It was my home number. Something must be wrong. Dad almost never called me at work and Jack didn't, either.

I hit the button to call home, my fingers trembling.

"Mom?" Jack asked. "I don't feel good. Can you come home?" He sounded drowsy and unlike his usual chatty self.

"Of course. What's wrong, Hon?"

"I don't know. I just keep throwing up."

"What does Grandpa think?"

"He left before it started. He took his car in to be fixed." He coughed, and a few seconds of silence followed before he spoke again in a weaker voice. "I tried calling him, but he didn't answer."

"Probably didn't hear his phone in that noisy garage. Hang in there. I'm already on my way."

I called the office before pulling out of the parking lot and was surprised when Ross answered. "Hey, I was expecting to hear Angie's voice."

Ross chuckled. "She needed to take an early lunch, so I told her I'd cover."

"I'm calling to let you know I'm headed home. Jack's sick. He called as I left my meeting, and he sounded awful."

"Sorry to hear that. Tell him I hope he feels better soon. Take all the time you need. I can cover the lesson you had scheduled at four."

"Thanks. Sorry to have to ask." I paused. "Oh, and Ross, I need to talk to you tomorrow after work. Can you write me into your schedule?"

"Why so formal all of a sudden? You're always on my schedule. We talk every day."

I laughed. "True, but this will take some time."

"Any advance hints?"

"No, things are still evolving. I'll fill you in tomorrow." I started the engine of my SUV. "Love you, see you soon."

As I drove home, my mind was a jumble of worries about Jack and conflicted emotions about my future plans with Ross. How would he respond to the proposition I'd been offered? I needed to call the lawyer in the morning. I'd ask him if Ross could accompany me to the meeting. With all the emphasis on confidentiality, I wasn't sure what I could and couldn't say to him. It was such a good deal I couldn't turn it down, but Ross might not understand my pulling back from the business, especially since our partnership had barely begun.

The house was quiet when I opened the door. I dropped everything on the kitchen table and ran upstairs to Jack's room. I found him in bed with Tiger and Piper beside him. The kitten was snuggled close to the dog's side.

"Hi, Mom," he said in a low voice.

"How are you doing?" I kissed him along his hairline and placed my hand on his forehead. No doubt about it, he had a fever. "Let me get the thermometer before I call Dr. Baker's office."

"I don't want to go see the doctor," he said with a quaver in his voice. He grabbed the wastebasket sitting beside the bed and added to its contents. "I want to stay here."

"Sure, you do. I wouldn't want to leave home, either. Let me call the doctor and see what he thinks."

After I went downstairs to get Jack some water, I dialed and spoke to the nurse practitioner in the office.

"He has a temp of 103 degrees and frequent bouts of nausea and vomiting," I explained.

"Sounds like a virus that's been going around," the nurse said. "How long has he been sick?"

"Just since this morning."

"Try giving him Tylenol, and let's hope he can keep it down long enough to lower his temperature. Meanwhile, I'll call in a prescription for some suppositories to control the vomiting. Encourage him to take sips of fluids. Any sports drink high in electrolytes would be good. Call us back if he's still vomiting tomorrow. We don't want him to get dehydrated."

"Will do."

"And hang in there. If it's the virus we've been seeing a lot of lately, the good news is that it probably won't last long."

"I hope not. Thanks for your help." I disconnected and dialed Dad's number. Fortunately, he picked up and agreed to stop at the pharmacy on his way home.

Now to offer Jack some comfort and a variety of liquids. I climbed the stairs to deliver a glass of orange juice with a quick sprinkle of salt added to Jack. It wasn't a scientific solution, but it would do until Dad arrived.

The next morning, Jack was up early. Aside from his disinterest in breakfast, he seemed to be getting back to his normal self. I was glad to see it'd been just a 24-hour bug.

"Mom, look! Piper's getting much stronger. He just jumped off my bed."

"Good. Looks like you're stronger, too." I tousled his hair. "We'll know for sure that Piper's strong when he can jump back up."

"But Mom, he's so little. That would be a gigantic leap."

"True, but cats are good jumpers. It won't be long before he can."

"Is Gramps up yet? He's gonna take me out to the driving range this afternoon. I can't wait to practice my golf again."

I chuckled. "I'm glad you're feeling better, but don't overdo it. Why not hold off a day or two for golf. You might still be contagious."

"I promise I won't sneeze on anybody."

Exasperated, I shook my head. "I'll check with the doctor's office and let Gramps decide this one if they give the okay. I have to leave for work. My meeting starts in less than an hour." A wave of guilt washed over me at leaving him, but I pushed it aside as I left the house to start what promised to be a long day.

Sully's bald head gleamed from the light streaming through the wall of glass behind his desk. He stood and took my hand in both of his. "Beri! So good to see you again."

"Same here. I really need your help to resolve this latest dilemma. You certainly managed to pull me out of my fracas with the FAA last year. Once again, I seem to be in over my head."

"So, I hear, so I hear. Have a seat and tell me about it."

I sat and pulled my chair closer to his desk. "I understand you're acquainted with Jason Heckenlively and the NGA."

"Oh, yes. We've worked together a number of times. I'm sorry I couldn't recommend that Ross join us today, but they require stringent security measures for all their operations."

"I understand. My situation is related to a business proposition Jason has made me on the agency's behalf. It's an offer that is hard to refuse in many ways, but…"

"Let me guess. It sounds a little too clandestine to you?" Sully steepled his hands and gave me a direct look.

"Exactly. I'm not sure I can trust what he's telling me. That, and if I accept, it will mean changing my business commitment to Ross, who is my partner now. Since I saw you last, I purchased a half interest in his flight instruction business, and he counts on me to carry my weight. If I leave, he'll need to hire another instructor. It's a tough decision, especially since NGA is such an unknown entity and requires secrecy."

"Beri, I can assure you that Jason Heckenlively is on the up and up. He demands discretion because many of his operations have potential national consequences. You have nothing to worry about. If you decide to go with his proposal, I've drawn up confidential documents to protect your interests while also meeting his standards. Jason has already signed them, but shall I ask him to join us while we complete the legalities?"

"Yes, please. It's too good a deal for me to pass it up. I hope Ross will understand."

My mind made up, fifteen minutes later, Heckenlively joined us, and we signed and notarized the documents.

Before leaving, I gave Heckenlively the list of office requirements I'd prepared and left reassured, though dreading how to explain my decision to Ross.

Once back at the office, Angie informed me that my only flight instruction student for the day was scheduled for late afternoon after the fellow got off work.

Good. That will give me most of the afternoon to try to connect with Ross.

Chapter Sixteen

My explanation to Ross had to be postponed. He was engaged with students all afternoon. I used the time to catch up on things at my desk until Angie came in with the mail.

"You seem to have some anonymous correspondence there. Whoever it's from apparently had a lot to say, but at least it doesn't clink when I drop it."

I picked up a thickly padded envelope. "Charlie, again?"

"That's my best guess."

I put the envelope in my desk drawer and turned to read the other mail.

"Aren't you going to open it?" Angie asked, sticking around to watch.

"Yes, but I want to get through my work first."

"Don't be cruel. You know I'm dying to know what's inside that envelope."

I looked up at her. "I know whatever it is, you'll be unable to avoid giving me your opinion about it."

Angie laughed. "I'm not that bad, am I?"

"That's a definite yes." I opened the drawer. "I have to admit, I'm curious, too. Do you promise to keep this top secret?"

"Of course." She quivered with anticipation as I reached for my letter opener and surgically sliced the envelope open. As much as she complained about Charlie, his antics had captured her imagination.

Inside, I found a short note attached to a stack of hundred-dollar bills.

"I wasn't expecting greenbacks," Angie said. "What does the note say?"

"He's still worried about Gina. I am, too. She seems to have vanished without notice of any kind. Charlie wants me to use the money to hire a local private investigator to search for her."

"That's it?"

"Yes. That's it." I stuffed the note back in the envelope with the money.

"Huh," Angie huffed and started out the door. "Well, at least he isn't expecting you to do the looking."

I didn't mention that Charlie had also written a page authorizing me to check their storage unit. He said he'd hidden the key in his sock drawer where I'd already found it and asked me to inventory the contents of the unit so he'd know what Gina had taken with her. Finally, he said he'd call me in a few days after-hours when no one could overhear. That raised my curiosity. As I recalled, the cabin didn't have cell service. Was he still there?

I sat and considered his requests. A private investigator I could trust. The only problem was I didn't know any PIs, trustworthy or otherwise. Where to turn? I rejected the idea of asking Sully. No need to involve him in Charlie's issues. The only person who came to mind as an expert was Norm Underwood, an FBI agent I'd dealt with and considered a friend—at least on the racquetball court. He could be hard to catch, but I picked up the phone and dialed, hoping to find him in.

"Special Agent Underwood."

"Norm, it's Beri Quinn. How are you?"

"Fine, Beri. What are you tangled up in this time?"

I laughed. "Nothing to do with the FBI, I hope. I'm calling to ask if you could refer me to a good private investigator?"

"Sounds like you're involved in something questionable. Another murder, perhaps?"

"Not this time. I'm trying to help a friend find someone."

"A friend, is it?" He sighed. "I haven't dealt with many investigators outside the agency, but I've heard good reports about Wallace Killion."

"Thanks, Norm. I'll give him a call. Any chance you'd be up for a game of racquetball soon? I need a chance to get even after our last match?"

"Sounds good. I'll call you as soon as I can take a breather from my current case."

"Fair warning. I'll be practicing my serve in the meantime. Thanks, Norm." I ended the call and breathed a sigh of relief.

I called and made an appointment with Killion for the next day. I think I was talking to the man himself, which caused me to wonder if it was a one-man operation? At least I'd found a PI as instructed.

After my lesson, I left the office. As I climbed into my SUV, it occurred to me to call Dad and update him on my plans in case I ran late getting home.

"You're on your way to Forest Lake Storage Units? Now?" he asked.

"Yes. I expect to be there about an hour. After that, I have a meeting with Ross scheduled and it might take a while. I expect to get home late."

"Hmph. Didn't know you had a storage unit, but can I ask a favor while you're there?"

"Of course," I said.

"Could you pick up some photos from my unit?"

"Didn't know you had one, but sure. I'll need your key."

He chuckled. "Guess we're even then. I've had mine for years. Nothing much in it that would interest you, but I did include your name on the contract. They should give you access. If not, have them call me."

"Will do. What do you need?"

"Some historical photos of Providence Hospital I took back in the day. Look in the file cabinet to the left side of the door as you face it. You should find the folder in the third drawer."

"I thought we sold the film library when we sold the business."

"We did. But I kept hard copies of some of the more interesting subjects. My history buff genes, I guess. Anyway, the hospital is celebrating their centennial anniversary soon, and I wanted to donate my pictures of the old building on Minnesota Drive and L Street. It was demolished a long time ago."

"I'm sure they'll be happy to have them. Will the file be easy to find?"

"No worries. It's labeled and near the front of the drawer."

A lone pickup truck of ancient vintage was parked outside Forest Lake Storage. I took this as a good sign. The attendant should have time for my requests. I entered and greeted the same young man I'd spoken to before.

"You're back." He held out his hand to shake. "I'm Dillon. What can I do for you this time?"

"Same as before." I smiled and held out Charlie's note. "I need to check out Charlie Greer's unit. He asked me to inventory the contents for him. He sent me his key and this letter of authorization to give you." I slid both across the counter to him.

"Huh. Looks like his signature all right, but why didn't he just do it himself when he was here?"

I frowned. "He was here? He's not in town."

"I thought I saw his name on the sign-in page from my day off. Let me check." He ruffled through several pages before announcing, "Here it is," and turned the page around for me to see.

"Strange. Charlie didn't mention he'd been here." I shrugged. "Maybe he forgot to check something important. While I'm here, I also need the key to my dad's unit. His name is Frank Quinn and he said I'm listed on the contract."

Dillon tapped some keys on his computer and turned back to me. "Your name is Beri Quinn?"

I nodded. "Do you need ID?"

"Sure, if you don't mind."

I showed him my driver's license.

"I can't be too careful these days. The number for your dad's unit is 2317. I'll get you the key while you sign in. Please return the key when you leave."

"Thanks." I grabbed a map from the counter and located Charlie's unit in the outdoor section. Might as well get his done first. It should take only a few minutes to pick up Dad's photos after I finished.

I wandered a gravel path through a maze of identical doors until I located the right one. I dropped my tote and notebook on the ground, inserted the key into the padlock, and lifted the latch. As I bent to pick up my belongings on the ground behind me, a flash of light and a blast of percussive force threw me off my feet. Stunned, I lay face down on the concrete slab, breathing in smoke and the acrid scent of scorched wool.

I'd climbed to my knees before I realized I was smelling my own burning hair. Panic struck, I tore off my jacket and smashed it around my head to make sure the fire was out.

Once assured I wasn't in danger of further combustion, I turned to see what had happened. A black hole stared back at me. All that was left of Charlie's unit. A few flames still licked at the ruined contents.

Dillon ran up to me, his mouth shaping words I couldn't hear. Using my hands, I signaled my hearing was gone. I hoped it was only a temporary result of the explosion.

It looked like he was trying to ask what had happened. I spread my hands and lifted my shoulders to indicate I had no idea. The new guard dog's barking and some sort of alarm ringing created a cacophony of background sound that seeped through to my damaged ears.

Fortunately, a light rain helped limit the fire. To make sure it was out, Dillon grabbed a nearby fire extinguisher and sprayed the area. After he finished, he took me gently by the shoulder and mouthed something to my ear.

"I called 9-1-1," I think he said.

Chapter Seventeen

First responders were everywhere. Police, firefighters, and bomb disposal unit personnel examined every inch of the storage facility. Relocated to the parking lot, I stood waiting for Detective Diaz to release me so I could go home. I'd told both he and the first officers on the scene everything I knew. Now, I was anxious to jump in the shower and change my clothes. Nothing much was happening, except an ongoing search of each unit to eliminate the possibility of more explosives. I shifted my weight from one foot to the other in exasperation and was about to ask again if I could leave when Norm Underwood drove up. Not the FBI, too. Would the questions ever end?

Norm exited his vehicle and headed straight toward me.

"Why am I not surprised?" Norm said. "This incident wouldn't have anything to do with that friend you mentioned, does it?"

I cupped my hand around my ear to signal he should speak louder. "Yes, it was their unit that exploded when I unlocked the door."

"Their unit?" He frowned. "More than one friend then?"

"Not exactly." I described the details of what happened one more time and sighed. It had seemed like an innocent enough request at the time.

"Has the bomb unit found explosives in any of the other units?" Norm asked.

"You'll have to ask them, but I don't think so. They've kept me out here away from danger. I've told them all I know." I clutched my tote to my chest to help stop the shivering. "I'm anxious to go home, get warm, and clean up."

"I'll find out what's going on and see if they'll release you."

"Please do. The detective suggested the paramedics take me to the emergency room, but I'm okay. I lost my hearing for a while after the blast, but it's coming back now." I shook my head. "I just want this to be over."

An hour later, I was home. Angie had locked up the office early and picked me up since they wouldn't let me move my car from the parking lot. Jack and Dad were out playing golf and apparently didn't hear their phones when I tried to call them. That was a good thing, because it allowed me to delay telling them about the explosion until later. I did text Dad to tell him there'd been an incident at the storage units, but I was fine. Didn't want to scare him if he heard about it on the news.

I showered, shampooed my torched hair, and dressed in fresh clothes. Looking in the mirror, I still looked a fright. I grabbed a pair of scissors and whacked off a good three inches of my hair. The lower part of what remained was still frizzled, but I wanted to leave my hair stylist enough to work with. I was doomed to have a stubby ponytail unless she could work miracles.

A quick glance at the clock reminded me I needed to get back to the office to meet with Ross. I called a taxi and practiced my explanation of the NGA offer in my head as we drove. Ross was no fool. It would be a challenge to describe the proposal I'd accepted without explaining exactly what I was getting into. I didn't want him to ask too many questions.

Ross walked up to the car and opened the passenger door after we came to a stop in front of the office. "Let's talk over dinner. I'm starved." He stared at me for a moment. "What happened to your hair?"

"Guess you haven't been listening to the news today. It's a long story. I'll tell you over dinner. Meanwhile, where do you want to go?"

"How about La Cabana? Tacos sound good, and it's usually quiet enough for conversation."

"Margaritas?" Ross asked after we'd been seated.

"Sounds wonderful." I dove into the chips and salsa, suddenly ravenous.

"If you'll slow down on those, maybe you can tell me what's going on. Angie was gone when I got back from my last lesson."

"That was my fault. I called her to pick me up after the explosion."

His eyes wide, he asked, "Explosion?"

"Yes. That's what happened to my hair. When I unlocked a storage unit door, it exploded. I wasn't hurt, but my hair caught fire."

"This promises to be a long story. Go on… Why were you there in the first place?"

"My former glider student asked me to inventory his unit at Forest Lake Storage while he's out of town. He's trying to locate his missing girlfriend and thought it might help to know what she'd taken when she left. He's desperate for any clue. Also, Dad asked me to pick up some photos from the unit he has at the same location."

"All very interesting, but not what I assume you wanted to talk to me about."

"No." I reached across the table for his hand. "First, I want to apologize for the problems we've experienced with our partnership. I didn't expect it to be…be so difficult to make our joint operation financially stable."

"No apology necessary. We can make it work; it will just take some time."

"I'm not so sure. It could take years."

"Don't forget we still have most of the money you contributed to buy your half in the bank."

"Yes, you have a cushion, but that money should be compensation for your equity, not used to cover our deficits into the foreseeable future." I gave his hand a squeeze. "Besides, I have another plan that I hope you'll approve."

"Tell me about it." He gave me a doubtful look. "This better be good."

I launched into my spiel. "I received an offer completely out of the blue, to start a new mapping business to provide some specialized services for a government agency. They already have space leased in the building next to ours and have ordered the high-tech camera equipment the project requires. That's part of the reason I sold my business last year. The new technology is so expensive, I couldn't afford to move with the changes in the industry."

"What government agency, and what specialized services? This sounds questionable to me, Beri."

I smiled to reassure him. "Wait, it gets better. The agency came to me because I have experience with both mapping and flying in the Aleutians. I also have the security clearance required from working for the military in the past. And, this is the good part, when their projects are completed, I can keep the equipment as part of my compensation. There's also a generous salary, and they'll include Angie and Dean part-time, which will lessen your expenses." I gave Ross a sheepish grin. "I already have the business license. Time is critical on their project. They'd like to complete much of the work this summer if the weather cooperates."

"I don't know. Too good to be true stories always raise the hair on my neck."

"I had doubts at first, too, so I ran everything through Sully, the attorney I worked with last year. He said the agency is legit and I could trust them."

"All this without saying a single word to me until now? I don't understand the need to be so secretive." Ross avoided my eyes.

I could tell he was upset. But I knew he'd try to see my point of view. "Yes, I know I haven't been upfront with you. It all happened so fast I wasn't sure I could take it seriously at first. And much of what they told me requires a security clearance." I looked down at our joined hands. "On a brighter note, we'll still be neighbors. I can work as a back-up instructor for your students if you need me. I can also pay half our current staff's salaries, if we share their time."

"That could get complicated, but we are underutilizing their talents now." Ross furrowed his brow, his lips pressed in a tight line.

"True. I think they'd be happier if they had more to do, and I know they'd like a bigger paycheck." I tried to read his eyes. "What do you think?"

"I think you've already made the decision. I hope it's the right one." He rubbed the back of his head. "We'll have a lot of work to do to make it work. Let's start by discussing the changes with the staff tomorrow."

"I did it again, didn't I? Made a decision without you. Thanks for being patient with me." I kissed him. "I do want this to be fair for all of us, and I hope this latest venture proves to be more successful than the last scheme I proposed to you."

"Me, too. I'd hate for you to lose your status as my favorite business partner."

Chapter Eighteen

The alarm went off the next morning, and I pushed the snooze button. Something I rarely do. I slept another thirty minutes before dragging myself out of bed. The events of yesterday must have taken a greater toll than I'd realized.

I showered and dressed in a hurry, ran a brush through my damaged hair, and stumbled downstairs.

"You look like you've been hit by a truck," Dad said.

"Good morning to you, too." I gave Jack a quick peck on the cheek as he stood at the sink helping his grandpa peel potatoes.

"We're making hash browns," Jack said and brandished his peeler with a flourish.

I wished I had a camera handy to capture this uncommon scene. Jack usually entered the kitchen only to find something to eat.

Dad dried his hands and slid a barstool over to me. "Thanks for the text you sent me yesterday. It was good to get a heads-up, but my curiosity has been killing me. Haven't seen much on television."

I filled him in. "The good news is the explosion didn't appear to damage any other units. Yours seemed fine, but the bad news is that I wasn't able to access it to look for your photos. I'll try again when they take the crime scene tape down."

"No rush. I haven't mentioned it to anyone on the anniversary committee yet. No one is anxious for me to deliver them."

"I'll get them soon. I have to go back anyway."

Jack looked confused. "What happened?"

"I ran into a little excitement at the storage unit yesterday. I'm late getting to work, so I'll let Gramps fill you in."

"Before you leave, Sarah and I want to invite you and Jack to a special dinner at the Crow's Nest on Friday. Be sure to bring Ross, too."

"What's the occasion?"

"You'll see." He turned back to his task.

I wasn't sure, but I thought he was blushing.

I called Dean and asked him for a ride. He arrived at my house and greeted me with a surprised look when he saw my hair.

"Please, don't ask questions. I'll explain later."

"You got it, Boss," he said. "Where to?"

"I gave him directions to the parking lot, thanked him after we arrived at our destination, and walked to my SUV to drive to visit my hair stylist. She had agreed to fit me in for a much-needed emergency appointment.

Afterward, looking human again, I arrived at the new office to meet Heckenlively for a walk-through. I'd already taken a peek at the Cessna 180 and turbo 320, both with camera holes in their bellies, moored in the adjacent tie-down area outside. Both were types of planes I'd flown in the past.

"You've been busy." I turned toward Heckenlively. "I'm impressed with how much you've accomplished in so little time."

He straightened his posture before speaking. "We have an excellent team. It helps that planning started some time ago."

"I like the reception area. Looks like you followed the schematic I gave you to the letter."

"The computer stations are even more impressive. Double triple screens on them all. I've set up a training to introduce you to the finer points of LIDAR—Light Detection And Ranging." He walked through the rows of consoles and entered a large room with layout tables and equipment storage.

My fingers moved reverently over the LIDAR and digital cameras. It was hard for me to comprehend the monetary investment they represented. "Impressive," I said. "I'm anxious to learn how their operation differs from my old film equipment. Do they require having a cameraman aboard the plane?"

"Yes, but we call them operators now." He smiled. "I'll introduce you to yours tomorrow. Most of the finer points will be handled by the operator, but you'll need to understand what's required. There'll be some adjustments to make with the laser technology, but it has many advantages. For instance, you can take pictures in the dark."

"Amazing," I said as I turned to face him. "I still don't understand why you don't use satellite photography."

"The laser technology we need isn't efficient from space. It takes too long for the laser beams to hit the ground and bounce back."

"How does the weight of this equipment compare to our old Zeiss camera?"

He paused. "I'm not sure. Together, they weigh in the 500-pound range."

"That could be a problem flying to the Aleutians, the distance there is so great. With my old camera, my total run-out range with a cameraman was about 1,200 miles. That equipment weighed about 280 pounds. With the turbo-charged Cessna 320 I saw parked outside, we could have a problem with the additional weight restricting our range. It's a long way between gas stops out there."

"Hmm... I'll get on that. Finding a longer-range airplane with camera hole already installed could take a while. I'll see what we can do." Heckenlively took his phone out of his pocket and dialed.

I left him to his call and walked next door to pack a few things to transfer to my new office. If I hurried, I could be semi-organized in time to leave for my lunchtime meeting with the private investigator.

Wallace Killion sat waiting for me at a table near the back of the restaurant. He'd told me to look for a redhead with glasses, and I spotted him immediately. His hair wasn't just red, it was an orange-red with accompanying freckles. He stood as I approached and held out his hand to shake.

"Wallace Killion. You must be Beri Quinn."

"Yes. Glad to meet you." I sat in the chair he'd pulled out and pondered how to explain my mission.

"You look perplexed. How can I help?" he asked.

"Sorry. I was wondering how you manage to be inconspicuous with your striking hair? I would think it could cause difficulties in your line of work."

He laughed. "At times, yes. I've found keeping it short and wearing a hat works well. Occasionally, I've resorted to wearing makeup to cover my freckles. Sounds like you may have undercover work in mind."

"Not really. At least I don't think so."

We were interrupted by the server who took our orders for coffee. "They have wonderful scones, if you're interested. I'm going to have a blueberry one." He smiled at the waitress who made a note on her pad.

"Sounds good. I'll have one, too," I said.

Once we were alone, I explained Charlie's request to find his missing girlfriend and summarized the situation. "Her name is Gina Figgins. I asked him for a photograph, but I haven't received one yet. I also didn't find one in their home."

"Let me get this straight. I'm looking for a woman we know almost nothing about, who was last seen leaving for a tennis lesson. No sign of her at their home and no communication with Charlie since the shooting at Birchwood. He asked you to inventory their storage unit to see if she'd taken anything when she left, but you were unable to do so because it exploded. An employee of the storage business told you Charlie himself had visited the unit a few days before the explosion, and you haven't been in communication with Charlie since that happened. He feels threatened and is keeping his location under wraps. He communicates with you only by Tundra Talk or mail. Does that cover it?"

"Yes. I know it sounds crazy, but that's what I'm dealing with. Will you give it a try?"

"I like a challenge," he said. "Ask Charlie for more details about Gina. Relatives or friends, quirks, hobbies, education, former places of employment, Social Security number, credit card numbers, if he has them—anything we can use to find her. And emphasize that I need a photo."

"I will, and I made a copy of his note with the information he's given me. I also met a neighbor lady who knew Gina, Caroline, I don't know her last name, at the house next door. I'll try to contact Charlie today. No telling when he'll get back to me, though."

"Save the envelope if he sends anything by mail." Wallace stood, took one last bite of his scone, and took a business card from his wallet. "Contact me as soon as you get a response."

"Of course." I glanced at the card. "You only have a phone number listed. Why no address?"

"I guess I'm a little like Charlie," he said. "I like to keep my whereabouts to myself."

Chapter Nineteen

Later that same afternoon, I stopped by the police department to give my official statement regarding yesterday's events. Detective Diaz asked all the same questions I'd answered before and videotaped my answers. I'd hoped to learn if they had any leads in the case, but they remained tight-lipped. Or maybe they were as clueless as I was. They asked if I thought anyone was intentionally trying to harm me, and who would know I'd be there. I couldn't come up with anyone unless it was the person who I believed had impersonated Charlie. I assured them that I didn't believe Charlie himself wanted to harm me.

I called home and asked Dad if he had started dinner. Since he hadn't, I suggested that I pick up Jack and take him out for burgers, followed by a trip to the unusual driving range he'd been bugging me about. I wanted to spend more time with Jack, and I might be tied up with work later when the new job was fully underway.

"You're taking him to Fox Hollow?" Dad asked in surprise.

"I think that's what he called it. Why?"

"That's the huge tent facility off Ingra. The same place that was so controversial when it went in some years ago. It might be expensive."

"Didn't know about the controversy. Guess I missed that news cycle. What was the issue with it?"

"I'm sure it's fine as a golf facility, especially for winter practice, but some people thought it was an eyesore and ruined the ambiance of the city. I've heard that's why the owners eventually painted it to blend in with a tree and mountain motif."

"I've wondered how they keep it from collapsing under a load of snow in the winter."

"Air pressure. That's how they manage to have the wide-open spaces they need to hit golf balls. No structural impediments. They just force air in to control the pressure and temperature inside the dome."

"Sounds more high-tech than it looks. It'll be interesting to check it out up close. Will you ask Jack to have his clubs ready when I get home?"

"Will do, Cupcake."

I'd no sooner parked outside the Fox Hollow tent painted in the blues and greens of the landscape when my phone's chime sounded. I accepted the call and motioned to Jack to go ahead, that I'd follow in a few minutes.

"I'll check it out, Mom." Jack jumped out of the vehicle, grabbed his clubs from the back, and dashed inside.

"Good news!" Heckenlively announced as I held the phone to my ear. "I think I've just solved our weight problem. Thought you'd want to know."

"Great," I said, surprised. "How did you accomplish that so fast?"

"Like I said before, I have a good team. I'll give you the details tomorrow."

"Sounds good. See you then." I ended the call and locked the car. As I turned toward the structure, someone shoved me against the side of the driver's side door.

A masculine voice behind me growled, "Where is Charlie Greer? Tell me. I've had enough of your meddling." He slammed my shoulder again, this time into an adjacent truck. The large man was dressed in a tan jacket and jeans. He had a dark beard and an intense dark-eyed stare. Was this the same guy who rang Charlie's doorbell? I didn't get a good look at him then before Caroline intercepted him.

"I don't know where he is," I said, keeping my voice steady despite my fear.

"Drop the act or you'll end up like that tow pilot of yours. You'd better…"

I looked past him to see Jack standing outside the tent entrance. He started coming toward the SUV. "Mom, hurry up. I need you to pay them so I can get started."

The bruiser who'd accosted me let go and disappeared behind vehicles parked nearby.

I double-checked to make sure I'd locked the doors and followed Jack inside. I thought fast. *How did this guy find me here of all places?* Either he followed me from the house or put a tracker on my car while it was parked at the storage unit parking lot. I'd have to call the police with an addendum to my report tomorrow. And ask them to check for hidden trackers.

Jack led me to the counter where I paid for his use of one of the driving stalls and a bucket of balls. He pulled his driver from his bag and shoved the rest of his clubs over to me. "Here, Mom. Watch these please."

Still a bit shaky, I found a seat and watched him whack golf balls with great enthusiasm. It did seem to me that he was hitting the ball a long distance for his size.

"That your boy?"

I turned to see Detective Diaz standing beside me. "Yes, my son, Jack."

"He has an impressive swing. Does he play much?" He sat down on the bench beside me to watch.

"Not as much as he'd like, but he plays more when he's with his dad in Arizona."

"That's golf country all right," he said. "I used to play there myself. I was a pro at one of the resorts there."

"You're full of surprises. I'd never have guessed you weren't a lifelong Alaskan."

"Not quite. Got here about ten years ago after I decided to join the force." He rolled the club he held between his palms. "Still love the game, though. Was glad when this place went up."

"I didn't expect to see you again so soon after giving my statement, but it's actually good timing. I had an uncomfortable encounter in the parking lot just now that might be related."

"What happened?" he asked, concern showing on his face.

I described what had transpired. "Whoever the man was, he knew about the shooting at Birchwood and threatened the same would happen to me if I didn't tell him where Charlie was hiding."

"Did you tell him anything?"

"How could I? I don't know. Besides, Jack came out looking for me and scared him off." I pulled my jacket closer around me. "I'm nervous about going out there with Jack when he finishes. For all I know, the guy may be waiting."

"I'll go with you," Diaz said. "I'd like to get a look at him."

"I'd appreciate that," I said.

Diaz, true to his word, waited with me until we were ready to leave. I introduced him to Jack, who was happy to meet a former golf pro.

Nothing happened as we approached the car. "Looks like all is well, but I wonder how he found me here. Anyway, thank you so much for your help."

"Be sure to let me know if anything else happens," Diaz said. "I don't know what's going on, but I know it's not good."

Once we arrived home, I scrutinized the vehicle carefully to see if I could find a tracker but found nothing. I'd forgotten to mention the possibility to Diaz. I asked Jack to slide under the car with a flashlight, but he didn't see anything odd, either.

"What are we looking for, Mom?"

"Just checking to make sure nothing is stuck under there." I wasn't convinced our search was thorough enough, but there wasn't anything obvious.

Chapter Twenty

It was official. Today was my first full day in my new office. It didn't take long to move my things. Less than two hours after I'd started, I stashed my last load, my survival gear, into a closet behind my desk. As I made a mental note to purchase a gun safe, Heckenlively entered the room, accompanied by a diminutive man in his early forties.

"Beri Quinn, I'd like you to meet Mickey Ford, your new sidekick."

The man flashed a smile that lit up his eyes. "Glad to meet you."

We shook hands. He surprised me with the firmness of his grip.

Heckenlively puffed out his chest. "I told you our team was stellar. We managed to find you a top-notch aerial photography operator who weighs in at an even one hundred pounds." He smiled. "Mickey is a former jockey. If you follow the horses, you may have heard of him. He's highly regarded in the sport."

I smiled. "Sorry, I haven't followed the racetrack circuit, but I'm happy you've agreed to join us."

"I'm excited to be here with y'all," Mickey said. "I'm anxious to check out Alaska. I've always wanted to see this state."

"As soon as Jason gets you oriented, I can help with that. I was born here. Meanwhile, I want to test-fly the aircraft outside. I'm familiar with both models but haven't flown either of these planes. You're welcome to come along."

"That would be great. I'd especially like to join you when you take the twin."

"Sure. I'll fly the 180 first to give you time to get settled. I'll let you know when I'm ready to take the twin out."

The sky was clear with unlimited visibility as the sun glistened off the waters of Cook Inlet. My spirits rose with the plane as I took off and made a wide circuit of Anchorage, then a short distance up toward Turnagain Arm, past the Alyeska Ski Resort. After thirty minutes, I forced myself to head back to Merrill Field. I hated to return so soon, but I had too much to do to fly for pleasure alone.

When I returned to the office, Mickey sat by the front door studying the operating manual for the digital camera. "Ready when you are, Beri."

"How about you meet me at the twin in fifteen minutes? That'll give me time to get my act together."

I transferred the survival gear to the baggage compartment of the twin and proceeded through my pre-flight checks.

Mickey walked out to meet me. "All set?"

"Sure am. Climb in and let's go." I called Merrill ground. "This is 7415 Quebec at AIA Mapping requesting taxi for takeoff. I have information, Bravo."

"Okay, 15 Quebec. Proceed to runway two-four."

Once at the run-up area, I checked mags, fuel mixture, trim, oil pressure, and flaps, then called the tower and was cleared for takeoff.

After we lifted off the runway and reached an airspeed of 110 mph, I pulled the gear up and continued climbing. I turned to the south and flew lateral to the Chugach Mountains.

Mickey gasped.

"Beautiful mountains, aren't they?" I asked.

"No. I mean yes, but I think I see smoke coming out of the wing on this side."

I looked back, and sure enough, a white cloud billowed from that side. I checked the left side and found the same was true there. The main fuel gauges looked okay. The auxiliary gauges were another story. They were dropping, even though the new tanks weren't engaged. *Must be a problem with the newly installed auxiliary fuel tanks.*

Keeping my cool, I radioed in. "Merrill Tower, 15 Quebec. Need to return for landing. I have a fuel leak problem."

"Cleared to land number one. Runway of your choice. Wind direction ATIS still current."

"Roger. Landing on two-four."

We landed without incident with two fire trucks chasing us down the runway. I explained to the fire crew what had happened and thanked them for being there for us in case we'd needed them. We taxied uneventfully to our old hangar. I wanted Dean, the mechanic I trusted most, to take a hard look at the aircraft.

Mickey opened the door and stumbled out. Once I'd followed him, he turned to face me. "Good job. You didn't even seem nervous, but I can tell you I was plenty scared. What do you think went haywire?"

"It wasn't smoke you saw. It was vaporized fuel. The main gauges were steady, but the new aux tanks were dropping. My suspicion is that the new fuel tanks weren't installed correctly." I shook my head in disgust. "I'm guessing the plane wasn't test flown after the job was completed. Once my mechanic takes a look, we'll know for sure."

I headed toward the open hangar door. Mickey followed close on my heels, rubbing the tension from his shoulder as he walked.

"Will you report the incident to the FAA?" he asked.

"I don't think it's necessary since I didn't declare an emergency."

"You could have fooled me about that." Mickey shook his head. "Have you considered using drones on this job?"

"Why?" I asked. "Did this experience scare you off airplanes?"

"No, I just wondered. We used them a lot in my previous job."

"I know they're popular for some projects, but I haven't heard them mentioned for this one. It may have to do with security issues."

I spotted Dean's small frame lying on his back working on an engine. When I spoke, he slid forward and rose to his feet, all five feet two inches of him. I introduced the two men and explained the situation to Dean. He wiped his oily hands on a rag and shook hands with Mickey.

"Can you give the plane a thorough overall inspection for me please?" I asked. "I don't know a lot about its history."

"Will do, Boss."

"Thanks, Dean. You're the best."

As usual, he avoided eye contact, but a grin spread across his face. "I'll call you when I finish."

While we walked toward the office, Mickey asked, "He's an Alaskan Native?"

"Yes, he's Yupik from Bethel. Grew up around airplanes, and he's saved my bacon more than once. He's not very talkative, but when he does speak, I listen."

"Nice to meet another vertically challenged guy. Hope I can get to know him."

Before leaving for lunch, I stopped by the hangar to check with Dean again about the plane. He filled me in on what he'd found and said he could fix the problem by tomorrow. I sighed with relief, thanked him, and went inside the old office to talk to Ross.

I found him sitting at his desk, poring over a stack of paperwork. He looked up and gave me a big smile. "Hello, stranger. I miss you already. Glad you stopped by."

"Hello to you, too," I said. "Thought I'd better touch base with you to confirm we're still on for the dinner with Dad and Sarah tomorrow night."

"Sure, it'll be nice to see them, and nicer still to spend more time with you. I'm already missing having you in the same building."

I laughed. "It's only been a day, but life has been hectic lately."

"I'm trying to give you the space you need for this start-up, but I have to admit, it's painful."

"Yes, I know. It's hard for me, too."

"It'll be good to see Frank again, but I have to wonder what's behind the sudden invitation?" He squeezed my hand and pulled me close for a kiss. "Now, that's more like it," he smirked. "What's behind the sudden invitation, anyway?"

"I'm not sure. When I asked, he was evasive, but I have my suspicions."

"Sooo?"

"I'm thinking it has something to do with Sarah. He's been seeing a lot of her lately."

"Unlike another couple I know." Ross stood and placed his hands on my shoulders and bent down to touch his forehead to mine. "Are we good?"

"We're good. Very good," I said as I moved into his embrace. The scent of his sandalwood after-shave made me hunger for something more than lunch.

After a quick stop at a fast-food drive-through, I returned to the new office and found Angie and Jason Heckenlively deep in discussion. Their conversation stopped when I approached.

"Everything all right?" I asked.

"Sure," Angie replied. "Mr. H. just asked me to pick up some documents from our competition across the runway."

"Do they know you're coming?" I asked.

"Yes, I talked to them about it," Jason said. "They're expecting her."

"Okay, I'm off," Angie said. "Just know it'll take me a while to get used to playing nice with the enemy." She grinned and headed out to the parking lot.

I turned toward Jason. "I just talked to Dean, my mechanic, about the problem we had with the twin. He said whoever installed the auxiliary tanks put them in backwards. He also said it was an easy mistake to make if the mechanic hadn't done it before, but it doesn't give me much confidence in your team's mechanic. The plane should've been test flown before handing it off to you. I'm planning to ask Dean to do any future mechanical work we need on the planes. We've already agreed to use him part-time."

"Agreed. It will mean more paperwork, but I can deal with it. I'll file an incident report with our maintenance office so they can provide some needed training for their guys."

"Thanks, you won't regret it. Dean's work is always top-notch."

Jason picked up a bundle of paper and handed it to me. "Since the planes are operational, I hope you can get to work on the proposals. This packet contains RFPs and other particulars you may need to complete them. Look them over and let me know if you have questions. It's also time to start keeping a keen eye on weather patterns in the Aleutians."

I cocked an eyebrow. "Here we go. I hope the weather cooperates, and we can get the job done this summer. I've lost track of how many missions I've had to scrub due to bad weather."

"At least the LIDAR will work in our favor. We shouldn't have as much trouble with light and weather conditions as we would with the old camera equipment."

"True, to an extent at least. The weather might not matter as much for pictures, but it's still critical for flying out there."

Chapter Twenty-One

Requests for grant proposals cluttered my desk. I'd sifted through them, choosing those that looked promising enough to consider. Tedious work, but Jason had annotated them with his suggestions which helped to narrow the possibilities.

I completed the most promising ones and asked Angie to submit them right away. The remainder I divided into two piles and stashed the more favorable ones on top of my desk for future reference and dropped the rest into a bottom drawer.

My cell phone chimed. Seeing Ross's name pop up on the caller ID, I answered.

"Beri, I'm picking you up for dinner tonight, right?"

"Looking forward to it. I'll have Jack with me, if you don't mind. Dad's taking Sarah."

"No problem. I haven't seen my buddy since he got home. It'll be nice to catch up with both of you."

"The reservation is for seven. Can you get to the house about twenty minutes earlier?"

"I'll be there."

I hung up the phone, finished clearing my desk, and stood to leave when Mickey walked through my office door.

"Have a minute for a couple of questions?" he asked.

"Anytime." I looked at my watch. "I'm at your disposal now for about fifteen minutes. I have to leave then. If you need longer, we can talk again tomorrow."

"Fifteen minutes is fine. I've been wondering just what kind of flying we'll be doing. Your conversation with the boss about my weight and the Aleutians confused me. What's that about anyway?"

"I don't know what Jason has told you, but the details of the job are vague due to security issues. He's planning a major project that will involve flying to Adak out on the chain. Your size is an advantage because it is a long flight to get there, and we won't be able to stop for gas midway. Since our equipment is heavy, we need to keep other weight aboard down to allow us to carry maximum fuel."

"Ah. Makes sense." He chuckled. "It's the first time other than horse racing that my size has been an advantage. It was always a thorn in my side growing up. Especially with two brothers over six feet tall calling me 'Pipsqueak'."

"It's definitely an advantage working for us on this job."

"My brothers will be jealous I'm working in Alaska. I was the sickly one growing up and had to take a medication that stunted my growth. I dreamed of becoming Mr. America when I grew up but only managed to grow to five feet tall."

"You look healthy now, and you got the fitness part right. I'll appreciate having some muscle along. Our equipment is heavy, even with the two of us."

"I became a gym rat. Tried to make up in muscle what I lacked in height."

I laughed. "I'll remember that when we have to load the planes."

"When do you expect we'll leave for the Aleutians?"

"I have no idea. The weather will be the deciding factor, and the area is notorious for marginal weather conditions. We'll have to watch and wait for a good pattern."

"Thanks. I think I understand the plan now, and I know you have to go. See you Monday unless you call me in this weekend."

"If the weather over one of our projects looks good, I'll give you a call. It doesn't seem likely right now, though. You'll probably have a chance to explore on your own for a couple of days." After Mickey left, I quickly got my things together and went home.

The doorbell rang, and I heard Jack run to the door. "Hi Ross. She's almost ready."

Ross shook his hand. "Great to see you again. Hear you shined up your golf game while you were down in the desert."

"Yeah. I played a lot. Thirty-six holes some days," Jack said. He stood straighter, proud of his progress.

"We'll have to play a round one of these days, so you can show me your skills. Probably teach me a thing or two."

I watched from the stairs as Jack's face brightened.

"That would be super, Ross. I haven't had many chances to play since I got home." He bounced on his toes in excitement.

I came down the last few steps and joined them. "You're a little early." I gave Ross a quick kiss on the cheek.

"Not that early," he said. "Guess I was anxious to see you all decked out. Love the dress. Black is definitely your color."

I felt my face flush. "Thanks. I ordered it online because I wanted something special for the occasion—whatever the occasion is."

We climbed into Ross's Jeep and drove to the Captain Cook, a premier hotel in the state built shortly after the 1964 earthquake by Wally Hickel, Sr., a former governor of Alaska. We parked and entered the lobby. Jack's eyes lit up as we passed a full-sized polar bear showcased in his acrylic habitat.

When we reached the elevators, Ross punched the button for the eighteenth floor. "Your dad's really going all out, treating us to dinner at the Crow's Nest."

"I think he wants tonight to be a memorable occasion," I said.

"It looks cool," Jack said after the elevator opened, and we walked into the nautically-themed restaurant with its view of Cook Inlet and the city below.

The host showed us to a table adjacent to the window, near the end of the dining room. A candle-lit lantern flickered in the center of the round table.

Dad was already seated next to an attractive woman who appeared to be in her fifties. He stood to greet us and introduced us to Sarah, a big grin on his face.

"I feel like I already know you," I said. "Dad has mentioned your name once or twice."

Sarah looked over at him, her striking brown eyes glowing in the candlelight. She turned to me, smiled, and said, "I feel the same about you and Jack. I've heard your names mentioned often, too, and Ross. It's such a pleasure to finally meet all of you."

The host stood, waiting to seat us. He pulled out my chair and distributed our menus.

After he left, I blurted, "So what's up, Dad?"

"Let's wait until we order," he said.

The server appeared, and we ordered cocktails.

"I don't want a Shirley Temple," Jack said. "Just a lemonade, please."

"Sure thing," the waiter said with a smile.

We ordered our food when he returned with the drinks. The men ordered steaks, the waiter wincing when Jack ordered his well-done with catsup. Sarah and I ordered dilled halibut piccata.

Dad glanced at the wine list. "Now, I have a dilemma. Do you want red or white?"

"May I suggest an excellent Pinot Noir?" the waiter asked.

"Whatever you think," Dad said, "and add a bottle of Dom Perignon following our meal, please. We're celebrating."

As soon as the waiter left, Sarah said, "I'm glad you are finally getting around to making the announcement. I'm tired of sitting on my left hand." She tossed her silvery curls and jabbed Dad with an elbow.

At our questioning looks, she held up her hand to show off the diamond engagement ring sparkling on her third finger.

"Dad! You finally popped the question. Congratulations!" I stood and gave Sarah a hug.

"Congratulations," Ross said. He shook Frank's hand. "I'm sure you'll be very happy."

Jack piped up. "Does this mean you won't be making me breakfast anymore?"

"Yes," Frank said. "I'm afraid it does. I'll be moving in with Sarah when we return from our honeymoon." He winked at his grandson. "You're getting to be such a good cook that you don't need me to cook for you now anyway."

I gave Dad a sideways look. "May I ask how long you've been keeping this secret?"

"Almost a week," he said. "It will cause one complication, though. We'll need to ask a favor."

"Sure," I said. "What can we do?"

"Remember that promise I made to Jack—to take him to Nome with me to make my annual gold claim visit? I'm hoping you can go in my place, Beri."

"Oh." My voice fell a couple of octaves. "Will the Jeters be okay with us going? Do we stay with them?"

"I'll let them know. I usually stay only a couple of days." He turned to Sarah and squeezed her hand. "We need to travel to Seattle so I can meet her two sons. She wants them to give us their blessing."

"I'm sure we can make it work," I said, wondering how I'd fit this unexpected turn of events into my already complicated schedule.

Chapter Twenty-two

The drive to Birchwood the next morning offered a peaceful interlude to reflect on the changes taking place in my life. First, I strained my relationship with Ross by making a major decision without consulting him. Fortunately, he'd forgiven me and had agreed to the new plan. Next, I learned I was about to acquire a stepmother and the inevitable accompanying change in my relationship with my father. I'd seen that one coming of course, but it still represented a major shift. Although I was in my early thirties, I knew I had an innate resistance to change. It was something I hadn't recognized in myself before, always associating the trait with senior citizens.

When I arrived at the Birchwood airstrip, I found my student waiting. I'd scheduled her for bi-weekly lessons before starting my new job. She stood beside the already assembled glider, waiting for me. She was always eager to get started and often arrived early.

"Hi," she said. "Since I got here first, I asked Pete, our tow pilot today, to help me attach the wings."

"Great." I walked around the sailplane and checked the connections. "Sounds like you're anxious to get into the air. I'll grab him, and we can move out to the runway, if he's ready."

"He's ready. I already checked."

I smiled at her. "You're making my job too easy." We checked for possible traffic before placing the glider at the end of the runway.

Pete approached and positioned his Super Cub ahead of the glider, attached the tow rope to the plane, and handed me the other end. I attached it to the glider, climbed in, settled into my seat behind my student, and closed the canopy. At our signal, the plane's pilot applied power. We sped down the runway and lifted into the air behind the plane. As we circled, gaining altitude, my student glanced back at me, her eyes shining with excitement. I felt a swell of pride as she flawlessly found lift, released the rope, and rose higher above the ridge.

I realized I'd chosen my career path for this very feeling. I enjoyed teaching others to fly and the sense of solitude and freedom it could bring. Soaring, so quiet and graceful, offered an even greater boost to my spirits than flying motorized aircraft. I hoped my students shared this sensation. It made me wonder though, why I was now choosing to move my career in a different direction.

I pondered this for the twenty minutes we stayed aloft without reaching a conclusion. Was it the friction with Ross, the financial straits we experienced, or a sense of duty to support my government? I had to admit the overall challenge played a role, but so did the high-tech equipment and potential financial reward the contract offered.

We landed the glider without incident and together returned the sailplane to its trailer. She thanked me and turned to leave. I touched her arm to stop her. "You won't need me as a backseat driver any longer. Your performance today convinced me that you're ready to be certified." I signed her logbook with my recommendation and handed it back to her.

"Thanks, Beri." She gave me a grin that lit up her face and waved good-bye.

I walked inside the office to ask if anyone knew of other glider pilots with instructor ratings in the area. I needed to find a referral before I discontinued lessons. To my surprise, seated inside the door was Sarah, my soon-to-be stepmother.

"Beri. You're back already. I didn't even see you land." She stood and hugged me, her curly hair tickling my chin. "Darn, I wanted to watch that."

"How did you know I'd be here?" I asked.

"Ross told me. I hope you don't mind my meeting you here."

"Of course not. I hope nothing's wrong."

Sarah smiled and shook her head. "No, nothing like that. I wanted to talk to you alone, that's all. Let's go for a walk, and I'll explain."

We traipsed side-by-side along the gravel road, inhaling the pungent scent of the wild onions growing along the edge.

"I sensed last night that we might be expecting too much to ask you to take Frank's place for the trip to Nome. I know you're under a lot of stress getting this new business of yours underway, and I wanted you to know we could delay our trip to visit my boys. Frank can go ahead with the Nome trip, and we'll schedule our visit to the Lower 48 after he returns."

"No need to wait," I said. "When my dad is on a mission, it's a mistake to get in his way. I'm sorry if I gave you the impression it would be a problem. You two should go ahead with your plans."

"Frank is the one who's in a hurry. Once he decided we should get married, he was suddenly in a rush."

I laughed. "He's like that, isn't he? Once a decision is made, he's raring to go."

"I'm flattered he's anxious, but I wanted you to know we can easily wait until he returns from checking his claim."

I stopped walking and draped an arm around her shoulder. "What do you say we head back to our cars and drive into town for some lunch? I'm hungry, and I'd love to get better acquainted with my new stepmom."

I felt a rush of affection for this sweet woman. I considered her the perfect person to make my dad happy, and she might help fill the void I'd felt most of my life after my mother deserted us years ago.

Jack was ecstatic when I gave him the news that we were leaving for Nome the following day. With a poor weather outlook in the Aleutians,

Jason had agreed with my plan to take a long weekend off work. "Family is important," he'd said.

Jack had settled down by the time Dad showed up to deliver the plane tickets and to advise us what to expect once we arrived.

"Gramps, I wish you were going with us."

"Wish I could, Jack. Next year, I hope the two of us can go, but I think your mom will enjoy meeting the Jeters."

Jack looked at me. "You haven't met them, Mom?"

"No, I haven't had the pleasure. See how lucky you are to get to go now?"

"Sure, but why didn't you go before?"

"They live a busy life, Jack," Gramps said. "I didn't want to disrupt their work, and they don't have much space in their cabin. It's quite rustic. I usually sleep in my tent, but Zeb insists they'll make room for you if you bring sleeping bags."

"Sounds fun," Jack said. "Wait! If you're going to be gone, too, who'll take care of Tiger and my kitten?"

"Don't worry," I said. "I've already made arrangements for Tiger and Piper to stay with Angie. Ross says he'll be a back-up if she has any problems."

"Good." Jack sighed in relief. "I'm ready then. I've already been checking my bird books so I'll know what to look for while I'm there."

"I think Zeb can help you out there. He'll show you where to look for the good ones. Now, I need to talk to your mom about how to handle the business side of things while you're there."

"Okay. I know when I'm not wanted," Jack said, and turned toward the stairs to head to his room. "I need to check the internet for a list of birds in the area anyway."

"At least he's interested in something besides golf for a change," Dad said when Jack was gone.

"Yes, he's definitely excited."

"Zeb and his wife are eager to meet you, so this trip will make a lot of people happy," Dad said and moved to the sofa. "There are a few things you should know before you leave. Zeb will give you my share of the gold they've recovered this season. You need to be careful not to let people know why you're in town. Zeb has made arrangements with the bush pilot he uses to deliver supplies to their camp and to deliver you and bring you out. He trusts him, so flying back to town with the gold shouldn't be treacherous."

"Treacherous?" I asked, surprised.

"If crooks find out you have the gold, you may be targeted for theft. Zeb's pilot will accompany you to the Bank of Nome. Go with him directly as soon as he lands the plane. They will assay the gold for you and convert it to a check, which will be safer for you to carry."

"Okay. Sounds like a good plan."

"Zeb usually gives me one leather poke of jewelry-quality nuggets that I don't cash in. Bring it back with you, and I'll add it to my safety deposit box stash here. Best not to mention it to anyone at the bank or anywhere else. Take a big enough carry-on so you can take it with you. Ross and I will meet you at the plane when you come home."

I nodded. "Will do."

"Sarah and I are leaving later tonight for Seattle. Should be back before you return. I'll text you the details." Dad handed me a paper bag. "Here, take these tomatoes from Sarah's garden with you for Zeb and his wife. Fresh produce is a treat out there." He gave me a hug. "I appreciate your doing this, Beri. Remember to be careful, and warn Jack not to mention where you've been when you return to Nome."

"I will, Dad. Thanks for the tips."

Chapter Twenty-three

The plane landed with a thump of tires on the asphalt runway. I'd scanned the small town's flat landscape edged by the Bering Sea and surrounded by treeless tundra from my window seat before landing. While large for an Alaskan village, it appeared small for a town, and like most rural Alaskan settlements, it was composed primarily of wooden structures. Wood was lighter to ship than other construction material.

Our plane was only half filled with passengers, the rear half blocked off for delivery of supplies to the village.

It didn't take long for our small group to descend a portable stairway rolled up to our Boeing 727, and we descended to enter a terminal adjacent to the taxiway. A DC6 and a cluster of mixed smaller aircraft were parked nearby.

Once inside, we waited for our baggage and waited some more. Staffing was minimal and no one seemed in a hurry. Standing to one side of the room, a fellow in his fifties with unruly gray hair, dressed in jeans and a puffy vest over a Pendleton shirt, held a placard with my name emblazoned across it. I smiled. It seemed so out-of-place in this bush environment.

"Mom, I think he's looking for you," Jack said.

"I think you're right." I waved in the man's direction. "Let's go meet him."

Jack ran across the room and reached him first. "You must be Jack," the man said.

I answered. "Yes. I'm Beri Quinn and this is my son, Jack."

"Howard Leech at your service." He held out his hand.

I put my bag down, and we shook.

"I'm your bush pilot. Zeb suggested we meet here so you wouldn't need to get a taxi or a hotel room. I'll drive you to my plane, and we'll go directly to the Kougarok. As soon as we get your bags, we'll get going. I'm parked outside."

The other passengers began jostling each other at the base of a baggage chute. Bags were dropping through a delivery window. We joined the crowd and soon had our luggage in tow.

Howard led us to a rusty blue pickup truck and tossed our bags in back. "Jump in," he said to Jack after opening the passenger door. "Your mom gets to sit by the window."

We drove a short distance to a smaller general aviation airport, passing a number of one- and two-story wooden buildings and a lot of telephone poles as we went. He parked next to a red and white Cessna 185. We climbed out. Howard stowed the bags while Jack climbed into the back seat of the plane and fastened his seat belt.

"You have him well-trained," Howard said. "I'd guess he's been in a small airplane before."

"Mom flies me all the time. I'm planning on getting my glider license as soon as I turn fourteen."

"Atta boy. Well, this will be tame for you. It's a short hop."

Less than an hour after landing in Nome, we were airborne and heading to Dad's Kougarok River claim located about sixty miles north. Twenty minutes after taking off from Nome, we were circling a small gravel landing strip adjacent to a couple of ramshackle, peak-roofed buildings and a weather-beaten wooden structure built along the river. I thought it resembled a Brachiosaurus with its long neck rising skyward over the river's edge.

Our plane had barely rolled to a stop before a thin, weathered man with a dark complexion walked up to meet us. He opened my door before the prop had completely stopped spinning. He grinned, his bright eyes sparkling below the brim of his Northern Outfitters baseball cap.

"Beri! Welcome. I'd know you anywhere, I've heard so much about you from your dad." He shook my hand, placing his sinewy free hand on top of mine. "And Jack, too," he said. "It's an honor to finally meet both of you. I just hope it's not because Frank is ailing?"

"No. Not unless being lovesick counts. It looks like he'll be getting married soon."

"Well, I'll be danged," Zeb said. "Never thought I'd see the day. Wait until I tell Mary. That news will make her day."

Mary met us outside as we approached the cabin, wiping her hands on a dish towel before shaking hands. She was petite with salt and pepper hair pulled into a ponytail, but what I noticed most was her smile. It appeared so genuine you hardly noticed her crooked teeth. She hugged first Jack and then me.

"Careful," I said. "Don't want you to squash this bag of tomatoes Dad sent you."

"That dear man," she said. "He definitely knows what will make me happy. I can't wait to slice some of these beauties. We'll have a real salad for dinner." She took my arm. "Come on inside. You must be worn out from your travels."

"I'll leave you ladies to get acquainted," Zeb said. "I have another visitor I can't abandon. He's here looking at the dredge and plans to fly back to town tonight with Howard." He turned to Jack. "Want to walk down to the river with me and get a look at an old gold dredging operation?"

"Sure," Jack said. "Can I see some gold or is it mixed into the mud from the river?"

Zeb grinned. "Come on, I'll show you how it works."

Mary held the door to her home open for me, and we entered a rectangular room smelling of freshly baked bread. Two loaves sat on a rack, cooling at the end of the room that served as a kitchen with a sink and small table. The other end of the room held a neatly made bed with a sofa and recliner serving as a room divider. Although the space was compact, I found it cozy and welcoming. Every inch was used with efficiency. Mary pulled a chair out from the kitchen table and motioned for me to take a seat. "Would you like some coffee?" she asked.

"Please, if it's not too much trouble."

"Not at all. I'll put some on and start dinner while we talk." She filled a beat-up percolator with water from a dispenser on a stand in the corner, filled the basket with loose coffee grounds, and placed it on an electric hot plate to heat. After, she washed and sliced two of the tomatoes, set the table for four, and pulled out a chair for herself.

"Our meals are simple out here. Tonight, we'll have tuna sandwiches and fiddlehead ferns with tomatoes and vinaigrette dressing. Sound okay?"

"Sounds delicious. Jack loves tuna and that bread smells good, but I hope we're not displacing Howard from the dinner table."

"Oh, don't worry about that. Howard is leaving in a few minutes to fly our visitor back to town."

Zeb returned with Jack soon after the coffee was ready. He poured himself a cup and joined us at the table.

Jack held out his open hand to me. "Look, Mom. Zeb let me pick this flake out of the gravel. It's real gold!"

"Better find something to put it in so you don't lose it," I said.

Mary handed Jack a small glass bottle. "Here, this should work."

"Thanks," Jack said as he dropped the flake inside and carefully replaced the lid before putting it into his pocket. "He's also going to take me birding in the morning. He knows all the best places."

Zeb laughed. "It'll give me a good excuse to take a break from the dredge," he said. "Mary keeps the books. She can review the finances with you while we boys go out with our binoculars."

Chapter Twenty-four

Early the next morning, Zeb rolled Jack out of his sleeping bag. I opened one eye and watched them slather rounds of Pilot Bread with peanut butter. Zeb filled a thermos with reconstituted milk from the refrigerator and grabbed the bag lunches Mary had prepared the night before. I was surprised Zeb managed to be so alert without his morning coffee. I wasn't sure what time it was, but after they left, I rolled over in my sleeping bag and went back to sleep. Jack had informed me birds are more active in the morning and evening hours.

The tantalizing scent of bacon sizzling woke me. I rolled up my bedding and since I'd slept in my clothes, pulled on my boots and headed for the outdoor facilities.

Mary smiled when I returned. "Good morning, sleepyhead. I waited as long as I could to wake you, but my hunger pangs were hard to ignore."

"I'm sorry. What time is it?" I asked as I ran a brush through my hair.

"Only seven. I'm used to getting an early start on the day."

"Me too, usually. Guess my subconscious thinks I'm on vacation."

"You are," she said. "Enjoy your stay."

"I am, but please don't feel you have to wait on me."

"No chance. It won't be all fun and games. We have work to do this morning."

As soon as we'd eaten and cleared the dishes, Mary pulled out her record books and sat beside me at the kitchen table.

"We log each day's 'take' in here. This column is for the weight of the loose gold, small nuggets go in this column, and a third column lists the larger ones, with a description of size. Zeb takes our share of the proceeds to the bank in Nome about once a month. Your dad's 20% share we store in a safe hidden here in the house. Zeb keeps all the nicer nuggets aside until the end of the year to make sure the division of these is equable. Sometimes your dad takes some of the promising concentrate back with him. He has a friend with some expensive equipment to help separate it."

"Dad didn't mention anything about that." My ears grew warm with embarrassment. "I'm not even sure what it is."

Mary laughed. "Don't worry about it. It would be awkward for you to try to haul it back with you anyway. If he wants, we'll ship it to him later." She sighed. "We've worked with your dad for so long that he's left the bookkeeping to us, but if you prefer, I can make copies of my records when I'm in town and send those to him."

"I'll tell him you offered, but I doubt it'll be necessary."

"He might want to see them this year. I'll explain what I mean later."

My pulse kicked up a notch. *What did Mary want to hold off telling me?*

We spent the rest of the morning going over the books. My brain was swimming with numbers by the time we finished.

"That's it," Mary said. "I think you have all the information I have. Now for the bad news. This has not been a good year." She paused. "Our overall take is down 34% from last year and that was down from the year before. We also worked harder and longer hours just to make that much. Zeb thinks the claim is about played out and has decided to retire after this year. We haven't told your dad, but I don't think he'll be too surprised. He knows the take is dwindling, and Zeb isn't getting any younger."

"I'm sorry to hear that. He's been at it for a long time now, hasn't he?"

"Yes, and he's not happy about quitting now, but his emphysema is getting worse. Too many cigarettes over the years."

I put my hand on her arm, and she pulled me in for a hug. After wiping tears from her eyes, Mary smiled.

"We've had a good run, but it's time for your dad to find someone else to lease this place. I'll warn you though, it won't be easy. A lot of people around here have deserted their claims and staked new ones on the coast of the Bering Sea. Underwater dredges are the more profitable trend now. I think our dredge is probably the last one still operating in Alaska. The visitor you met earlier was here researching the history of mining in this area."

After a moment of silence, she looked up at the clock on the wall. "It's getting late. The guys will be getting back soon. I'd better get started on dinner."

"What can I do to help?"

"We'll get to it in a minute. Let's finish up our accounting first." She picked up a small leather poke marked "Bank of Nome" and handed it to me. "This is your share of the nuggets we collected. Truthfully, I think I found more of them with a metal detector checking through old tailings than we found with the dredge."

She pushed a second larger poke across the table to me. "Here's the rest of your take. Sorry it isn't more."

"I'm sure Dad will understand."

Mary went to the refrigerator and pulled out a ham. "I wanted to have a caribou roast for you instead, but I didn't have any caribou. Zeb hasn't gone hunting yet this year. I thought we'd heat the ham up and serve it with a cheesy rice dish. We have some blueberries I canned last summer since fresh ones aren't ripe yet. I'll throw a cobbler together for dessert and we'll call it dinner."

"Sounds delicious, but sandwiches would be fine and a lot less work."

"Not to worry, it's all simple. You notice I didn't say scalloped potatoes or blueberry pie. Rice doesn't need peeling and cobblers are much easier than pie."

I laughed. "A woman after my own heart. I've been spoiled by my dad doing most of the cooking in our household. Guess that will change now that he's getting married." I tied on the apron Mary handed me. "Give me a job, I'm ready to go."

An hour later the bubbling cobbler came out of the oven and the aroma of berries and ham pushed my appetite into overdrive.

"I'll open a can of green beans when I see the whites of their eyes," Mary said. "The guys shouldn't be more than another hour."

The hour came and went with no sign of them. "Do you think something's wrong?" I asked.

"No, they still have plenty of light this time of year. They've probably lost track of time. Besides, Zeb would call me if he needed help." She rinsed and dried her hands. "How about a game of Kings in the Corner to help pass the time?"

"Sure. I think I remember the rules."

Mary moved to an end table beside the sofa to get a deck of cards. "Uh oh!"

"What's wrong?"

"Zeb forgot his phone again. He has a bad habit of doing that."

"Oh no." A frisson of fear shot through me. "I hope they're all right."

"I'm sure they are. Zeb wouldn't take any chances with Jack along. You watch. They'll walk in that door any minute now." She moved to the stove and took the food out of the oven. Even after she'd reduced the heat earlier, the ham looked dried out.

After we played three rounds of cards, Mary rose and slipped her arms into a jacket. "Guess we'd better go take a look. You want to come or stay? On second thought, you better stay so you can feed them and tell them which way I went if they get back before I do. Besides, we can't leave the gold sitting out with no one home." She opened the door and turned back to face me. "There's a shotgun behind the door if you need it."

I agreed, although I felt torn. I should go with her in case Jack needed me, but I should be here when he made it back, too. I decided to trust Mary's judgement and stayed behind.

"I'm taking our other ATV, and I'll follow the river in the direction of Kougarok Road," she said as she left.

Chapter Twenty-Five

The minutes dragged by with no sign of the guys. I stashed the gold inside my bed roll for safe-keeping and played solitaire until I actually won a game. I returned the deck of cards to their box, walked to the refrigerator, and stuffed our dried-out dinner inside. I picked at a small piece of ham, but it stuck in my throat.

After I closed the door to the fridge, a scratching sound at the window caught my attention. I froze, then turned to look and found myself eye to eye with a black bear. Now I understood why Mary alerted me to the shotgun. I'd thought she'd wanted to warn me about possible thieves, but she probably had this critter in mind. He was small, but apparently had a big appetite for ham or maybe blueberries or both.

I debated if I should fire a warning shot out the door to scare him off, but I didn't see any extra ammo. I decided to hold my fire and wait to see what he'd do next. He continued scratching at the glass for a good half hour, snuffled around the perimeter of the cabin, and finally threw his weight against the reinforced door. I watched him as best I could from the window, shotgun at the ready, until he ambled off toward the creek and out of sight.

I replaced the gun behind the door and sighed in relief. At least the animal had provided a distraction from my fears for Jack and Zeb. I looked at my watch. The light outside had faded to dusk. Eleven-fifteen. *Where could they be until almost midnight?*

Waiting was torture. I considered calling Dad, but what could he do? I didn't want to worry him unnecessarily, and I felt sure Mary would call if she had anything to report. I'd just turned on the radio for distraction when Zeb's phone rang.

With shaking fingers, I punched in the password Mary had given me before she left. As soon as I answered, Mary's calm voice came through. She explained she'd found our guys. Zeb had caught a tire in an unusually deep hole disguised in the muskeg and flipped his ATV. Jack was fine, but Zeb had injured his leg. She'd be back with them soon.

Relief flooded through me. It didn't sound like Zeb was in any danger, and Jack was okay. I went to the kitchen and started pulling dishes from the fridge figuring they would be famished by now.

Mary drove up to the cabin and parked her ATV as close to the cabin as possible. When I opened the door, Mary and Jack were already struggling to help Zeb out of the vehicle. I grabbed a kitchen chair and pulled it close enough to the ATV for them to slide him onto it. Mary and I dragged the chair inside and Jack closed and locked the door.

Mary grabbed some scissors from the kitchen and cut Zeb's pant leg off at the knee to expose his injured lower leg. "It's swollen, but let's hope it's not broken."

She applied two instant ice packs from her first-aid kit and wrapped a towel around his leg to keep them in place. "Looks like he's going to have to fly back to Nome with you tomorrow morning and check in with the doctor," she said.

Zeb moaned. "Could you get me some aspirin or something in the meantime?"

"Coming right up," Mary said, hurrying into the kitchen for a glass of water.

Zeb looked at the trio of pills she delivered to him with suspicion. "What's this other pill?"

"Just something to help you sleep. Relax and swallow them. I'm not going to poison you." Mary winked at me. "It's amazing he wanted aspirin. He absolutely hates to take medicine."

We slid him off the chair onto the sofa, and Mary put a pillow under both his head and his leg. "Look at that. He's already asleep. That blessed pill worked fast."

Jack's face crumpled. "I tried to help him. I couldn't lift the ATV off of him. I tried and tried."

I pulled him close. "There was nothing you could do except stay with him. I know he appreciated that."

"And don't forget," Mary said, "you waved me down. If you hadn't yelled and jumped up and down, I might have driven right by and not seen either of you."

Thinking I'd divert Jack's concerns, I asked, "Does anyone want some ham? I almost lost it to a visitor I had while you were gone but managed to hang on to it." I shrugged. "I was glad you left me that shotgun, Mary."

"Oh, no," Mary cried. "I forgot to warn you about PeeWee. He's a frequent visitor, especially if he smells food cooking. You didn't shoot at him, did you?"

"No, it didn't come to that."

"PeeWee?" Jack asked.

"A small black bear," I said. "I met him face to face peering through the window. He thumped against the door a few times and eventually left without breaking in."

"Sounds just like him," Mary said. "He kinda grows on you. I just hope he doesn't get larger and more aggressive."

"Boy, wish I could have seen him," Jack said. "When do we eat the ham? I'm starved."

The next morning, Howard arrived to ferry us back to Nome as scheduled. Jack and I climbed into the back of the plane while Mary and Howard helped Zeb into the front.

"Thank you for everything, Mary. I'll make sure Dad sends you an invitation to the wedding, although I'm sure it will be a low-key affair."

"Wouldn't miss it," she said with a smile. "Please tell him thanks for the tomatoes."

"Will do."

Howard started the engine and ran through his checklist before he taxied to the end of the gravel strip and took off. I admired the way he maintained control on the narrow strip.

Once in the air, Jack started rattling off the names of the birds he'd seen the day before. "See back there?" He pointed to the left.

"That bluff?" I asked.

"Yup. We went there hoping to see some nesting birds and we did. I saw a couple of crested puffins. Even Zeb was surprised. Altogether, I added eleven birds to my life list. I just wish we could have stayed longer."

"You might add a few more while you're in Nome," Howard said. "I'll give you a list of the best places to look, but the harbor is always a good bet for sea birds. The east side of town has a park that's known for birding, too."

"Great," Jack said. "Thanks for taking me, Zeb. I'm sorry you got hurt."

Zeb shook the sleep from his eyes. "That Mary. I think she slipped me another sleeping pill." He shook his head again. "Don't you worry about me. My own stupidity caused the accident. I've driven that area lots of times and know to watch for holes. I wasn't paying close enough attention, that's all."

A few minutes later, Howard landed the plane in Nome. Two men emerged from a red van parked next to Howard's tie-down.

"Howdy," the driver said.

"Glad to see you," Howard said. "Guess you got Mary's message that Zeb needs a little help getting to the doctor."

"Sure did. How're you doing, Zeb?"

"I'm fine. Just a little busted up."

"Doc Watkins is expecting you," one of the men said. They positioned themselves on each side of Zeb, so he could put his arms around their shoulders and hop to the van.

Howard finished tying down his plane, then turned to us. "Jump into my truck, and we'll get you to the bank. Maybe after that you'll have time for some sightseeing."

"We should be good," I said. "Our plane doesn't leave for home until this evening."

Howard's company was reassuring as we walked to the bank. Was it paranoia or was the feeling we were being watched real? I looked around, but saw nothing suspicious. We finished our business and left the bank without incident. I thanked Howard and turned to Jack. "Okay, where do you want to go first?"

"To see the birds, of course, but Howard said he'd drive us to look for them tonight on the way to catch our flight." He thought for a moment. "How about checking out the giant gold pan and the finish line for the Iditarod Race?"

"Sure. We might as well play tourist for a while. We can take pictures to show Gramps and Sarah."

We headed down the street where I snapped a few shots of Jack by the enormous gold pan that greeted visitors to the city of Nome. I looked behind me, once again feeling like we were being watched, but realized I was being silly. *Where would anyone hide on the streets of Nome? And why would they bother?* No one knew about the poke of nuggets I had in my tote. I pushed my nerves aside and tried to enjoy the sunny afternoon.

As Jack stood grinning at the finish line of the Iditarod dog sled race held every February, he announced, "Mom, let's start our own dog team. I'll bet Tiger could pull a sled."

"Uh, I'm not sure how he'd feel about that. Besides, building a team is a lot of hard work. You'd need to dedicate most of your free time to it, and that would be hard to do if you're in California going to golf school."

Jack tilted his head and considered. "I guess you're right," he said.

"When you do come back to Alaska for winters, you might talk to my friend, Kaitlyn, about skijoring."

He wrinkled his nose. "What's that?"

"It's when you train a dog to help pull you on cross-country skis. You could try it out and see if you like it before you think about training a whole team." I stopped walking and held up my camera. "Hey, go stand over by the arch so I can take some more pictures."

"Okay. We can send some to Dad in Arizona, too."

A tap on my shoulder caused me to jerk to attention and turn around. "Charlie! What are you doing here?"

"I was about to ask you the same thing. Why did you follow me here?"

"Follow you? I had no idea you were even in Nome. Why are you?"

"Not important," he said. "Don't you know they're following you to find me? You and Gina are their only leads." He grabbed my shoulder. "Have you found Gina yet?"

"Not yet. The PI asked me for more information about her. And he wants a photograph."

He opened his wallet and pulled out a snapshot. "Don't lose this. It's the only one I have. She didn't like her picture taken." He took a step back and replaced his wallet in his pocket. "Be careful, Beri. I'll be in touch," he growled. "Don't try to contact me. I've got to disappear again."

After he stalked off, Jack turned to me. "Mom, he scares me. Who is he?"

"Just a former student I've tried to help. Don't worry about him. I don't expect to see him again."

"I took a picture of you talking to him. I can delete it if you don't want to remember him."

"No, it's okay. He can be nice when he isn't scared. I hope the police catch the bad guys chasing him soon."

I gave him a little shove. "Come on, let's go find something to eat."

Chapter Twenty-six

The flight back to Anchorage didn't take long once we'd completed the interminable TSA screening process. You'd have thought Nome was a hotbed of terroristic activity by the number of personnel and the thoroughness of the process. I worried that my poke of nuggets might not be compatible with the x-ray screening, but it didn't raise any alarms.

Once aboard, Jack immediately dozed off, still exhausted from his bird-watching misadventure with Zeb. I used the quiet time to ponder my unexpected encounter with Charlie. Surprised to see him in Nome, I found his demand "to stay away from him or I'd get him killed" statement shocking. The intensity of his voice still echoed in my head. After all, he was the one who initiated our encounters. Why did he think his enemies were following me in their effort to find him? I hadn't noticed anyone tailing me to Nome or anywhere else, except possibly to the golf tent. I'd felt someone watching me in Nome, but now I knew it was Charlie.

I glanced around at the other passengers on the plane but saw no one suspicious. Was Charlie being paranoid? Maybe, but that didn't make sense, either. Undeniably, someone had killed our tow pilot, and someone had sabotaged the storage unit.

The plane began its descent, and Jack awoke from his nap. He rubbed his eyes with his fists. "We're back already?"

"Yes. We'll be on the ground in a few minutes." I lifted his seatback tray and fastened it closed.

"I hope I can go again next year. Zeb is so cool. I hope he'll be okay."

"I'm sure he'll be as good as new if he takes it easy. We'll have to wait and see about going next year, but Grandpa will keep in touch with them and let you know."

Ross had texted me that he'd be home late. Angie would meet us at the airport and drive us to her house where I'd left my vehicle. Tiger and Piper greeted us with much tail wagging and purring when Jack gathered them both in his arms.

"I missed you guys," he said into the fur of Piper's back.

"My kids are going to miss them now," she said. "Believe me, they didn't lack for attention while they were here. I see a campaign for adopting a pet coming my way soon," Angie said with a laugh.

"Thanks so much, Angie. We knew they'd have a good time with your family."

After loading kennels, food, and other pet paraphernalia in my SUV, we headed home.

The answering machine light blinked on our landline phone, but I waited until we were settled in after a dinner from the freezer to check the messages. The only one of interest was from Wallace Killion, the private investigator I'd hired for Charlie.

"Beri, if you're back, give me a call. Some developments in our inquiry I'd like to discuss with you."

I checked the clock. A little after nine. Late to call, but my curiosity couldn't wait until morning. He answered and agreed to stop by the house to fill me in on his progress.

When the doorbell rang, Tiger let out a single "Woof" and ran ahead of me to the door.

"Sit, Tiger. It's okay," I said.

Wallace smiled when I opened the door and held out his hand for Tiger to sniff. "Hi there, fella. Aren't you the handsome one?"

Tiger's tail wagged, and he looked up at me with pleading eyes, afraid I'd put him in his kennel. He rubbed against our visitor's knees.

"I see you have a way with dogs," I said.

"Love 'em. Believe me, it's an asset in my profession."

"I can see that. Come on in." I led him to a chair adjacent to the unlit fireplace. "Can I get you anything to drink?"

"No thanks," Wallace said. "What I have to tell you will only take a few minutes, and I know you're still decompressing from your trip."

"It was interesting, but I'm glad to be home. I'm curious about what you've found, though."

"It's more what I haven't found," he said. "I've looked into the neighbor you spoke to, and apparently, she doesn't exist. I've talked to everyone who lives on that street and no one knows anything about her."

"That seems odd. Any ideas why she would pretend to be the neighbor?"

"I'm wondering if she isn't Gina herself. Perhaps she followed you and posed as a neighbor to figure out what you were up to."

"But wouldn't the neighbors have recognized her?" I asked.

"I wondered about that, too, but Gina is somewhat of a mystery to them. A few had spoken to Charlie, but none of them had ever talked to her. One lady saw her back out of their garage in a gray Toyota SUV early one morning, but she was wearing a white visor or hat and the lady didn't see much of her face."

"Strange. The woman I spoke to who called herself Caroline was outgoing and friendly. I doubt she would have been reclusive with the neighbors."

"One reason might be that most of the families are middle-aged working people with children who lead busy lives."

"We might have more luck talking to their kids, maybe."

"Good idea. I'll look into that. Did Charlie ever send you that photograph he promised?" he asked.

"I almost forgot. He didn't send it, but I ran into him in Nome. He gave one to me. It's in the bedroom. I'll go get it."

I dug the photo out of my carry-on and studied it before taking it downstairs. The quality of the picture was not very good, but I could easily discern that the woman in the picture was not Caroline. Something about her eyes looked slightly familiar, but I couldn't place why.

When I handed it over to Wallace, he looked at it for a few seconds. "Not great quality," he said.

"No, Charlie said she didn't like to be photographed."

"Hmm. That in itself is interesting. I'll make a copy and return it to you." He shifted in his chair. "Did you learn anything else talking to Charlie?"

"No, not really. It was a strange meeting. He seemed irritated that, as he put it, I'd followed him to Nome. He said I'd exposed him to his enemies as he felt sure I'd been followed there."

"Were you?" he asked.

"I didn't see any sign of it. The bigger question for me is, why was he in Nome? I've never understood why he doesn't just leave the state. Alaska is a big place, but a stranger sticks out in a relatively small village like Nome, even though it is tourist season."

"Maybe it has something to do with Gina."

"Whatever his reason, neither of us seem to have made much progress in finding his girlfriend."

"No, but I'll follow up with your idea of interviewing as many of the neighborhood kids as I can manage without setting off alarms with their parents. I'll also look into the possibility of using facial recognition software now that I have a photo. Unfortunately, the quality may not be good enough, but it's worth a try."

Tiger followed Wallace to the door for one more pat before he left.

Chapter Twenty-seven

Angie handed me the mail. "He's at it again, I see."
"What?" I looked up at her in confusion.

She pointed to the envelope on top of the pile.

Sure enough, I recognized the envelope. It was postmarked from Nome.

"What else could it be?" Angie asked. "I shudder to think what Charlie wants now."

She was right. The letter had all the hallmarks of Charlie's earlier letters. I ripped it open, forgetting my intention to keep Angie's nose out of my business.

"Just a note," I said as I unfolded the half sheet of paper inside. I hoped it was an apology, but Charlie only said he'd been shocked to see me in Nome. In answer to the questions about Gina, all he knew was that she was an only child and her parents were dead. She grew up back east someplace and had accounting and public relations degrees. She didn't talk much about her past. He'd try to call me next week and hoped the PI would have some leads on her whereabouts by then. He'd enclosed another small photograph from the company brochure that he'd forgotten he had.

The photo fluttered to the floor when I pulled it from the envelope.

Angie bent to pick it up and studied it. "I've seen her before," she said. "Over at Northern Mapping when I went to pick up the package for Mr. H. She was coming out of the boss's office."

"At Northern Mapping? Why was she there?"

"I don't know," Angie said. "But she seemed familiar to everyone. I just got a glimpse of her as she was leaving, but she talked to the people there like she knew them."

"Interesting... Wish I knew how she's connected to them."

"One thing I do remember," Angie said, "when the boss lady said goodbye, she didn't call her Gina. It was some other name."

"Can you remember what it was?"

She cocked her head to the side. "Something that started with the letter V. Maybe Vivian, Victoria, Vickie? That's it, Vickie!"

"Good work, Angie. Thanks."

Angie left my office patting herself on her shoulder. She stopped in the doorway and turned back to face me. "Don't use this as an excuse to get mixed up with that Charlie guy again. He's still trouble."

Exasperated, I ran my hand through my hair. *What kind of connection could Gina have to Northern Mapping?* I unfolded the note and read it again. I noticed I'd overlooked the postscript he'd written at the end.

> *Remember, you're their best way to find me. Stay clear. If you have news, leave a message as before.*

I shook my head again. Not much of an apology after scaring us half to death. He seemed to think he was the wronged party because we *dared* visit Nome. Angie was right. He was trouble.

I picked up the phone and arranged to drop off the picture to Killion. I described Angie's encounter at Northern Mapping and asked him to look into her relationship with them.

From now on, he could deal with Charlie. I was done.

Later, Jason found me outside standing next to the twin Cessna. I wanted to check the plane's logbook to see what Dean had entered about the fuel tank repair.

"Didn't expect to find you out here," he said. "I've got possible good news on two fronts. The big news is the weather pattern looks optimistic for the chain. I need you and Mickey to be ready to go in the morning if it continues to look good."

"That's our job. Always a slave to the weather," I said with a smile. "I hope we get the go-ahead. It would be nice not to have it constantly on our minds. What's your other news?"

"I just got word we were awarded the contract on the Ketchikan mapping proposal you submitted. Northern Mapping is steaming about it. They'd assumed their proposal would be selected."

"That will keep us busy for a couple of years," I said. "It's a massive project."

Heckenlively clapped me on the shoulder. "Looks like you're staying on top of things."

"Say, I have a question for you about something else." I replaced the logbook in the plane's cabin. "That package you asked Angie to pick up at Northern Mapping? I'm curious what kind of relationship we have with them, since we haven't exactly been on friendly terms in the past and probably won't be in the future after winning this job."

"Purely business," he said. "I wanted to get copies of Aleutian photography from their old film library. I'd tried to get it from the military, who'd originally contracted for the job, but due to some kind of snafu in their archives, they couldn't put their hands on it. My contact suggested it might be available from the film library you sold with the business. I think the images dated back to the '80s when your father ran the company."

"Interesting. So did they give them to you?"

"They sent me copies of some old photography, along with a big invoice. Unfortunately, they weren't what I needed."

"What are you after?"

He paused. "I wanted original photos of the Adak Naval Base before it was decommissioned."

"Hmm, I do remember Dad talking about being there. They treated him very well. Put him up in officer quarters while he watched the weather.

He said they had quite a community and was surprised the place even had a McDonalds." I closed the door to the twin and hopped off the wing to the ground. I looked him in the eyes. "Is that what we're after now? More pictures of Adak?"

"Yes. I'd hoped to have both before and after photography for comparison, but it looks like we'll make do with what we can get."

"I know Dad kept some photos for historical reasons. I can check with him to see if he has the ones you want."

"I wish Ms. O'Hara would try a little harder to find them."

"Elinor Chen?" I asked.

"Yes. I think she uses her married name for business purposes."

Chapter Twenty-eight

I checked the weather in Adak one more time. Scattered clouds, good visibility. For Adak, that was as good as it gets. I shouted to Mickey, "We need to get a move on. The weather's clearing over the Aleutians."

Mickey ran into my office. "Finally! What do you need me to do?"

"Grab Dean and have him help you load the equipment into the plane. Fortunately, it's already fueled. I'll be ready to go before you finish."

I'd given Dad a heads-up about my plan so he knew he and Jack were on their own. I left messages for Jason and Killion with Angie and asked her to check on accommodations for our stay.

"How long do you plan to be there?" Angie asked.

"I have no idea. It will depend on the weather. Try to make it open-ended. I imagine Adak residents will be used to that."

I grabbed my laptop pre-loaded with flight maps and pulled my survival gear and travel bag from the office closet. Once I'd completed my exterior checklist of the plane, I tossed my bags into the storage lockers and climbed into the left seat of the cockpit, keeping my laptop with me.

Mickey slid into the seat beside me and closed the door. Meanwhile, I double-checked that we were within max gross weight and gave Mickey a thumbs-up.

"All set, Captain," he said. "And in record time, too."

I started the engines and called Merrill Ground Control to request taxi instructions. "This is 7415 Quebec, I'm at AIA Mapping and departing to the south."

"Okay, 15 Quebec, taxi runway six."

"Roger." I taxied as instructed, ran through my checklist in the run-up area, and called the tower. "15 Quebec ready for takeoff."

After departure, I made a right turn to the south and asked the tower to open my flight plan with flight service.

"Roger. Will do, at eight past the hour."

We climbed to cruise altitude VFR and tuned into the VOR at King Salmon.

"Now, can you sit back and relax a bit?" Mickey asked after we'd leveled out. "I'm full of questions. I was beginning to wonder if we'd ever make this trip, but I've been studying up some."

"I'm a novice, too. I've only been out as far as Cold Bay, myself."

"Oh, I thought you were a veteran. You sounded so familiar with the conditions in the region."

I glanced his way. "If I did, it's because I grew up hearing my father's stories about flying out on the chain. He stayed in Adak for over a month one summer."

Mickey stretched both arms over his head. "Don't know about you, but I'm ready for some action. Not that our local jobs haven't been interesting, but I'm itchin' for some adventure. My brothers keep asking what I've been doing. I need some good stories to tell them."

"You can start by telling them it's a 1,200-mile trip from Anchorage, and we may have to do it without refueling. You can also tell them that the town of Adak is the westernmost town in the U.S. and it's the southernmost town in Alaska."

"Thanks for the statistics. They'll be duly impressed." He gave me a lopsided grin. "We'll have to ask for a mint julep at the local bar."

"Speaking of that, did you ever ride in the Kentucky Derby?"

Mickey laughed. "No. Nothing that grand."

"Do you miss the sport now that you're retired?"

"In some ways. I miss the adrenalin rush of a good race and the joshin' with the other jockeys. I miss the horses most. I grew up around them, you know."

"We do have horses in Alaska. Not a lot, but we can find you some."

Mickey dozed after a few hours passed. He was sound asleep by the time we flew over Dutch Harbor. I regretted he wasn't awake for the clear view of the cluster of volcano cones on Atka Island as we neared them. I first noticed the weather starting to close in when the cones became less distinct, even though we were getting closer. Surely, we hadn't flown all this way to be stymied by the weather after all.

I checked my instruments and noted the RPM drop on the right engine. A check of the magnetos revealed we'd lost one on the left side. The second one continued to function, but power had diminished in that engine. I kept a close eye on the instruments because we were past the point of no return. I had no choice but to continue to Adak since I didn't have enough gas to head back to Dutch. I changed the ADF station and tuned it to Adak.

The ceiling and visibility continued dropping until it fell below the minimums. It was like flying inside a gray ball of cotton. Mickey wanted excitement, but I was glad he was sleeping through this. He'd ask questions, and I didn't need distractions right now. I contacted Adak Approach Control and asked for weather.

"Below 200 feet and a quarter mile. Hold east. Will need to make ILS approach to runway five when cleared."

"Roger," I said.

After two turns, the tower gave the go ahead. "Weather at minimums. Cleared for approach, runway five. Report procedure turn inbound."

On course, I descended, watching the altimeter drop lower and lower, but was forced to pull up when I reached minimum altitude and still didn't have the runway in sight.

"Weather has dropped back below minimums," I said. "Had to make a missed approach."

"Hold over Adak beacon. We'll get weather update."

"Reporting 300 feet and one mile visibility. Cleared for ILS runway five approach. Report procedure turn inbound."

"Okay, 15 Quebec. Procedure turning inbound."

"Report runway in sight."

I dropped to minimums. No runway was visible. I drew a deep breath; I had no choice but to blindly descend still lower. Finally, I caught a glimpse of the runway through a small break in the fog.

"Runway visible! No choice but to find it. I was too low on fuel for another approach. I'm now on the ground."

"Congrats, 15 Quebec. Welcome to Adak."

I slowed the plane and followed taxi instructions to tie-downs, wisps of fog parting before me. I sat still for a few minutes, rolled my head to relieve the tension in my neck, and heaved a huge sigh of relief. We'd made it.

Mickey stretched and opened his eyes. "We're here already? What did I miss?"

"Not much." I shrugged. "One thing I know for sure, though. We're sending our equipment back on Alaska Airlines when we finish this job. I want to take maximum fuel on the way back."

Chapter Twenty-nine

Grateful that Angie had prearranged our housing and car rental through the Aleut Corporation, we picked up the keys to a gray sedan and a map of the island. Mickey drove as I navigated. The fog had dissipated due to a growing wind and a drizzle of rain had replaced it. My job was simplified by the small size of the town. Not a freeway in sight.

Mickey pulled into the garage of our rental, and we dropped our bags inside the former Naval housing unit assigned to us. A quick walk-through of the place revealed a typical government construction with living room, kitchen, two bedrooms, and unfortunately, a shared bathroom. Mickey checked out the inside of the empty refrigerator.

"Looks like we'll need to find a grocery store, right quick," he said.

I pulled out the local resource guide we'd picked up at the airport. "There's one not far from here and a couple of restaurants, too."

"That's a relief. At least we won't starve." Mickey tossed his bag into one of the identical bedrooms. "Let's go explore. I'll drive."

"Wait a minute. I need to grab my rain slicker. The wind's so strong now, the rain's blowing sideways. Glad the wind didn't pick up until after we landed."

"Guess that's what we can expect in a place known as 'the birthplace of the wind,'" Mickey said.

"Sounds like you've been reading that guidebook."

Mickey chuckled. "Yeah. I'll be in the car. Don't expect we'll get much sightseeing done in this downpour, but at least we can find that grocery store."

I climbed into the car, and Mickey backed out of the garage.

"Which way do I go?" he asked.

"Left, I think. We'll see where the road takes us," I said. "The map is so small, it's confusing."

"Interesting place. There's military stuff everywhere, all just gone to pot, but there isn't much else. It has a ghostlike quality in the blurry light of this storm."

I shared what I knew. "The U.S. Navy closed their base here in the late '90s and left a lot behind. Too expensive to remove it, I guess. The population fell from a peak of around nine thousand to only about a hundred full-time residents. That explains the blight you see. Most everything belongs to the Aleut Corporation and the city now, and I understand they're working to clean it up." I swiveled my head to check a passing sign.

"Hey, there it is, we just passed it," Mickey said. "See those two cars parked out front?"

We turned around, parked and ran inside, hanging our rain gear on hooks by the entry.

The establishment was small and cozy with a register and cashier at the front and rows of cans and boxes lined up inside. A lone table of produce was stationed near the check-out area and a glass-fronted refrigerator stood against the back wall.

Mickey looked the place over. "Not exactly a Safeway or Fred Meyer."

"Shh. It has fresh milk, canned goods, and a little produce. What more do we need?" I picked up a box of Pilot bread, peanut butter, apples, and a chunk of cheese.

Mickey added some cereal and instant coffee to the basket I'd picked up at the door. He turned to the cashier as we were checking out. "Any chance you have grits in stock?"

The clerk smiled. "Afraid not, but we do get fresh stuff in twice a week. If you want home cooking, I'd recommend you try the Blue Heron Café down the street. They serve breakfast, lunch, and dinner. The coffee and conversation are free, but they don't serve booze. The internet and TV are a bonus, though."

"Thanks, we'll be sure to give it a try," Mickey said.

I added a couple of decks of playing cards to my purchases, and we dashed to the car, threw our bags into the back seat, and headed out.

"Not much we can see in this rain. How about we go back to the rental, and I'll challenge you to a game of gin rummy?" I asked, smiling.

"I'm more of a poker guy, myself, but we'll probably have time for both. I didn't see a television in our quarters. Should have brought a good book. Maybe I can find one tomorrow."

Before settling in for the night, I called Dad to check on him and Jack. All was well.

My eyes popped open early the next morning. A peek out the window revealed the rain had stopped. I checked the weather forecast for pilot's reports and winds aloft and learned it was a no-go for taking our photos. Too much turbulence. Mickey was still asleep, and a breakfast of instant coffee and cereal didn't sound appealing. I left a note for him and headed out to look for the Blue Heron Café, hoping they opened early.

Sure enough, several cars were parked outside what looked like another military housing duplex with a propane tank out front and an oil tank on the side. An 'Open' sign was visible both on the garage door and above a sandwich board sign beside the recessed entrance. Inside, the captivating aroma of coffee and something sweet drew me in.

"Good morning, stranger. Can I pour you some coffee?" The proprietor, a tall middle-aged man wearing a black apron gave me a questioning look accompanied by a smile.

"Sounds wonderful." I took a seat at the small table closest to his counter. It was one of a handful of small tables in a room not much larger than the living room of our rental.

I sniffed the air. "Anything good to go with the coffee?"

"You're probably smelling my doughnuts. I don't make them as often as my wife does. She's off cooking for the fish processing plant right now." He turned and placed a glistening doughnut on a plate for me. "These won't last long. Good thing you came early."

I took a bite, savoring the still warm pastry. "It tastes wonderful."

"We're kinda' famous for them. Even had a write-up in a magazine a while back." He left when the only other customer walked up to pay his bill, then headed back to face me.

"What's brought you to our chunk of rock in the middle of the ocean?" he asked.

"I'm here to take aerial photographs, if I can catch some good weather."

"Good luck with that. It may take a while."

"I'm afraid you're right. Since my son's a birding enthusiast, I'm planning to get some birding in during my down time. He'll expect a full report of what I see here when I get home."

"How old is he?"

After a sip of my coffee, I said, "Just turned twelve last month. He wanted to come with me, but it wasn't possible."

"Yeah, we have the birds all right. Today's probably too windy for good birding, though. I'd wait until it dies down."

"Good advice I'm sure, but when the weather improves, I won't have the time. I'll have to get to work."

"I imagine you'll have plenty of waiting time." He picked up my empty plate. "You know, there's a new bird research center that opened up recently. One of our regulars, Billy Ivanoff, an Aleut fella, got a job out there. You might check that out if it's open to the public. I'm not sure whether it is or not."

"Sounds like a great idea."

"Haven't seen Billy since he started work out there. While you're going, take him a bag of doughnuts. He loves 'em." He sketched a rough diagram of the location on a napkin and handed it to me with the bag. "It's off the road a ways. I'd take an ATV if I were you."

"Thanks, I'll head over there later this morning. Maybe these will be the ticket I need to entice him into giving me a tour."

Chapter Thirty

Mickey sat at the kitchen table crunching down a bowl of cereal when I returned.

"Good morning, sleepyhead. Sorry I left without you."

"No worries. Felt good to sleep in." He yawned. "Where'd you go?"

"I needed some real coffee, so I checked out the Blue Heron Café. Can't stand that instant stuff, and theirs definitely passed muster. It's a friendly place. I give it five stars."

"Good. Maybe I'll try it for lunch."

"Meanwhile, I have a favor to ask."

"Sure, what's that?" he asked.

"I want to rent an ATV to visit a bird research center outside of town. Could you drive me to the rental place? That way, you can take the car, and we won't have to share." I picked up the keys from the counter and extended them to him with a smile.

Fifteen minutes later, I followed the map drawn on my napkin north toward the new research center. The staff at the ATV rental didn't know much about the place but warned me to be careful when I drove off-road. They advised me that there were still unexploded military ordinance scattered throughout the island.

Sure enough, after leaving decaying buildings behind, I spotted several 'DANGER Unexploded Ordinance' signs along the hilly landscape of green tundra dotted with wildflowers. I steered around tall grasses as much as possible to avoid hidden hazards and made my way without incident to a fenced-in enclave of concrete, windowless buildings. I couldn't tell if they were new or re-purposed old military bunkers. If they weren't newly constructed, they'd definitely been thoroughly remodeled. A large multi-branched antenna rose from the right rear corner.

I parked and read the signs attached to the closed gate. The top one read 'Avian Migratory Research Center' and the second one in larger letters read 'NO TRESPASSING!'

Hmph. Not exactly welcoming. I turned off the engine and tried unsuccessfully to reach them by phone. I'd heard phone and internet reception could be iffy on the island. After about five minutes of frustration, I decided to head back to town to ask around about how I could contact them.

I turned the key to start the ATV, but the engine only sputtered and stopped. After a few coughs and rattles, the engine quit altogether. *Now what?*

I tried my phone again but had no bars. Out of options, I honked my horn hoping someone inside would hear me and come outside.

It took six blasts before the front door opened and a fellow about my age and height with shoulder length black hair came out and walked up to the gate. "Is there a problem?" he asked.

I explained my situation and asked if I could come inside to use the phone.

"Sorry Miss, but we are off-limits to the public. I can call for assistance if you like. Why do you want to visit us anyway?"

"My son is into birding and made me promise I'd give him a full report when I get back home to Anchorage."

"I see," he said. "Why don't you visit Clam Lagoon? That's where birders usually go."

"I will, if I'm here long enough, but it's too windy to go there today."

"That is true. Sorry I can't help you."

"My son is very interested in science. I thought he'd love to hear what kind of research you do here."

"That's good he likes science."

"Yes, I'm proud of him. Thanks, anyway. I'll wait until the ATV company can get here." I'd climbed back into my seat when I spotted the paper bag next to me. "Oh, I almost forgot. You're Billy Ivanoff, aren't you? I have something for you."

He nodded. A big smile spread across his face as he opened the bag of doughnuts.

"Your friend at the Blue Heron sent them. He said he made these this morning and asked me to deliver them because I told him I'd planned to drive out this way. He's missed seeing you lately."

"Sam? He sent them to me?" Billy asked.

"Yes. In fact, he's the one who told me how to find this place."

Billy opened the gate and led me inside to a small office. "You can sit down and make a call here."

Once I'd completed arranging for a repairman and giving directions, I looked at Billy. "They say it will be about an hour before they can get here."

"That's not good. I hope it's before the boss gets back."

"I'm sorry to be such a problem for you. My name is Beri Quinn, by the way." I held out my hand and shook his. "Glad to meet you."

"Come with me, Beri. I'll give you a quick tour while you wait. Thanks for bringing me Sam's doughnuts."

I followed him into a large plain rectangular room lined with computer screens covered with scrolling displays of data. "Who analyzes all this information?" I asked.

"Just the boss and a couple of helpers. One flew home to see his sick mother, and the other one is with the boss in town. The boss doesn't like to leave me here alone. They collect the data while they're gone and read it after they return."

"What kind of data do they collect?"

"I don't know." He shook his head. "Lots of numbers and Chinese letters, but I don't read Chinese."

"Do they collect birds so they can study them?"

"No. We don't keep birds here. Just study computers."

I noticed many of the computer screens displayed Chinese characters and snapped a few photos with my phone. I was glad it worked at least for pictures.

"Your son also likes computers?" he asked.

I smiled. "Not as much as he likes birds, but I have to have something to prove to him I came here. I'll take a picture out front for him when I leave."

"The rest of the equipment is underground to keep it safe in storms, but it looks about the same as…?" He abruptly stopped speaking and his body jerked to attention. "Someone just drove in. We must go back. Quick!"

We were seated in the front office when two Chinese men came through the door.

"What's the meaning of this?" the lead man shouted.

"This lady's ATV broke down. She's waiting for the repair man to arrive."

"You know the rules. She must wait outside," he said. "We do not allow visitors."

I rose from my chair. "I'm sorry. He was kind to let me use the phone and wait out of the wind." I felt terrible about causing Billy trouble. He was such a nice person.

"Get out. Get out now," his boss ordered.

Chapter Thirty-one

Shoved out the door by the larger of the two men, I stumbled to my inoperative ATV. Help to fix it was on the way, but sitting here for an hour or longer was not a pleasant prospect with those two goons inside. I tried the ignition again without success.

This was ridiculous. Maybe I could fix the darned thing myself, at least well enough to limp back to town. I only wished I knew more about ATVs.

Where to begin? No hood to lift. I climbed off and probed the workings of the machine. Under the seat I located the battery, which seemed a good place to start.

Sure enough, a cable to the battery felt loose. A small tool kit located adjacent to the battery provided a pair of pliers. I used it to tighten the cable.

I climbed back aboard, crossed my fingers, and tried the engine again. The resulting roar brightened my mood considerably.

Anxious to get out of there, I drove a short distance away from the building, stopping only long enough to snap a photo of the sign for Jack. While stopped, it occurred to me that the repairman would make a trip out here for nothing unless I contacted him.

I checked my phone. Still no service. Spotting a nearby ridge, I started uphill in an attempt to get better reception. Once I got there, the signal was strong enough to call and cancel my service request. That accomplished, I looked down at the research center below. The elevated vantage point afforded a better view of the antenna I'd noticed before. The lower part had been hidden by the building itself. It was enormous. I'd never seen one quite like it. I snapped a few photos of both it and the entire facility. There wasn't much else to see except the blocky building itself.

The wind velocity grew in intensity, making me even more uncomfortable. My hair whipped my face hard enough I felt sure it could slice open my skin, making me glad for the first time that I'd singed some of it at the storage unit fire.

I pulled off my helmet, twisted my hair into a knot on top of my head, replaced the helmet to hold it in place, and proceeded to retrace my route back to town.

The trip hadn't been very productive, but at least Billy got his doughnuts. I hoped he wasn't in too much trouble with his boss.

Mickey wasn't home when I entered our duplex, but I could see he'd been grocery shopping again as a bunch of bananas rested on the kitchen counter. He ate a lot for such a small person.

I undressed and jumped into the shower, feeling the tension in my neck and shoulders ease in the hot luxurious spray. Afterward, I changed into fresh jeans and a thermal shirt before turning on my laptop to take a closer look at the area we needed to cover when the weather cleared. Now that I had an up-close look at some of the land from the ground, I could better grasp the scope of our mission. Interesting that the area I'd just visited was at the center of our assignment. It would be good to take a more comprehensive look at the area from the air.

My stomach's grumbling reminded me I hadn't eaten since breakfast. I made a cup of tea and was taking my first bite of the sandwich I'd made when Mickey came through the front door.

"Good, you're back," he said. "Please don't eat too much lunch. I just told Sam we'd be at the Blue Heron for dinner. His special tonight is prime rib, and I don't want to miss it." He smacked his lips. "You were right. That's a great place to eat."

"Dinner sounds good, but I'm starving now. Could I have a banana with my egg sandwich?"

"Help yourself. I bought plenty for both of us. A fresh produce delivery just came in, and I couldn't resist."

He ducked his head and frowned. "I got into a little trouble today. I went exploring in the area with all the disintegrating buildings and got stopped by a city official. I didn't realize I needed to check in with them first. Anyway, he was nice, and I apologized. Guess I should have read those tourism brochures they gave us at the airport more carefully."

"Glad you worked it out with them. Did you see anything of interest while you were exploring?"

"Lots of buildings full of mold. Even a dried-up swimming pool. This place must have been a bustling military base when it was operational. Now, it's sad to see everything gone to ruin. I saw rusted vehicles, decaying barracks and other buildings, even some rats. It's probably dangerous to poke around too much. I can understand why the city has rules."

The doorbell rang, startling us both.

"Who can that be?" Mickey asked. He rose and walked to the door.

Billy stood outside shifting from foot to foot and scanning the road behind him. "Can I come in?"

"Of course, Billy," I said as Mickey stood aside, giving me a questioning look.

"Please close the door fast," Billy said. "I don't want them to know I'm here."

"Them?" Mickey asked.

"It's a long story," I said. "I met Billy today at the bird research facility. Billy, this is my team member, Mickey."

"Nice to meet you." Mickey shook his hand.

"Come on in and have a seat," I said.

Billy paused and looked down at his feet. "Could I talk to you alone for a minute, Beri?"

Mickey walked toward the bedrooms. "I was about to take a nap anyway. It was nice meeting you."

Billy nodded. "Same here."

"Come into the kitchen. I can make some coffee, or maybe tea might be better. We only have instant coffee."

"Thanks, but no time. Just wanted to warn you Mr. Chou is furious. They don't think I know Chinese, but I learned to understand the language from my grandmother. I can't read it, but I know what they say."

"What did you hear them say?" I asked, heating up water for us despite him saying no.

He hesitated. "Maybe they kill you. At least force you to tell them what you're really after." He shook his head. "I don't know. It makes no sense to me."

"As I told you, I'm only interested in birds." I swallowed a sip of tea, but my throat still felt dry. "Why are they so suspicious?"

"I don't know. I told them your son loves birds, but they found out you have an airplane here, and you want to take pictures. They don't like that."

"Why does that bother them? I'm sure people take pictures all the time—satellites do, too."

"I don't know. I just want you to be careful. They are not nice people."

"Thank you, Billy. I appreciate the heads-up. How about you? I'm sorry if I caused you trouble with your job."

"I quit already. I didn't like it there anyway. They probably hired me so local people wouldn't bother them." He put his still full teacup down after a tentative sip. "I have to go."

As soon as Billy left, Mickey poked his head around the corner. "What was that all about?"

I filled him in on the events of the day. "Something sketchy is going on at that place. Billy came to warn me that they may be out to get me. They were very suspicious to begin with, but when they learned I planned to take aerial photographs, their paranoia intensified. I'm not sure why."

"Guess I can't trust you to be on your own for one morning," Mickey joked. "Don't worry, I'll be your bodyguard."

I clapped him on the shoulder. "Thanks. I feel so much better."

The Blue Heron was packed. Apparently, the menu tonight was a town favorite. Other than a few kids eating burgers, every table ordered the prime rib. If Adak had any vegetarians, they knew better than to come in on prime rib night.

I'd ordered the petite cut, but Mickey chose a full serving along with salad and a baked potato dripping with butter and sour cream.

"I hope you don't mind my asking, but how do you keep from gaining weight? If I ate as much as you, I'd double in size."

Mickey grinned. "It's my one talent in life. I can eat as much as I want and never gain an ounce. I've been this way since I was sick as a child." He stopped for a sip of cola before continuing. "My jockey friends all hated me for it."

"I can understand why they'd be envious. Don't tell me you're going to order dessert, too."

"Tempting idea, but no. I think I've had enough. I'll ask for the check if you're ready to go."

"I'm ready. Better ask for a receipt. I know we have per diem to cover expenses, but I'm not sure how government agencies calculate Adak prices."

"Good idea."

While he paid, I slid into my jacket, grabbed the backpack I'd brought for safekeeping and gave Sam a wave good-bye.

We'd barely stepped out the door when two police officers stopped us.

"Beri Quinn?" one of the officers asked.

"Yes," I responded.

"We need you to come down to the precinct with us. We have a few questions for you."

"Me? Why?"

"There's been a murder, and we think you may be one of the last persons to see the victim alive."

Chapter Thirty-two

Mickey and I drove back to the rental from the police station in near darkness. "What I don't understand," he said, "is how the police knew you were one of the last to see Billy Ivanoff alive. And so quickly?"

"I think they found his body near our place, and he had a slip of paper in his pocket with my name and address written on it."

"That explains it. I thought maybe one of our neighbors had a front door camera that showed him arriving here. They're everywhere these days. Why not Adak?"

"What's amazing to me is that the killer found Billy so fast. Either the small-town grapevine at its best, or more likely, he was followed."

Mickey pressed the garage door opener and parked the car inside next to my rented ATV. He jumped out and opened the door to the kitchen. "What the hell? Someone ransacked the place."

I followed him inside. Cereal boxes had been dumped on the floor along with the contents of every other food container from the cupboards. The refrigerator door hung open, milk puddled on the tile floor.

"Looks like my new friends paid us a visit while we were at the police station. Brazen of them," I said. "Too bad the police didn't stick around to watch our place."

"Considering the size of the local population, and the station we just left, I'm sure the police have limited manpower. How many officers can they have?"

Mickey walked into his bedroom and emerged red-faced and steaming. "Everything I brought is in a heap on the floor. My iPad and electric razor are both smashed."

The mess in my room mimicked Mickey's. It was a good thing I'd taken my backpack with me to the restaurant. My laptop and maps were safe inside. I pulled out my phone and called the police.

"They'll send an officer right over," I told Mickey. "Don't think we'll get much sleep tonight. I'll call Jason and update him on the situation."

"Good idea."

After the officer finally left, promising to watch for future intruders, we straightened our meager belongings, swept and mopped the kitchen floor and headed to our bedrooms to try to get a few hours of sleep.

Unfortunately, my mind wouldn't slow down. I couldn't stop thinking about Billy. What had I done? I'd barged ahead without much thought about consequences. Now Billy was dead. Skip, too, although my decisions weren't the cause of his death. I still didn't know why Skip was killed other than it had something to do with Charlie. I hadn't had any warning that trouble could be ahead. This time, though, I should have known better.

When I awoke, Mickey was already in the kitchen drinking coffee. "I'll make you a cup," he said. "You look like you could use one. Hope you don't want milk in it."

"Thanks. Just black is great. I didn't get much sleep."

"What's the plan for today?" he asked.

"I just checked the weather. It's looking better, but not good enough to fly the project yet." I sighed. "What I want to do is put yesterday's events out of my mind, so I'm going to take the ATV out to Clam Lagoon. Might as well do some birding while I have the chance."

"Not by yourself, you're not," Mickey said. "I'm coming, too."

"Sure, if you're up for it. I could use the company, but I think I'll swing by the airport and get my shotgun from the survival gear, just in case. I want to check on the plane, anyway."

"Good idea. Think we could also swing by the Blue Heron? Maybe Sam would make us a couple of sandwiches to sustain us on the trip."

The plane appeared untouched. I pulled my shotgun, ammo and a flashlight from the survival duffle bag and stopped on the way out to chat with the security guard. After I described our situation, I asked him to keep a close eye on the Cessna. He agreed to watch it and said he'd tell the other guards to do the same.

"Don't worry," he said. "The tie-down area is fenced and visitors have to show credentials to enter. What do these suspects look like?"

I described the two men I'd seen. "I'm not certain if there are others involved."

We climbed back into the ATV and lurched along the road toward Clam Lagoon. After bouncing in one particularly nasty pothole, Mickey piped up. "Tell me again why we're taking this piece of junk instead of the car?"

I smiled. "There is road access, but I understand the area around the lagoon is sandy with some dunes. We can get a lot closer to the best viewing areas if we're driving an ATV."

"Where is Clam Lagoon anyway?"

"It's here on the north end of the island. The drive isn't long."

"Look!" Mickey pointed at an eagle sitting atop a light pole beside the road. "We don't have to even leave town to find birds."

"You can find eagles everywhere. Especially scavenging around dumpsters and at the dump."

He ignored my lack of excitement. "How much farther?" Mickey asked.

"It's less than ten miles from here."

"That's good news." Mickey lifted himself up from the seat to stretch his back.

"C'mon, this can't be as bad as riding a galloping horse."

"I'll take the horse any day."

Two volcanoes, Mount Moffet and Mount Adagdak, rose ahead. We passed Snow Pond on our left as we drove through hills covered in wild rye and meadows of anemone and lupine. Fireweed grew along the side of the road. Nature's artistry was evident in every direction.

Once we arrived at our destination, the water was at low tide and algae-covered mud flats flowed to land's edge. The road skirted the lagoon, and we drove the length of it before climbing off the ATV to walk the edge of the beach.

I pulled my binoculars, sketch pad, and phone from my backpack and snapped pictures of birds when I could get close enough. A group of plovers cooperated, running along the mud nearby. Birds that were too far away to photograph, I checked out with my binoculars and sketched as best I could. I wrote a description of colors and outstanding features of each. Jack could try to identify those when I got home. A few were totally unfamiliar to me and may have been visitors from Asia.

We watched a bald eagle dive and scare off a pair of green-winged teal.

"I got it!" Mickey said. "I got a picture of him swooping down on them."

I leaned over to look at the photo. "I'd love to get a copy for…"

A shot rang out and an explosion of mud and plant matter splattered us. Birds startled and flew off in all directions.

"Get down," I shouted. "Someone's shooting at us!"

I'd left my weapon in the ATV. We signaled each other and crouched down to run back to retrieve it. We waited for more shots, but nothing happened. I only heard the sucking sound of our footsteps in the mud tracking our movement.

Maybe it was meant as a warning shot, but why?

After we reached the ATV, I shouted, "Let's get out of here."

Mickey agreed. "You don't have to tell me twice. I'll drive. You can hold the gun."

CHAPTER THIRTY-THREE

Mickey headed the ATV back toward town, expecting another gunshot any minute. We detoured off the main road onto the adjacent dunes and hillocks of a meadow. "I think we're safer staying away from the main road. Better to take a chance with ordinance than bullets that we know will explode."

"I agree," I said. "Besides, the main danger with the unexploded stuff is when you dig down and run into an old minefield or ammo dump."

"Yeah. I heard a couple of contractors talking about needing permits to dig before they could start on their project. Some areas are completely off limits." Mickey swerved to miss a large rock.

"I don't understand why someone shot at us in the first place. Or why Billy was killed. What do they think I saw at that place?"

"I don't know. What did you see?" Mickey asked.

"Nothing much. A lot of computer screens with Chinese characters. Nothing I could understand. What I found more interesting was what I didn't see."

"And what's that?"

"Birds. Strange that an avian research place wouldn't have any birds or even a migration map."

"What are you saying, Beri? Do you think the place is a front of some kind?"

"Maybe. They certainly didn't want visitors. But a front for what?"

The tires hit a canyon of a pothole causing the ATV to lurch. Ahead was a larger than usual warning sign. Mickey checked behind us and swerved. "I'm thinking we could get back on the road now. Don't think anyone's following us."

"Good idea. The terrain is getting rough, and the last thing we need is to flip over or have a breakdown out here." I looked up at the sky, then at Mickey. "Do you see what I see?"

He swiveled and shook his head. "I guess not. Can't see the beach from here, just potholes and sky."

"Exactly. The sky is clearing. I think we can get our job done. It won't take us long if we can get moving. Let's head to the airport, and I'll get a weather advisory there."

"Won't it be awfully late in the day to start?" he asked.

"No, it's LIDAR, remember. We don't need light. It's the fog, clouds, and wind that get in the way. I think we'll have enough light to take a few digital photos, too, if we do them first."

"Assuming we'll have a short weather window at best, we might as well take maximum advantage of the ground control. I know I'm anxious to finish and get back home."

"Sounds like we have our work cut out for us."

"Let's calibrate in the air. The weather report shows only a brief clearing. We need to hustle." After takeoff, we flew the flight lines Jason had drawn on our maps. "Unusually low altitude project," I said.

"Yeah, I'm surprised he didn't have us do the job by drone or helicopter. I'm a lot happier when I'm not so close to the ground in a plane. Especially when someone might decide to shoot at me."

"Fortunately, it's a small job, and a good portion of it is over the port and the runway area. I already contacted the tower for clearance to take pictures around the runway. We'll only fly over the research area for a few lines and should finish before their eyes adjust from their computer screens."

"Sounds good."

I turned to look back at Mickey. "Here we go, we're about to fly over the area now."

We flew the lines over the Avian Center in less than five minutes and with no sign of anyone emerging from the building.

"Who knows? They may still be out at Clam Lagoon. Let's finish up and send the data to the computer in Anchorage tonight. If Jason says it looks good, we can crate up the equipment and send it back on the Alaska Airlines flight tomorrow. We might even be able to leave for home. Weather permitting, of course."

"Aren't we going to contact the police about our getting shot at?"

"We'll see. If everything goes well, I might wait to contact them after we leave."

Mickey frowned. "If you say so, but I don't think they'd be happy about it."

Chapter Thirty-four

Despite the iffy communication system available on Adak, our data transfer went through without a hitch on the first try. We got the go-ahead to crate up the equipment and return it to the Anchorage office.

Afterward, I couldn't stop thinking about Billy. We swung by the police station to check on the status of the investigation and say good-bye. The officer on duty looked up as we entered.

"No further problems, I hope." He stood up from his desk to face us. "Actually, I'm glad you stopped by. We interviewed Billy's employers. They were shocked at his death and claimed to know nothing about it or about the break-in at your quarters."

"Do you believe them?" I asked.

He shrugged. "I'm skeptical. Crime here is mostly limited to looting or drunkenness. Murder is very unusual. I have to admit I'm more suspicious of newcomers. No proof, though."

"You won't have to worry about watching our place after tonight if the weather is good enough for us to leave in the morning."

"Thanks for the heads-up. If anything develops after you leave, we'll be in touch. We may need you to testify if this goes to court."

Mickey gave me a sideways look.

"There is one more thing we need to report." I sighed. "We drove an ATV out to Clam Lagoon yesterday afternoon, and someone took a shot at us..."

"And you're just reporting it now?"

"We didn't have phone service out there. As we returned to town, the weather cleared up, and we didn't want to waste a second. We jumped in the plane to take our photographs and didn't return until just now."

The officer shook his head. "I'll report it to my supervisor. I hope this isn't the start of a new trend." He typed a few words on his computer. "Just the one shot?"

"Yes. I assume it was a rifle. We ran to our wheels and left immediately from the mudflats where we were bird-watching." I stood, ready to leave. "Please keep us informed if you make any progress on Billy's killer. We'll be happy to help in any way we can. Billy seemed like a great guy," I said with a catch in my throat.

Once back at the rental, we entered cautiously to find everything as we'd left it. Mickey used our few remaining provisions to hustle up grilled cheese sandwiches along with some canned tomato soup. We packed our belongings and tidied up.

We managed to sleep a few hours. I woke, checked the weather and roused Mickey at five A.M."

Mickey rubbed his eyes and stretched. "Short night. Too early to stop for breakfast?"

"Afraid so. The Blue Heron won't open for another hour. Let's get underway now and we can get something to eat in Cold Bay. We'll be stopping for gas there anyway, if we can."

All was quiet when we arrived at the airport gate. When we tried to enter the tie-down area, the security guard was not in sight. I grabbed my phone and called the number listed on the sign attached to the fence. Thankfully the phone worked, and a sleepy voice answered. He arrived a few minutes later with a sheepish look on his face. "Just went inside to make some coffee," he said. "Sorry."

The plane appeared undisturbed, but I ran through my preflight checklists with great care. Since I'd gassed up after returning last night, it didn't take long.

I climbed aboard and called to Mickey to tell him it was time to leave. While I waited, I stood in the plane's doorway and scanned the panorama of Adak one last time. It appeared both beautiful and forlorn in the early morning light. The ocean, mountains, and rugged cliffs on the one hand and the desolate skeletal vehicles and decaying buildings on the other. My favorite parts, the birds and the people weren't visible at the moment, but I'd never forget them or this place where they live.

I slid into my seat and called Flight Service for the current weather forecast for Anchorage and Merrill Field.

The radio crackled: "8000 broken with visibility unrestricted. Be aware there may be volcanic activity en route around Mount Shishaldin. Please give pilot report on activity if you encounter any."

"Roger," I said.

Seeing his arrival, I said, "It's a go, Mickey. All aboard. Weather looks good."

"What about that volcano?"

"I don't expect it to be a problem. It rumbles a lot."

He climbed in off the wing and latched the door. I began my run-up of the left engine, followed it with the right and contacted the tower.

"Okay, 15 Quebec runway five, altimeter 2992."

"Roger. Adak tower, 15 Quebec ready for takeoff, right turn on course."

"Cleared for takeoff. Right turn approved. Have a nice trip."

Once in the air, Mickey asked, "How long until we stop to get something to eat?"

"It's about three hours to Cold Bay, depending on the wind."

"Three hours! That's not breakfast, that's lunch." He scrabbled around in his jacket pockets and brought out two candy bars. "Good thing I made a stop at the vending machine at the airport. I filled my thermos with coffee. too. Let me know if you want some."

"Glad you came prepared. I can use some coffee. Where did you find it?"

"I smelled it. Followed my nose and asked the security guard. He led me to it."

"Good work." I poured a cup, took a sip, and pointed out to the right. "We're over Great Sitkin Island now. We'll follow the chain all the way to Cold Bay."

"How many islands in the chain altogether?"

"About three hundred. Some are quite small. A lot of them are volcanic, part of the Pacific Ring of Fire."

Mickey stretched his arms over his head and yawned. "I'll try counting islands instead of sheep. Wake me if there's anything interesting to see."

The flight went uneventfully. The light turbulence we occasionally encountered didn't disturb Mickey's slumber. Visibility wasn't bad, although I flew IFR anyway. Conditions changed rapidly out here.

I elbowed Mickey when we neared Umnak Island and Shishaldin Volcano. "Wake up. We're about to fly by Smokin' Moses. You'll want to take a look."

"'Smokin' Moses'?"

"Yes. The locals' nickname for Mount Shishaldin. It's the large dome-shaped mountain puffing smoke down there."

"Is that the one that's about to erupt?"

"I doubt that it will. It's been belching smoke like that since the Russians first discovered it back in the 1700s. It does erupt occasionally, but I'm willing to bet it's another false alarm."

Mickey took out his phone and snapped a few pictures. "Thanks. That was worth waking up for. Must say, I'm glad you're not worried, but I do smell smoke. Actually, it smells like matches burning. We're not on fire, are we?"

"No. I think you're smelling sulfur from the volcano. I might be wrong about my forecast."

He snapped another photo.

"Look at that!" I pointed to the peak now spouting fire. Lightning flashed from the flames.

Mickey's jaw dropped. "We can't fly through there!"

"We won't. I'm going to move as far away as fast as I can."

"I felt the percussion of the blast, but why didn't we hear it?" Mickey asked.

"I'm no expert, but I think the engine noise disguised it. Our headphones probably helped, too."

As we continued to fly on the edge of a plume of ash, I clung to the yoke to stabilize the aircraft as it bucked, bounced, and rattled in rapid-fire jolts. After one dramatic drop in altitude, I managed to get the plane under control and headed away from the volcano. Landing in Cold Bay was no longer an option. I set a direct course for Anchorage and was supremely thankful for our auxiliary fuel tanks. We should be able to make it to Merrill unless we encountered strong head winds.

The radio came alive with a flight advisory: "Attention all aircraft in Umnak area. Mount Shishaldin has erupted. Advising all aircraft to stay outside radius. Plume moving to north, northeast to an estimated height of 18,000 feet."

"That's a surprise. Even though we were warned of the possibility, I didn't believe it." I let out the breath I'd been holding. "Glad we weren't any closer, but we're still going to have to deal with this cloud of ash. It's far too abrasive for an airplane engine. If I fly through too much of it, Dean will never forgive me. And, that's assuming the engines will fly through it."

"What can we do? It's starting to look hazier already."

"I'll try to get above it." I glanced at Mickey and noted the pallor in his face. "You can help by getting the oxygen tanks operational. I need to increase our altitude. We'll require oxygen at 12,000 feet and the sooner the better, so we don't have to breathe this stuff in."

"I'll get it going now. How long will we have to use it?"

"For the rest of the flight. We'll need to stay above the plume all the way to Anchorage. If I can't get above the ash, we may have to divert to Homer, but I'm hoping that won't be necessary."

We donned oxygen masks and watched as the air grew increasingly dust-colored and ash-laden.

Mickey coughed. "Hey, it's getting dark, and you weren't kidding about it getting hard to breathe."

I picked up my mic. "Anchorage Center, 15 Quebec at 12,000 feet encountering poor visibility. Volcanic activity is apparent. Need to change altitude. Requesting change to 18,000 feet."

"Okay, 15 Quebec, altitude change approved."

As the manifold pressure decreased noticeably, I increased the props to 3300 RPMs and pushed the throttles forward as far as possible, being careful not to over-boost the engines. We had enough power to climb slowly. Good thing I'd had the malfunctioning mag replaced in Adak. "Looks like the air filters are getting clogged."

The light gradually increased as we climbed from the ash cloud until daylight returned. My eyes, however, still irritated by the grit, blurred with tears.

I leveled out at 18,000 feet and continued to Anchorage. Fortunately, the winds were from the southwest, so the ash drifted more toward Prince William Sound.

"It's clear out the side windows, but I still can't see anything out the front," Mickey said.

"The plexiglass windshield's been pitted by the ash particles. Fortunately, the side windows were spared."

Mickey turned to me with an anxious look on his face. "How are you going to land this thing? The windscreen is so frosted from the ash you won't be able to see the runway."

"I'll look out the side window." I caught Mickey's eye roll in my peripheral vision.

After picking up my mic, I contacted Anchorage Center for an approach to Ted Stevens International Airport and requested an instrument landing. I informed them I'd have minimum fuel and limited forward visibility due to ash abrasion from the volcanic eruption.

"Why not Merrill Tower?" Mickey asked.

"I can't make a full instrument landing there. I'd rather err on the safe side."

As we approached Anchorage, the radio came alive. "Roger, 15 Quebec. Hold for traffic. Standard holding. Cleared to enter the hold."

I glanced at my fuel gauge after multiple turns in the hold. Below a quarter in both tanks. Hopefully, it wouldn't be much longer or I'd have to declare an emergency.

Mickey shifted in his seat for the third time in as many minutes.

"Nervous?" I asked.

"I'll be glad to get on the ground. It's been quite a trip."

"Don't worry. We're delayed because we're not the only plane affected by the volcano. The tower's dealing with a lot of traffic."

"Okay, 15 Quebec, this is Anchorage Approach. You are cleared for ILS runway approach. Emergency vehicles will be on stand-by due to your impaired visibility on landing."

I made the approach to minimums. Once I was over the threshold, I spotted the runway through my side window, lined up the plane between the light fixtures, and landed uneventfully. I waved at the fire truck and taxied to the transient tie-down area.

Chapter Thirty-five

Mickey and I disembarked and walked to flight service. I closed our flight plan and called the office to ask for a ride back to Merrill Field.

Angie answered the phone. "You're back? Great. We've been worried since we heard the news about the volcano. I'll send Dean right over to pick you up." She paused. "Why did you land at Ted Stevens International?"

"I'll explain later. Please warn Dean that we got the plane back in one piece, but he'll have a few challenges to deal with before we fly it again."

Angie had apparently called Dad as well as Dean because both Frank and Jack were waiting at the office when we drove up.

"Mom!" Jack yelled and raced into my arms. "We were so scared."

I hugged him tight. "I was anxious to see you, too, but I'm sorry you were frightened."

"I knew you'd make it, but am still relieved to see you," Frank added, his voice gruff. He clapped his hand on my shoulder and turned toward Mickey. "And who is this young man?"

"I'm sorry," I said to Dad. "This is Mickey Ford. He's my camera and LIDAR operator. He just arrived in Alaska earlier this month."

"Glad to meet you. Don't know much about that LIDAR stuff myself. I retired before it was invented, I guess. Doesn't take long to get behind the times." He shrugged and shook Mickey's hand. "Anyway, I guess you had a good initiation to flying in Alaska on this trip."

Mickey grinned. "I reckon I did. Good to meet you, sir."

We walked into the office together and dropped our bags beside the door.

"Okay, enough suspense," Angie said. "Why didn't you land here like you usually do?"

"You'll understand when you see the plane," Dean said and shook his head. "And it was our new plane, too."

"Yes," I added. "You could say we were sandblasted. The windscreen is so pitted that I couldn't see to land. I came in on instruments and once I crossed the threshold, I managed to see enough out the side window to stay within the width of the runway. Merrill Field didn't have the localizer I needed."

"That bad, huh?" Frank said. "Reminds me of when Mount Redoubt erupted in the late 80s. An Alaska Airlines 747 flew through that plume and lost all four engines. The pilots barely got them restarted or they would've crashed into the mountains before reaching Anchorage."

"We did lose some power, but we managed to climb above the cloud of ash to make it back okay."

"A little more excitement than I anticipated," Mickey said, "but I'll have some good stories to tell back home."

"Mr. H. is stranded in Fairbanks," Angie said. "He flew down yesterday morning to meet with someone at the university and planned pre-volcano to fly back today. Now, I think he's planning to rent a car instead. Assuming of course, that they're renting them during all the hubbub. Ash isn't that good for cars, either, I hear. Anyway, he said to tell you he'll meet with you first thing in the morning, conditions willing. Otherwise, he'll call."

"Thanks, Angie," I said.

"Let's get you home," Dad said to me. "I'll cook some fresh salmon for dinner." He turned to Mickey. "You're welcome to come, too. If I say so myself, I'm a darned good cook."

"Thanks, I'm sorely tempted, but I need to get home. Maybe I can get a raincheck." He picked up his bag and waved good-bye as he left.

Angie handed me a stack of mail. "You might want to check this before you leave." She patted the envelope on top as I took the pile.

Staring up at me was another letter from Charlie. Pushing curiosity aside, I handed the pile back to her. "Thanks, but I think I'll wait to go through it tomorrow."

Chapter Thirty-six

We arrived home to find Sarah bustling around the kitchen. Frank moved behind her and pulled her shoulders back against his chest into a backward hug. "Taking over my job?" he asked.

"No. I just threw some potatoes in to bake and washed some greens for a salad. The fish is all yours," she said.

While the lovebirds worked on dinner, I went upstairs, took a quick shower, and changed out of my gritty clothes. When I returned, Ross was setting the table, and Dad had pulled the salmon and French bread from the oven.

Ross leaned down and gave me a quick peck on the cheek. "You timed things just right. Dinner is ready to serve." He kissed me again, lingering this time as I melted against him. "I missed you. Seems like you were gone a long time."

"A little over a week, but it seemed longer to me, too. I'm glad Dad called to tell you I was back."

"We'll have to go out for a night cap later so you can fill me in on your escapades."

"Sure. As long as we don't stay out too late. I'm looking forward to sleeping in my own bed for a change."

Ross pulled me close and whispered in my ear. "We'll have to see about that."

Frank cleared his throat. "Dinner is on the table. Hold the shenanigans until after we eat."

We'd taken about two bites when the phone rang.

"I'll get it." Frank picked up the receiver from the counter.

"Hello. Yes, Dennis. Hey, we just started eating dinner. Can he call you back in a few minutes?"

After returning the receiver to its holder, Dad came back to the table and said to Jack, "That was your dad. He wants you to call him after we finish."

"Oh," Jack said. "Probably about the school."

My heart stopped for a second. "What school?"

"Okay, I haven't had a chance to tell you, but I was accepted by the Stellar Golf School for this coming year. I'm super happy because I didn't think I'd make the cut. Dad took me to San Diego to try out before I left."

"San Diego?" *That damn Dennis. What has he done now?*

"Dad says I'll be close enough to Scottsdale that I can spend a lot of time with them on breaks."

"You can't leave." My appetite had vanished. "Not again! You just got home."

Sarah gave Frank a questioning look. He turned to Jack. "It's not fair to your mom to spring this on her at the dinner table. Let's postpone the conversation until after we've eaten."

Jack nodded but couldn't hide his excitement as he squirmed in his chair.

I picked at my salad, leaving my salmon untouched. "Dennis has done it again," I muttered to Dad as I cleared the table and slid my fish into a ziplock bag to save for tomorrow's lunch.

Jack left and ran upstairs. When he returned, he handed me an envelope. "This came while you were gone, Mom. My acceptance letter."

I opened it and read that Jack had scored in the top ten percent of applicants. The school was anxious to offer him admission and a small scholarship. My heart swelled and sank at the same time. Of course, I was proud of him, but I'd already spent one difficult school year without him due to my ex-husband's maneuvers to take Jack to Europe last year.

"Wow, Jack. Looks like you made quite an impression on them."

Jack ducked his head and grinned. "Yeah, I guess."

Dennis was so manipulative and knew me so well, he placed me in these impossible situations. I looked at Jack. "The school's not that close to where your dad lives."

"It's about a five-hour drive from Scottsdale, but since it's a boarding school, he'd only have to come get me for breaks, or I could get a plane ticket."

"I hope you could also fly up to spend some holidays with us."

"Mom! You know I would."

"You're okay with living at the school?" I asked, concerned.

"Sure. It'll be worth it to play golf. It's the only sport I'm good at, Mom."

"It sounds like the school really wants you. I'll have to do some research to see if I can afford it, though. Boarding schools are expensive."

"No problem. I have a scholarship, and Dad said he'd pay for the rest of it." He ran for the phone. "Let's call him back."

I sighed. *Déjà vu.* I called Dennis and expressed my displeasure about being left out of the decision process.

"I knew you'd object, and I didn't want the headache," he said. "You can't deny it's the best thing for Jack. He's beyond excited."

"You're right about that, but I wish you'd play fair and include me in the discussion before making plans. He is my son, too, you know."

"We're discussing it now, aren't we?"

"After the fact, yes." I paused before I said something I'd regret.

"Hey, you still there?" Dennis asked.

"Yes, I'm here, just thinking. You have to realize other people have made plans, too. If Jack leaves for school, he'll miss his grandpa's wedding."

"How was I supposed to know that? I didn't even know Frank was engaged."

"Just one example of why two-way communication is important." I took a deep breath. "Since you've worked out all the details, send us his itinerary, and we'll see what we can do on this end."

Dennis confirmed the schedule, and Sarah and Frank agreed to move the date of their wedding up a week to accommodate Jack's timeline.

Frank said sooner was better than later as far as he was concerned, and Sarah said she'd call Kincaid Park to make sure the venue would be available a week earlier.

Ross turned to me after the arrangements were made. "Well, that was intense, but I'm glad you've worked it all out. Are you ready for that nightcap now?" He grabbed my hand and gently pulled me toward the door. "I thought maybe we could drive down to Alyeska."

"Sounds good, but let me make a cup of coffee first, or I'll fall asleep before I can tell you about the trip."

Once in the car, I leaned back against the headrest and slumped down in my seat, exhausted both physically and emotionally. I hadn't anticipated losing Jack for another year. He was almost a teenager. Time was moving too fast.

It annoyed me that Dennis had managed to get his way. It was one of his most irritating qualities. But Jack was so happy, how could I say no?

Ross reached over and squeezed my knee. "I was proud of you back there. Jack is a lucky boy to have such a good mom. Many people would stand in their child's way just to thwart their ex. Dennis doesn't play fair when he excludes you from decisions."

"I think he feels it's his right as long as he's willing to foot the bill, but I'm happy to cover my part if only he'd quit shutting me out."

"My guess is he doesn't want to involve you. He enjoys having the power to control you. And to be fair, he has given Jack opportunities most kids wouldn't have, but he fails to recognize that you have done that, too."

The drive along Turnagain Arm was pleasant despite the heavy traffic so common this time of year. Tourists flocked to the pull-outs along the road, hoping to get a glimpse of a bore tide or maybe a beluga whale.

We arrived at the ski lodge and found a secluded table in the darkened bar. We ordered snifters of Frangelico and sipped the liqueur slowly to fully appreciate the complex hazelnut flavor. We didn't talk much, just savored the alone time together.

Ross nuzzled my neck, sending goosebumps through my body. *Damn, I loved this guy.* He suggested we rent a room for the night. I called Dad to let him know our plans while Ross made the arrangement with the desk. We left our unfinished drinks and moved to a cozy room decorated with an unlit fireplace and prints of skiers hurtling down the slopes.

After a shower for two, we tumbled into the king-sized bed for a much-anticipated night of togetherness.

I awoke early the next morning to find Ross staring intently at me. "What?" I asked.

"I'm memorizing this moment," he replied. He pulled me into his arms and said, "You are the best thing that's ever happened to me."

That's all it took. Afterward, we showered together again, resisted the temptation of staying another day, dressed, and headed home.

Chapter Thirty-seven

Ross had to leave early to meet his first student. I was wide awake and asked him to drop me off. The lights were already on at the office. Surprising, since I was over two hours early for work. An unfamiliar car sat outside. I quietly unlocked the door and crept inside with my phone in hand, ready to call 9-1-1 if I found an intruder. Instead, I discovered Jason sitting at his desk.

"Beri, what are you doing here at this hour?"

"Guess I've adjusted to Adak's time zone." I smiled. "I could ask you the same question. You're here early yourself."

"Yes. It took me awhile, but I finally found a rental car. Figured I might as well get to work when I arrived." He stood and stretched. "I hear you had volcano problems."

"I'll say. Smokin' Moses erupted minutes before we arrived in the area. Mickey and I were caught in the aftermath and couldn't land in Cold Bay for fuel as we'd planned. I was never so grateful for auxiliary fuel tanks and a light load."

"It pays to take precautions, especially flying out there, but a volcanic blast is hard to anticipate. Anyway, I'm glad you're here early. I wanted to go over your Adak data with you."

He pulled another chair over to his desk, sat down and tilted his computer screen so I could see it.

"Our primary area of interest is the portion of the island around a former bunker left by the military. Satellite images revealed unusual digging and construction adjacent to the structure and what appears to be some sort of antenna. The current occupants are Chinese nationals who we know little about at this point."

"Yes, I met a couple of them. Friendly, they were not. A local man employed by them was found murdered shortly after he broke their rules and allowed me to go inside while they were out."

"You were inside?" he asked, making eye contact.

"We're talking about the Avian Research Center, aren't we?"

"Yes, although we suspect they're researching something besides birds." He gave me an intense look. "What did you see inside?"

I described my impressions of the brief visit, then grabbed my phone. "Wait, I have a few pictures I took while I was there." I scrolled through my photos and handed him my phone.

He looked at me in astonishment and reached to take it. After a few moments of studying the images, he pointed to one. "What's this?" He indicated one of the outdoor shots.

"I have no idea. It looked like some strange antenna. I snapped the picture for my son. He's fascinated by electronics so I thought it might interest him. He's also a birder, which is why I went there in the first place."

He chuckled. "These pictures you took for your boy will keep our analysts busy for weeks. Our satellite images of this contraption were ambiguous. And while your aerial data is excellent, these close-ups are a gold mine."

He held up the phone, opened to a picture of the room full of glowing computer screens. "And this shot! We'll get a translator right on this. Does your son study foreign languages as well?" He pulled out a thumb drive and downloaded the photos from my phone.

"No, he doesn't read Chinese. I just thought the composition was interesting. Billy, my guide, mentioned there was another lower floor that held even more computers." I reached out and took my phone back. "So, what exactly are your analysts looking for, and why didn't you brief me about all this before I left?"

"We didn't ask you to investigate them on the ground because it was potentially dangerous. Our plan was to gather preliminary remote data and send experienced operatives later. As you probably noticed, Adak isn't a place where an undercover person is likely to go unnoticed. It turns out, you've accomplished far more than we expected."

He was right about the dangerous part. If I'd realized I was risking Billy's life, I'd never have finagled my way into the place. It made me wonder again if I was the cause of his death. "If they aren't studying birds, what do you think is going on there? I believe they murdered the Aleut employee who let me in."

"Yes, I heard. We're talking about classified information here. While you have security clearance to work with us, I'm limited in what I can tell you. Essentially, we think China may be planning to expand their island fetish beyond the South China Sea to include northern waters. They have long-term plans to dominate the Pacific. Our theory is they don't want to cede this strategic area to the U.S. and Russia."

"I still don't get it," I said. "What would they be looking for with some weird antenna in Adak that they couldn't see on a satellite image?"

"Good question. Hypothetically speaking of course, they might be looking for ways to better communicate with submarines. Right now, technology for communication at certain depths is limited to code transmissions and even that capability is mostly limited to the U.S. and Russia. Otherwise, submarines usually surface to receive transmissions. This can be a distinct disadvantage during military maneuvers."

"Is that what you think they're up to?"

"It's one possibility. To our knowledge, huge antenna fields are required for extremely low frequency (ELF) transmissions and for transmitting to lower depths. From what I can determine, we're not looking at anything like that. I'm guessing this is a test-run of some sort, possibly of a new technological communication advance they've made."

"But why Adak? Why wouldn't they choose Attu or another island closer to the end of the Aleutian chain?"

"I don't know. Adak does have the advantage of a world-class port that doesn't freeze in winter and an airport that can handle commercial air travel. Then of course, there's all that old military infrastructure that could possibly be of use." He shrugged. "They may be looking at something connected to those attributes or something else altogether. Maybe they thought they'd be less conspicuous on Adak because birding and hunting visitors would allow them to blend in. Or, they could see Adak as a stepping stone to using other islands."

"Who'd have suspected possible espionage in Alaska, especially in such a tiny town? Will you send operatives to check out the facility?"

"Possibly. I can't reveal specifics, but I'm sure immediate plans are in progress."

Tires crunched outside in the parking lot, interrupting our conversation.

Jason looked at his watch. "We've talked the night away. I'm hungry and you must be, too. How about we go to Peggy's for breakfast?"

We greeted Angie at the door as we put on our jackets and got ready to leave.

"Why were you two here so early?" she asked.

"I guess I'm still on Adak time. I couldn't sleep any later," I said.

"And I'm just in from Fairbanks. We'll return as soon as we grab some breakfast."

"Hurry back, Beri, I want to hear about Charlie's letter," Angie said with a wink.

Jason raised an eyebrow and gave me a questioning look.

I shook my head as I walked out the door. "It's nothing important," I said.

I was halfway through my omelet when my phone rang.

Angie sounded breathless. "Beri, you need to come back to the office. Quick!"

"We're almost finished. I won't be long."

"No. It's an emergency. You need to come now!"

"Okay, okay. Can you tell me…?" I asked.

"Now," she repeated. "You need to be here."

"I hear you. I'm leaving."

Jason stood. "I gather we need to get the bill."

"Yes. I'm not sure what's up, but Angie's in a dither and that's unusual for her." I stood to leave, my unease growing by the minute.

He signaled the server for the check, took one last sip of coffee and pushed back his chair.

I headed for the exit. *Why was Angie so unwilling to tell me what was going on?*

Chapter Thirty-eight

Angie rushed to me the moment I entered the office. She threw her arms around me. "It's Ross. He's had a heart attack!"

"What? Where is he?" I looked frantically between Angie and Jason, trying to absorb the news.

Angie moved me to a chair. "Here, sit down and I'll explain everything."

I fell into the chair, feeling completely numb. How could this be? Ross wasn't even forty years old. "He was fine last night."

"It happened while he was in the air with a student this morning. She said he didn't say a word, just moaned and when she looked back at him, he'd slumped over, unconscious."

"She? Who was he with?" I asked the question, though in my heart I already knew the answer.

"Megan. She'd failed her last lesson and needed more practice before he thought she'd be ready to go solo."

"So, what did she do?" I asked, trying to remain calm.

"She contacted the tower and explained the situation. They grabbed another flight instructor, put him on the mic, and he directed her through her pre-landing checklist. I guess she did a good job getting the plane down. Meanwhile, the tower notified 9-1-1 and had an ambulance waiting. They rushed him to the hospital." Angie smiled and gave my arm a reassuring pat. "Word is he's in the Coronary Care Unit and he's stable for now."

"Thank God!" I said. "I've got to go see him." I stood up and turned toward the door.

"Of course. Go, now," Jason said and waved me out. "Good luck and keep us posted."

I dashed through the front doors of the hospital and asked the receptionist for directions to the CCU.

"Are you a member of the patient's family?" she asked. "They don't allow other visitors, but there is a waiting room on the third floor."

"Thanks." I took the elevator and followed the signs to the Coronary Unit waiting area. Chairs were grouped outside two large closed doors.

One woman sat waiting, and I walked over to her. "Thank you, Megan. I hear you did an incredible job getting the plane down and saving Ross."

She stood and threw her arms around me. "Oh, Beri. I was so scared. I knew how to land the plane, but I was so afraid I couldn't get help fast enough. I mean, there was no way I could climb in back to give him CPR if he stopped breathing."

"No, but you did exactly the right thing and got him down so the paramedics could. You're a hero, you know."

She gave me a weak smile. "I guess."

"Have you been in to see him since he was admitted?"

"No. They're still doing tests and I'm not family." She pointed to a button outside the doors. "If you want to talk to the nurse's station, press that button."

"I wonder if they'll count a fiancée as family?" I pushed the button and asked.

It turned out I could see him as soon as they finished a procedure. They suggested I remain there until they called me.

I sat next to Megan and marveled at how much my attitude toward her had changed. I was in her debt for saving Ross.

She turned toward me, glanced at my left hand and asked, "Fiancée? When is the wedding?"

"I'm not sure. It's still up in the air. We decided to establish our partnership in the business first."

"I'm sorry," Megan said, blushing. "I didn't know he was off limits."

"Not your problem. We didn't exactly advertise our relationship. It didn't seem like the professional thing to do. Anyway, I'm very grateful you were with him when this happened." I took a deep breath and squeezed her hand. "And, I'm glad you're here with me now."

Chapter Thirty-nine

After an hour-long wait, Megan left, saying she'd come back tomorrow. I called Dad to update him, then sat alone in the waiting area, praying Ross would recover, and twisting the locket around my neck. Another hour passed, and my stomach growled. It seemed odd to be hungry at a time like this, but a sandwich sounded good. Just as I stood to find a vending machine, the doors opened and a nurse emerged.

"You can go in. He's awake and appears stable for now." She led me to a glass-enclosed cubicle containing a bed, an IV drip, and multiple pieces of monitoring equipment. My eyes swept past all that and focused on Ross, smiling and looking pale, but otherwise almost normal. I sighed in relief. I didn't know what I'd expected.

"I've been wondering when you'd get here."

I leaned over, kissed him on his cheek and ruffled his hair. "They kept me waiting outside the unit since this morning. Said the doctors were doing tests."

"They were right about that. I've been prodded and poked until there couldn't possibly be anything more to discover." He squeezed my hand. "Anyway, I guess I passed muster. The doc says I should be okay if I take care of myself. After this warning and with my family history of heart disease, I need to make some lifestyle changes apparently."

I bent over the bed and hugged him gently, tubes and all. "I'm so glad you're okay. You scared me."

"I'm sorry. Didn't mean to." Ross turned a somber face toward me. "I'll live alright, but you know what this will mean for us, don't you?" His shoulders slumped back against the pillow.

I sat in the chair next to the bed but kept hold of his hand without the IV port in it. "That you'll be good. That's what's important."

"Yes, but it also means I can't work as a flight instructor anymore. I won't be eligible to pass the medical after a heart attack, and no one would want to fly with me if I could."

"We'll worry about that later. Meanwhile, my Adak job is finished. I'm sure I can fill in for you until we figure things out."

His face crumpled. "It's my life, Honey. I've got to be able to fly again."

"You will. Maybe not as an instructor, but if I remember correctly, you can apply to restore your flight eligibility in six months."

"Yeah, maybe." He sighed. "I'm tired. I think I need some sleep."

I smiled for the first time since hearing the news from Angie. "Probably a good idea."

"Thanks for coming. Go home and catch up from your trip. I'll try to be in better spirits when you come back."

"I'll call the nurse later to check on you, and come by early tomorrow so I can be here when your doctor arrives. Call me if I can bring anything for you besides the essentials." I stood and kissed him good-bye.

"Don't know if you realize you had another visitor who tried to see you today. Megan saved your life, but they wouldn't let her in since she wasn't family. I think she'll try again tomorrow."

"The doctor filled me in on what happened. Guess she was ready to go solo after all, just lacked confidence in herself."

I kissed him again. "Glad you're doing well. I love you."

"I know." He winked and managed a smile. "As I nod off, I'll be remembering last night."

Jason ushered me into his office. "How's Ross doing?" He pulled out a chair. "Have a seat."

"Actually, he looked much better than I expected. Tired, mostly."

"Glad to hear it. Have the doctors given him a prognosis?"

"Favorable, as long as he takes care of himself. His main concern is the business. He'll be ineligible for a medical certificate for at least six months and flight instructing probably not at all. Which brings me to my question for you. Can you spare me to help cover his students now that the Adak job is finished? I'd like to help out until he can hire another pilot."

He grimaced. "Angie's over there now rescheduling students. We can work something out for you to share your time, but we can't give you up entirely. We still have a number of mapping projects to complete. I wouldn't object to your filling in after checking the weather over our sites. I'd trust you to keep a log of your hours. Oh, and Angie asked me to give you this." He handed me a list of possible instructors she'd compiled for me to contact.

"Go home for now; you've had enough stress for one day and you haven't even had a chance to recover from your trip. Take the rest of the day off. We'll see what tomorrow brings."

I drove home, wondering what would happen to the business. We couldn't schedule students only to cancel if the weather over my project looked good. I could fill in, but I couldn't be the primary instructor while still fulfilling my other responsibilities. Angie must be scrambling to figure out what to tell the students she was rescheduling now.

I pulled into the parking area at Potter's Marsh and turned off the ignition. I'd always loved coming here when I needed to sort things out. Something about the combination of water and birds relaxed me. It wasn't the isolation or quiet as the highway and railroad track both ran across the front side or that it was also a popular tourist spot. It was just peaceful.

I sat in the car and glanced at Angie's list of possible instructors. They were mostly newbies trying to build hours. While there was nothing wrong with that, I preferred experienced pilots who taught to share their love of aviation. Who did I know that fit that description?

My friend Kaitlyn came to mind. I gave her a call, and she sounded interested.

"Only one problem, Beri. I have a commercial license, but I'd have to get a flight instructor endorsement. It would take a little time. I could use the work, though."

"Great. Let me know when you can start."

I hung up, optimistic that Kaitlyn would be a natural for the position. If only she could start yesterday. Who did I know that was already qualified? When the answer came, it was so obvious I couldn't believe I hadn't thought of him first.

Richard Toledo had been a part-time instructor and a very good one for my former business. A retired military pilot, he'd liked the part-time hours and the notion of giving back to the aviation community. I called him, but he didn't answer. I left a message asking him to call me as soon as possible.

I got out of the car and walked onto the wooden walkway fronting the marsh. I watched as a goldeneye bobbed his head beneath the surface of the water, hoping for a quick snack. Resting my arms on the wooden railing, I leaned over for a closer look when a hand rested on my shoulder. I jerked upright and came face-to-face with Charlie.

"What are you doing here?" I asked.

"I followed you from your office."

"This is ridiculous, Charlie. You can't just keep popping up in my life."

"You don't give me much choice. I wrote and asked you to meet me last week, but you didn't show up."

I took a step away from him. "I was out of town and just got back. Your letter is probably sitting unopened on my desk."

"We need to talk. Let's drive to the back of the marsh where we can have some privacy. It's too exposed here."

I threw up my hands in exasperation. "Look, I have a lot on my plate right now. I'll go with you, fill you in on what little news I have, but then I want you to go away and stay away. I can't help you anymore."

"You might want me to fill you in on a few things first." He shrugged and headed for the parking lot. "Mind if we drive together in your car? It will be less noticeable that way."

"No problem. You know where I'm parked."

Chapter Forty

I parked my SUV off the shoulder of the old highway that skirted the back of the marsh. Charlie scanned the surrounding area before stepping out of the car. We stood briefly in knee-high vegetation before heading to a slight clearing that hinted at a narrow trail.

"Let's walk further; I think better when I'm moving," I said.

"Sure, anything to avoid attention." He pulled a pair of binoculars and a birding book from his jacket pocket.

We walked in silence for a few minutes, the only sound the hum of traffic on the distant Seward Highway. A slight breeze moved the air enough to keep most of the mosquitos at bay.

Charlie stopped and raised his binoculars, looking into nearby trees at the edge of the marsh. "It's hard to know where to begin, but in a nutshell, I need to leave Alaska. Before I do, however, there are some things I need to share with the authorities."

"They want to talk to you, so that shouldn't be much of a problem."

"More than you'd think," he said. "Let me explain. Before coming here, I was CEO and owner of a major investment firm in Texas. I preferred to stay in the background, leaving the public face of the company to others, but certain things were coming to light that made me uncomfortable. I'd just decided to meet with my CFO and take a close look into things when he was killed in a car accident. That's when it occurred to me to do some undercover work and fill his position myself using a pseudonym. I only informed the head of my board of directors of the plan."

"Sounds intriguing."

"It was. No one recognized me, and I took full advantage of my access to learn more about various accounts. After a few weeks, staff began to speak freely around me, and I learned a lot. Much of the time, the information was disturbing. I discovered our business had been used to launder money in staggering amounts for both foreign and domestic accounts dealing primarily with geologic enterprise. Money was moved offshore and off the books. It was during this same time that I got to know Gina.

"Was Gina in on this scheme?"

"No, she worked with the same clients, but in customer relations. Her job was to keep the clients happy, and she was good at it. I'd been living an almost hermit-like existence, always working without taking time for a social life. When I fell for Gina, I fell hard."

He looked away towards the trees but continued his story.

"After my suspicions were raised, I thoroughly researched our high-value clients and didn't like what I found. That made me dig even deeper, and in the process, I apparently set off some alarm bells. I noticed my car being followed, and that someone had been in my house. This scared me.

"I turned in my "resignation" as CFO the next morning and called Gina to ask her to go to Alaska with me. My primary reason for choosing Alaska was simply because it was far away, but I also wanted to take a close look at a business here. To my surprise, Gina agreed to the plan. She even seemed excited about it."

"Had you worked with the same clients and shared what you'd uncovered with her?"

"Only in the most general terms. I never told her who I really was. I felt guilty about that but didn't want to lose her trust."

He made eye contact with me before lifting the binoculars up again.

"Before we left, I transferred several of the questionable offshore balances to new account numbers in the same banks. I made copies of the company's books and stashed them in a storage unit once we arrived here."

"And Gina, now?" I asked.

"My best guess is that she was involved in the scheme all along. She knew I'd stashed copies of the records and wanted to destroy them, but when she learned the account numbers had been changed, she realized it wasn't that simple. She had to get the new numbers. My pursuers switched from trying to kill me to trying to capture me."

"Was she behind the explosion at the storage unit?"

He shrugged. "I think so. When she discovered what she wanted wasn't there, the group she worked with blew it up to destroy any records they might have missed."

"You hid them somewhere else?"

"No. The records are still at the storage unit, but in another location. They'll never find the account numbers because the only place I keep them is in my head. I have a photographic memory, something else Gina didn't know about me."

After a few minutes digesting all this, I turned to him. "Why are you telling me all this?"

"Because Killion confirmed my suspicions about Gina. When he reported she was working with Northern Mapping, it opened my eyes. I knew they were associates of a Chinese company deeply involved in the scheme I'd been investigating, but I wasn't aware of other details. I need to disappear, but first, I need you to take my records to the authorities."

"Why don't you go to them yourself?"

"Because I've undoubtedly broken a few laws along the way, and you've already been involved—both with the company and the storage unit."

"What difference does that make? Your unit was blown up."

"That one was, yes. My guess is Gina didn't realize I also had a second unit on the other side of the complex. It's small, barely large enough to hold the records. I've also provided the account numbers they'll need to recover the money. That was my intent all along." He handed me his birding book. "You'll find the key and everything they need inside. I only ask you to wait until tomorrow to call the authorities. I'll contact you later in case they have questions."

The sound of a car approaching on the nearly deserted road interrupted us.

"I have to go! Please do as I asked, and don't take any chances with the key." He turned off the path and headed away from the road.

Chapter Forty-one

What to do? Could I in good conscience follow his instructions and wait until morning to contact the authorities? And which authorities?

The police? My employer? The FBI? Yes. The FBI was my best choice. The police would contact them if they did anything at all. Might as well skip straight to the ones who would take action. Besides, Norm was already involved in investigating the explosion at the storage unit, and I had worked with him before. Jason could be filled in later. Charlie implied he was knowledgeable about Northern Mapping. Was there a connection?

I took the turn-off toward home, planning to call from there.

Dad stood at the kitchen counter, chef's knife in hand, chopping vegetables for dinner. The pungent scent of onions and garlic permeated the air.

"Cupcake. Glad you're home early. Thought I'd make my famous lasagna tonight." He pulled me close for a hug. "Jack should be home from his friend's house soon, and of course, Sarah will be coming. She liked the lasagna when I took some to her fish fry a while back."

"Sounds great, Dad. I'm home early, but I do have some phone calls to make. I'll head upstairs and get those out of the way so I can help you with dinner." I plunked my backpack on the floor by the table, pulled out Charlie's bird book and hid it in a cupboard beneath a stack of casserole dishes.

Upstairs, I pulled my phone out of my pocket and dialed Norm's direct line at the FBI. After several rings, the call went to voice mail.

"Damn!" I sighed, and left a message asking him to call me as soon as possible.

The doorbell rang and I heard Tiger let out a woof before Dad opened the door.

"Where are they, old man?" a voice said.

"Hold on, sonny." Dad's voice grew louder. "No need for a gun! Who are you after?"

"Get back." The door slammed.

I dialed 9-1-1. "Send help. Armed intruders broke into our house and my father is being held at gunpoint downstairs." I rattled off our address and ignored the dispatcher's advice to stay on the line.

With my Glock shoved into the waistband of my jeans, I pulled my shirt over it and headed downstairs. A tall, rangy man and an attractive woman with long dark hair, both in their late thirties and casually dressed, stood inside the living room door with guns pointed at my dad's chest.

Halfway down the stairs, I stopped when I heard Dad say, "I'm the only person in the house. Who are you looking for?"

The woman looked up in time to see me retreating back from sight. "I see you, Bitch. We just saw the two of you together down the road."

"Oh, you're looking for Charlie," I said and descended the remaining stairs to face them. "Charlie stayed at the marsh. He was determined to spot the yellow-rumped warblers he'd heard were in the area."

"Little Miss Innocence, huh? You're not fooling us. He left his car in the parking lot to throw us off. Now, get him downstairs or we'll kill the both of you, and Gramps here, will be first in line."

"I can't. Charlie's not here and I've already called 9-1-1. The cops are on their way."

The man nudged his companion. "Get up there and find him. Hurry!"

She ran up the stairs, gun extended. We heard doors slamming into walls as she searched.

I turned to the gunman. "Look, the fellow you want took off across the marsh. That's the last I saw of him. He's probably still there."

"Don't expect me to fall for that. We have binoculars, too, you know. Besides, we saw him give you a package. Where is it?" He picked up my backpack and threw it at me. "Find it. Now."

The shrill of sirens screamed in the distance, the sound growing steadily louder.

"Get back down here, Sister. We've got to leave while we still can."

The woman tore down the stairs and threw open the front door. She glared at her companion. "No one's upstairs and I'm not your sister."

He turned to me, snatched my backpack from my hand and smirked. "That package better be in here or we'll be back, Bitch. You can count on it."

He followed his partner outside, taking my backpack with him.

I watched as they raced away from the house to where they'd presumably left their vehicle.

The two young police officers who responded to my call interpreted the incident as a routine burglary attempt. I hadn't even drawn my gun. They assured me they'd keep a close eye on the area and left.

"What was that really about?" Dad asked.

"It's a long story." I gathered the remnants of the dried floral arrangement that had been upended when my backpack was snatched.

"What's in the package they were so anxious to find, Beri? They threatened our lives. I have a right to know."

I sighed. "It isn't a package, it's a book. It contains information about a crime and a key to a storage unit. I stashed it in the kitchen when I first got home and think I'll leave it there until tomorrow morning when I hand it over to the FBI."

"Why wait? They may come back during dinner when they figure out it's not in your backpack. Hope you didn't have anything valuable in there."

"No, just incidentals from my trip. I left my laptop at the office. Good point about dinner, though. Why don't you move dinner to Sarah's place? Take Jack when he gets back. I'll stay here and try again to reach my FBI contact."

"Alone? Are you sure?"

I pulled my shirt away from my side to expose the Glock. "I'm not defenseless. Besides, I don't think they'll be back so soon after the police left. For all they know, the police may be watching for them." I inhaled deeply. "Your lasagna smells delicious. Promise to save me some."

"Of course. Please be careful."

"I will, Dad." I kissed his cheek.

After he and Jack left, I called the hospital for an update on Ross and asked if he was awake. Since he was, I dialed his cell phone.

It was reassuring to hear his voice. I wished him good night and sat at the table with a sigh.

I tried Norm at the FBI again, but could only leave another message. Unsure if the "burglars" would come back, I ate a sandwich and called Dad to ask if he and Jack could stay at Sarah's.

I awoke the next morning to the ding of a text from Ross telling me he was scheduled for a procedure this morning and would be moved out of the Coronary Care Unit afterward. He said he'd let me know when I could stop by. His doctors were telling him everything continued to look good.

Nice that he'd given me a heads-up. Saved me an unnecessary trip to the hospital this morning on an already complicated day.

I showered and dressed, called to check in on Dad and report that nothing had happened. I called Angie at the office to let her know I wouldn't be in this morning. Finally, I called Norm Underwood at the FBI. This time he answered on the first ring.

"Just reaching for the phone to call you," he said. "What's so urgent?"

I summarized the situation and suggested we meet at the storage unit.

"No," he said. "Judging from your experience last night, I think it would be wiser for me to pick you up, and we can drive together. These people might try to intercept you. Give me your address. I'll be there in a few minutes, and I'll call for back-up to meet us at the storage facility. Just in case."

Chapter Forty-two

Norm Underwood pulled up in front of the house. After giving Jack a peck on the cheek as he and Dad walked through the door, I grabbed my things. "See you tonight, Big Guy."

"Love you, Mom."

"Love you, too. Be sure you keep the doors locked and remind Gramps to do the same."

"Don't worry. We'll be safe, and Tiger will bark if anyone tries to sneak in."

"We probably don't have anything to worry about, but it pays to be careful after what happened last night." I opened the front door and headed out to the car.

The FBI agent had his door half-open when I ran out to meet him. "I'm ready. No need for you to get out."

He pushed the unlock button on the passenger side to let me in.

"So, this is what FBI agents drive?" I asked, eyeing his Land Rover.

"Not during work hours, but I figured an official vehicle might arouse curiosity in the neighborhood." He turned his head from side to side. "Not that you have many neighbors."

I clicked the seat belt in place and glanced out the window. No neighbors in sight. "I like it that way."

He turned the SUV around in my driveway and headed back to Rabbit Creek Road. Once we'd arrived at the storage facility, Norm parked near a Toyota Highlander. He turned to me. "You brought the key and note, I presume."

I pulled the birding book from my jacket pocket. "Don't expect too much from the note. It's brief and doesn't provide much context." I handed it to him and dropped the key into his hand. "I have a more detailed version he sent to the office. I can get it to you later."

He glanced at the two vehicles parked at the end of the parking lot before extracting the note, reading it, and examining the key.

"Okay, let's go." He handed both items back to me. "You'll need these to authorize your access since I don't have a warrant."

"I'll go sign in. Since I've been here before, they'll probably recognize me."

"Yes, I'm sure they'll remember you from that day. I know I do."

Dillon stood behind the counter and greeted me with a grin. "Hey, good to see you. I thought you'd given up on this place."

"No. I'm back to check another unit." I picked up a copy of the map from the counter to help me figure out where Charlie's unit was located but couldn't find the number. I looked at Dillon. "Can you help me locate unit 5183? I don't see anything starting with the number five."

"Oh, that's one of our smaller units. It's not on the map because those units are back behind the counter. Come, I'll show you." He led us to what looked like a locker room with three-by-two-foot units, each with a padlock on the door.

After opening the designated door, Dillon left and Norm joined me. He extracted two thick ledgers from the unit. "That was easy."

"Since it was, would you mind if I grab something from another unit? My father asked me to pick it up some time ago."

"Go ahead. Meet me outside when you finish. I want to release my back-up guys anyway."

I glanced at my map to locate Dad's unit. It turned out to be near the blackened area where Charlie's other rental had been demolished. Fortunately, the explosion had been limited in size.

I pulled Dad's key from my wallet and entered the approximately eight-by-ten-foot space filled with cartons and camping equipment.

A file cabinet stood on either side of the entry door. I pulled open one of the four drawers in the first one but found only paperwork and old documents. The other three drawers were filled with more of the same. Moving to the second cabinet, I found the photographs I was looking for.

I sifted through until I found the Providence Hospital file. If we were lucky, there'd still be enough time for them to be useful for the anniversary event.

I shut the drawer and turned to leave, but curiosity caused me to turn back and leaf through some of the remaining photo files. Near the back of the third drawer were a group of folders labeled "Aleutians." I flipped through them until I found one labeled "Adak" and pulled it out. Thirty or forty prints were tucked inside. Dying to examine them closely, I restrained the impulse and locked up. I knew Norm would be anxious to get the ledgers back to headquarters.

Dillon was nowhere to be seen when I returned to the front office. I signed the register documenting that I'd visited Dad's unit and pushed through the door to find Norm. Two agents loaded a man in handcuffs into the back of their official vehicle. Dillon stood watching the process.

"Where's Norm?" I asked as I tossed my folder of photos on the passenger seat of his Land Rover.

The agent shook his head. "He's still inside. This guy's been keeping us busy. We found him pointing a gun at Dillon demanding to know which unit the two of you had requested."

"That's strange. I left Norm inside after we retrieved the ledgers and expected he'd head back to his car."

"We haven't seen him, but I'm sure he'll be here in a few minutes."

I frowned. "He couldn't possibly have gotten lost. Did he say anything to you, Dillon?"

"No, I left before you had the locker open."

"I'll go check on him." I patted the Glock in my shoulder holster.

The older of the two agents said, "I'll be right behind you as soon as I call this in. My partner here can watch the prisoner."

Dodging the counter, I entered the back room and headed for the area where we'd located Charlie's second unit.

A gunshot rang out, followed by a second blast.

A dog barked frantically outside the building. Pressing my back against the wall, I drew my gun and peered around the corner.

Norm lay sprawled on the floor, a small pool of blood beside him. The woman from last night was clutching the ledgers while leaning heavily against the wall. Her left kneecap was missing and blood drenched her lower leg. She tried to slide along the wall, hopping in my direction.

I stepped around the corner to face her. "Stop. Drop your gun or you'll lose your other knee."

She staggered and raised her gun toward me.

I shot. The bullet hit her in the shoulder.

She dropped her gun and screamed. "Shit." She inched down the wall to the floor and sat, legs outstretched, glaring at me.

I kicked her gun across the room, ran to Norm and found him unresponsive. He did have a pulse.

"I heard a gunshot," the newly arrived agent shouted. "Is he alright?"

"No, he needs help fast. Call an ambulance!" I waved toward the woman. "She could use one, too." I bent down and picked up the blood-soaked ledgers.

"Hey. Put those down. They're evidence." The agent gave me a look that indicated he thought I was an idiot.

The ambulances pulled out of the parking lot together. Norm had suffered a head wound that bled a lot, but the paramedic said it looked superficial. He probably had a concussion, but he was already regaining consciousness.

The woman's status appeared more precarious. I hadn't had much choice but to shoot her, and I prayed she wouldn't die. I wondered if she was Charlie's Gina.

I turned to Dillon. "Glad you missed the excitement."

Dillon laughed. "I didn't realize the storage industry could be so exciting until I met you. I thought our guard dog was going to have a stroke after the gunshots, but I finally got him calmed down."

One of the FBI agents tapped me on the shoulder. "You need to come with me to headquarters," he said.

He walked me to his cruiser and held the passenger door open for me to get in.

"Where's your partner going to sit," I asked.

"He already left in the ambulance with Norm," he said.

Two different hospitals. Why couldn't both men be in the same one? It meant I'd need to spend most of what was left of the day in healthcare facilities. Ross was scheduled to be discharged from Alaska Regional later this afternoon. Fortunately, the FBI agent drove me back to my SUV in time for me to visit Norm before I needed to pick Ross up.

Norm's condition worried me. I headed to Providence to check on him. I'd just finished spending several hours at FBI headquarters giving my statement. Lunchtime came and went before they let me go. When I called to check in with Dad and Angie, all was well.

The first thing I noticed when I entered Providence's lobby was a large poster advertising anniversary events planned for next month. The date was encouraging. Dad's photos might still be useful.

After determining Norm's room number from the reception desk, I proceeded to the elevator, but not before receiving a warning that access to the patient was restricted.

When I reached his room, one of the back-up agents sat outside the door.

"Hello, again. How's the patient doing?"

"You mean Van Gogh?" He laughed at his own joke and opened the door. "You can go in if you like."

"Thanks."

Norm sat upright in the bed, an empty lunch tray on the table beside him. A large bandage covered the left side of his head.

"You're looking much better than when I last saw you. How are you feeling?" I asked.

"Anxious to get out of here, but otherwise fine." He patted the bandage. "I'm missing a chunk of my left ear and they say I have a mild concussion, but I don't even have a headache."

"I'm glad. Do you think the pain meds they gave you might have something to do with that?"

"Naw. They just gave me local anesthesia." He reached for my hand. "They tell me you saved my life. Apparently, you're quite the markswoman."

"I've had lots of practice, although usually not with a human target."

"Anyway, Beri, I'm grateful."

The agent at the door motioned to me. "You're wanted back at FBI headquarters. They have a few more questions for you."

What could they possibly ask now?

Chapter Forty-three

I finished at the FBI and went to the office. The grilling had been intense. Questions about Charlie, the person at the root of the events at the storage unit were particularly difficult to answer. It would have been easier if I fully understood his involvement myself. At least, both Norm and the woman I'd shot were recovering. I can only imagine what it would have been like if someone had died from the shooting.

I leaned back in my chair and called Dad. He didn't answer, but I left a message telling him I'd picked up his Providence photos.

The unopened pile of mail on my desk caught my attention. Halfway through the stack of envelopes, I came across the letter from Charlie.

He wrote on a page dated a week and a half ago that he was back in town. Something I already knew. He'd given directions and the time and place for a proposed meeting that didn't happen. He also spelled out a brief description of how he'd gotten into the mess he was in, and what he planned to do next. I wished I knew how to get in touch with him. I had so many questions.

The FBI would be interested in seeing the letter, although it was light on specifics. I'd have to give Norm a call tomorrow. He should be home by then, although probably not at work yet.

The clock on the wall opposite my desk read 2:15. Ross was scheduled to be released from the hospital soon. I slipped Charlie's note inside the pages of a regional airport directory lying on my desk and stopped at the front to ask Angie for an update.

"When's Jason expected back?"

"He didn't say. Sorry."

I left for the hospital. On my way out, I noticed Mickey with a bored look on his face thumbing through a magazine. I realized I'd been so absorbed in my problems that I'd neglected to provide him any training or direction since we got back. I'd need to make that a priority tomorrow.

Ross, packed and dressed, greeted me with enthusiasm when I reached his room. It was so good to see him on his feet. "Looks like you're ready to go."

"Let's get out of here. They've finished all the paperwork."

"You're awfully energetic for a convalescent," I said. "I can tell right now it's going to be hard to get you to follow doctor's orders." I picked up his bag. "What are the orders anyway?"

"Nothing much. Take it easy, resume my usual activities."

"Really? Right off the bat?"

"Yeah, mostly. Can't fly, of course. Take it slow on vigorous exercise. They want me to go to cardiac rehab so they can monitor my heart while I increase intensity. Sounds like a gym with a stethoscope attached."

I laughed. "Probably a little more high-tech than that, but it sounds like a good idea."

"Hmph. I think I can manage to figure out how much to exercise on my own."

"Okay, smart guy. Just don't plan on going overboard your first day home."

With Ross situated in his living room watching a sports channel on television, I called Dad again. This time he answered.

"Hi there, Cupcake. I just noticed I missed a call from you. I must have been in the shower." He coughed. "Is Ross okay?"

"He's home, watching television and raring to go. It's going to be hard for him to take it slow. I called you because I wanted to drop those Providence photos off. Would now be a good time?"

"Sure. Maybe I can deliver them later this afternoon and get them off my conscience."

I loaded both sets of dad's photos in my SUV and decided to check in at the hangar on my way. I hated that I'd been neglecting my job responsibilities so much lately.

Perched on the fuselage, Dean was applying pressure on the newly installed windshield of the twin. He gave me a head nod in greeting.

"How's it going?" I asked.

"Making progress." He dropped down from the plane to speak to me.

"Mickey needs something to do. Would he be in your way if I asked him to get the twin's interior ready for our next project?"

"Tomorrow morning will work. I need a little more time to finish this up." He looked down, avoiding eye contact in his usual indirect way of communication. I needed to remember to mention this to Mickey so he wouldn't misinterpret the Yupik mannerism.

"Thanks, I'll let him know."

I popped my head in the office door and found Mickey bent over a stack of boxes adjacent to Angie's desk.

"Hey, Mickey," I said, "I talked to Dean a few minutes ago. He said tomorrow morning would be a good time for you to start organizing the twin's interior for our upcoming projects. Why don't you go home for the day, and check in with Dean then?"

"Thanks, but I told Angie I'd finish unpacking and inventorying these deliveries. She had to leave because one of her kids is sick. I'll close up if Mr. H. isn't back by five."

I laughed. "Sounds like you've caught on to Angie's nickname for the boss. Okay, thank you."

Dad met me at the front door, took the folders from me and carried them into the house. "Guess I saved more of these pictures than I realized."

"You do have quite a few, but they're not all of the hospital. I brought another folder I wanted to ask you about." I hung up my jacket.

"Let's sit here at the kitchen table. I'll bring coffee, and we can take a look at them."

"Sure, sounds good. I'll grab a notebook and pen from the desk while you work on the coffee."

"Didn't take much work," he said as he placed steaming cups and napkins on the table. These new-fangled machines are fast. What do you need the paper for? Didn't know you were interested in hospital history?"

"I'm not, but I am interested in the Adak photos in the other folder."

"Aha, you found them in the file cabinet, too?" He smiled. "I didn't think I'd actually saved them. The military probably wouldn't like that I did."

"Why not?" I asked, taking a sip of the steaming liquid.

"They may have been classified. I know they were considering possible missile and communication sites at the time." He shuffled through a stack of pictures as he spoke.

"Do you think having them could get you in trouble?"

"I doubt it. They're copies for my records, but who knows? I don't see what good it would do for them to prosecute a doddering old man for a few keepsakes."

I pulled a couple of shots from the stack. "Look at these. They were taken in the area we flew while Mickey and I were there."

"One of those World War II bunkers, I think."

"Probably." I looked closer. "It's changed, though. It looks a lot different now." I jotted down the reference numbers of the prints. "Not surprising that it *would* change after all these years."

He glanced at the photo. "If I remember correctly, we flew these sometime in the late seventies or early eighties. I'd have to check my reference number log to know for sure."

"Do you still have it?"

"I think so. Likely, I stashed it in the same folder as the pictures. He held a stack of photos and flipped through them. Wouldn't have these in today's digital age. While it may be nice to be able to skip film processing with everything computerized now, it's unlikely anyone would have hard copies to save."

I leafed through the rest of the photos. "My boss might be interested in some of these. Would you mind if I gave him a call?"

"Of course not."

When I tried to phone Jason, the call went to voicemail. I left a message. "Hi, this is Beri. Could you please meet me at the office when you finish? I came across something you should see. I'll wait for you there."

Chapter Forty-four

The sound of a vehicle pulling into the driveway caught my attention as I gathered the Adak photos from the kitchen table and rose to leave.

"Sounds like Sarah's back," Dad said. "She ran down to Carr's pharmacy to pick up my allergy medication."

"It's her car all right." I stepped back from the window.

The front door opened. "Glad you're still here, Beri. I saw you drive in as I was leaving."

She gave me a hug. "I've been wanting to talk to you about the wedding."

Just what I needed—another distraction, but she seemed so enthusiastic I couldn't disappoint her. "Sure, how can I help?"

"We're keeping it simple, but I mainly need to talk to you about your dress."

"My dress?" I asked, surprised.

"Yes. You're my maid of honor, remember."

"I remember, and I'm honored to be asked. What do you recommend?"

She held out her phone with a picture of a small girl in a floral print dress. "This is what the flower girl is wearing. I hoped you could find something that would coordinate with it." She smiled. "So, the wedding photos will look like we planned it."

"I don't wear much pink, so how about I look for something blue or green?"

"That would be perfect. Maybe a coordinating tie for Jack?"

"You got it." I frowned. "I may have to look online. Wish my favorite boutique hadn't closed a few years ago. It was my go-to place for this kind of thing."

"Oh, I'm sure you can find something locally if you look."

"It's finding the time that's the problem. I need to swing by and see Ross tonight, but I'll try to shop soon."

Sarah's eyebrows shot up. "I have an idea. You're so busy, how about I do the shopping and bring some possibilities for you to try? That way, you can give Ross the attention he needs, and we can get everything settled. Just give me your measurements, and I'll scour the town."

I laughed. "Are you sure you have the time?"

"What else do I have to do? I need to get this wedding right. I always wanted to be a bride, just didn't imagine it would happen so late in life. I eloped before."

I gave her a hug. "You've done a bang-up job choosing the groom. That's what counts most."

From across the room, Dad smiled and gave Sarah a thumbs up.

"How about the flowers?" I asked. "Something native to Alaska would be nice. Maybe even fireweed blooms?"

"Only if you want me sneezing throughout the ceremony," Dad said.

"You're allergic to fireweed? I never realized that," I said.

"At the moment, I think I'm allergic to everything," Dad said with a sniff.

Sarah hugged him. "I'll talk to the florist about using something hypoallergenic."

Anxious to share the Adak folder with Jason, I headed to the office. It was almost five o'clock. I expected he'd be back.

I noticed Mickey's lone car still parked outside the office, but no sign of Jason. Inside, I found a massive mess—file drawers hanging open, papers strewn about, boxes of supplies upturned.

"Mickey? Are you here?" My unease grew with the silence as I searched throughout the rooms until I spotted him on the floor in the break room. His mouth was gagged, his wrists and ankles tied. He wasn't moving.

I dodged a puddle of coffee and broken pieces of a mug lying beside him to kneel and check his breathing. Alive, but unconscious. For the third time in as many days, I dialed 9-1-1.

The police and the paramedics arrived almost simultaneously a few minutes later. By then, I'd carefully removed the duct tape from his mouth, but waited until the police arrived to untie him to avoid destroying evidence.

Mickey didn't deserve this. I hoped he wasn't badly hurt.

Jason arrived shortly after the police and ambulance. While Mickey was examined and untied, I described how I came on the scene. Mickey was loaded on a stretcher and carried out to the ambulance.

"Is he going to be okay?" I asked.

"Nasty head wound," one of the paramedics said. "He's starting to come around now, though." He announced they were taking Mickey to Alaska Regional Hospital and rolled him out the door.

"What do you think went on here?" one of the officers asked. "Any idea what they were looking for?"

"Not really," Jason said. "Whatever it was, it's probably related to one of the jobs we're working on." He spread his hands. "At this point, we'll need to go through this mess to see if we can make sense of it."

"We'll see if we can get any fingerprints that will help, but this is a public place. We'll need to get both of yours and the rest of the staff to rule them out. We'll need the victim's, too. Think there's any chance he can identify who attacked him?"

"That's a remote possibility," I said. "Maybe if you had a line-up. He's new to Alaska, so it's unlikely he'd recognize anyone."

"Two tough guys," Mickey said, propped up on pillows in his hospital bed. "Tall, thirties, buff. One had a beard. I don't remember much more." He grimaced. "It happened so fast; I didn't have my guard up. I was in the break room when I heard them enter and called out that I'd be right with them. They came at me like gangbusters. I threw my coffee at the first one and that's all I remember. Obviously, the other one hit me with something."

"We're glad you're going to be okay," I said and rested my hand on his shoulder.

"The doctor said I could go home tomorrow. He wants to keep an eye on me overnight." He shifted in the bed. "I hope they didn't take anything important."

"We're not sure yet what they took," Jason said. "They left such chaos behind that it'll take some time to go through it all. I'm lucky I had my copies of the Adak pictures you took with me at the Federal Building. Beri, I'll meet you back at the office."

He slipped out and I continued to explain things for Mickey. "We don't know yet about computer files," I said. "Angie left the computer on her desk open. The files are encrypted, so we're probably alright. We'll know more after the cyber security guys take a look. Do you need me to bring anything here for you?"

When he said he didn't need anything, I told him good-bye and returned to the office. I'd spent far too much time in hospitals lately. Thankfully, everyone was expected to recover.

Jason was already busy repairing the damage to the front office when I walked in.

"We have a lot of work to do to even figure out what to include in the police report. They weren't that thorough checking things out while they were here. They did take a few fingerprints, but that's about it." He slapped a pile of documents on the corner of Angie's desk. "Amazing how much paper we've accumulated in such a short time. And this is supposed to be the digital age."

"Now we have both, and I have more out in the car. I found Dad's file of Adak photos to add to your collection."

"Thanks. That's good news, considering our current situation. I'll bring them home with me tonight, take a quick look, and return them in the morning. Later, we can examine them more thoroughly together."

"Sure, I'll get the folder for you, but I think I'll stay long enough to sort out my office before I leave."

"Are you sure you want to stay here alone?"

"I'll lock the doors, and I won't stay long. I want to take Ross some dinner in about an hour."

"See you tomorrow, then. Good work tracking down the old Adak info."

I walked with him to my car and handed him the sheaf of photos.

After he left, I took a hard look around my office. Pages of job proposals and flight maps were strewn everywhere and the locked closet door where I kept survival gear had been pried open.

Sure enough, both my 357 Magnum and my shotgun were missing. Black fingerprint powder blotches dotted the door and frame, but the police wouldn't know what had been inside.

I sat at my desk and called the station to inform them about the guns. As I clicked off, I noticed I had a voice mail message. Richard Toledo had returned my call. Finally, some good news. He'd asked when he should report for work. I called him, and we scheduled a time the following Monday.

As I stood, I noticed my Regional Airport Directory splayed on the floor below my chair. I picked it up and flipped through the pages. They'd overlooked Charlie's letter, but I didn't think it would have mattered much now anyway.

CHAPTER FORTY-FIVE

I pushed the doorbell with one knuckle while balancing two large take-out bags and a bottle of Merlot in my arms. Without waiting for Ross to answer, I opened the unlocked front door and walked inside.

"It's me," I called. "Stay put while I drop these bags off in the kitchen."

Never one to follow orders, Ross met me at the kitchen table. He opened a bag, lifted the lid of the take-out container, and inhaled deeply. "Yum. My favorite Cajun chicken fettuccini from Simon's. I feel so special."

"You are special. I figured you were probably tired of bland food after a few days in the hospital."

"Am I ever." He grabbed me around the waist and pulled me toward him. "Here I was sitting in front of the television feeling sorry for myself, and you come in and chase the blues away."

"Wait until you hear my news, and you'll feel even better." I opened a cabinet and pulled out a couple of wine glasses. "Since I'm not flying today, I can join you in a glass or did the doctor restrict alcohol for you?"

Ross raised his eyebrows. "He didn't mention it. I'm sure it's fine in moderation. I also like the sound of good news. Let's have it."

"Richard Toledo is reporting for work first thing Monday morning. I'm hoping you'll feel well enough to orient him. He's already familiar with me, so it would give the two of you a chance to get better acquainted."

"That is good news. I already have a serious case of cabin fever. A few more days, and I'll be going completely stir-crazy."

"You have met him, haven't you?" I poured the wine and set the table with napkins and forks.

"We crossed paths a few times when he was working for you. I had the impression he was sweet on you."

"Richard?" I recoiled. "We had a completely professional relationship. Besides, I'm fairly sure he's a happily married man. He has at least one grown son in the military."

"That doesn't mean he's currently married. You have Jack, but you're single now."

"Do I detect a hint of jealousy?" I shook my head. "Strange coming from you, the same Ross who gave me a hard time about Megan? I don't think I like it."

"Sorry. I'm not jealous. Maybe just aware of possible competition."

"So that's what you call it. Well, you don't have to worry about that. I love you, and have absolutely no romantic interest in Richard. I'm also sure he has none for me."

"Good, I'm glad we've got that settled." He gave my hand a squeeze. "Will he want to work part-time like he did a few years ago for you?"

"That's up to the two of you to figure out. We haven't talked about the particulars, but my impression is that he'll be flexible."

"He sounds perfect. Thanks. That's a stress off the list."

I pulled a chair out from the table and sat next to him. Changing the subject, I said, "You must be hungry. Let's eat."

While we ate, I gave him a brief re-cap of the break-in at the office and explained I'd be tied up most of tomorrow getting everything straightened out.

"Did anyone get hurt?" he asked.

"Mickey was there alone when the two guys broke in. They hit him over the head, but he'll be okay."

"That's a shame. Any idea who they were or why they broke in?"

"Some suspicions, but no names. The police took fingerprints, but didn't seem to have much confidence they'd result in anything."

"Why didn't you tell me sooner?" he asked, taking my hand.

I smiled. "Probably because I didn't want to get your blood pressure up."

"Be careful, Sweetheart. Make sure you're not at the office alone in case they come back."

I got up to take care of the leftovers. "There you go, getting overprotective. I'll be careful." I leaned over and kissed him good-bye. "Get some rest. I'll try to stop by tomorrow for lunch."

I put the wine bottle in the fridge. "Better not finish this off. I'm not sure if your doctor would approve of mixing alcohol with your meds."

I walked with him, and he held the front door open. "Hope to see you tomorrow, but if you can't, I have plenty of PB & J on hand."

The following morning, Jason placed two stacks of photos on the conference table. "I think a good approach should be to locate similar shots from each era and compare them to demonstrate what has changed over time." He slid one stack of prints over to me. "I've already removed the photos outside our area of interest. That eliminated more than half the total. Your father's project was more comprehensive than ours."

"That's good. There were a lot to go through."

"We're lucky he flew at the same scale of 200 feet per inch. I'm glad we don't have to adjust for altitude differences, only the few you flew at the lower altitude. Let's each take a flight line and check from beginning to end. They won't be identical, but similar."

"Wouldn't it be faster to whittle it down further to just the bunker area?" I asked.

"Yes, but I want to be sure we don't miss anything."

I looked down at the pile of photos in front of me. He'd given me the ones we'd just sent him from Adak. That would make it easier for me, but I'd be surprised if I found anything unexpected. The process was tedious. I didn't find anything during the first hour but noticed

Jason slid a stereoscope over a couple of his photos. If he found anything of interest, he didn't mention it. He began to compare prints of the harbor area and grunted, but didn't comment before moving on.

When I eventually arrived at the shots covering the bunker and antenna, I studied them more carefully. Nothing new jumped out at me. I turned to him. "Have you reached the bunker yet?"

"Getting close. Why don't you take a short break while I catch up?"

"Sure." I went to my office and called Ross to let him know I'd be tied up for lunch. "Why don't you order something and have it delivered?"

"Nah. I'll make a sandwich and finish off that bottle of wine from yesterday. After that, a nap sounds good."

"Easy on the wine," I said. "Okay, I'll call to check on you later. Love you."

I struggled to find an empty space for my coffee on my cluttered desk, so I set it on the floor and began organizing the mass of paper by category. Most of it was comprised of pending Requests for Proposals – RFPs. Quite a large number had accumulated while I'd been gone.

I noticed many of the RFPs originated from geology research firms. While geologists were frequent customers of ours, there seemed to be more of this type than usual. The job sites varied, but many were located across the inlet from Anchorage. Another location was in the Southeast near Ketchikan, and a third was in a different area of the Aleutians I'd just flown.

As I flipped through, I noticed one submittal date had already expired. I assumed the contract had already been awarded to a competitor. Two others were due in the next few weeks. I put those on the top of the pile.

Jason appeared in my office doorway. "Ready to get back to work?"

"Yes, Sir." I returned to the conference room and settled next to him at the table. "Sorry, I lost track of time."

"Cleaning your office was that absorbing?" he asked.

"The more I organized, the more I realized that the bulk of the pending RFPs were from geologists. Is there a resurgence in mining exploration going on?"

"Hmm. I must admit I didn't keep up with those while you were gone." He chuckled. "Guess it was easier to save them for you."

"The majority are for projects across the inlet, not that far from here. Would you mind if I snooped around a bit? I could talk to a few geologists to get a sense of what's going on?"

"Not at all. In fact, a friend of mine recently retired from U.S. Geological Surveys in Alaska. I'm sure he still knows which way the winds are blowing. I'll give him a call and ask him to meet with us."

He picked up his cell phone and dialed. "I'll put it on speaker, so you can hear. Don't be surprised if I use a little subterfuge setting this up."

"Okay." I wondered what he meant, and why that would be necessary, but kept my questions to myself.

"Hey, Spence. This is Heck. Heard you took retirement recently. Congratulations."

"Good hearing from you, Heck," the man said. "Yes, I'm taking life easy, doing a lot of fishing. What are you up to these days?"

"Enjoying being assigned to Alaska. We'll see how I feel about it when winter comes." He coughed. "Say, I have a favor to ask."

"What's that?" Spence asked.

"An old college buddy asked me to look out for his daughter. She's starting a small business here, and he worries about her inexperience with all things Alaskan."

I raised an eyebrow but kept quiet. *Didn't he know I was born here?*

"Anyway, she's got some geology questions I can't answer. I thought maybe you could help."

"Sure, if I can."

"How about meeting us for an early lunch. Say at 11:00, at the Moose's Tooth? It'll be on me."

"Lunch sounds good, but why so early?"

"It's a busy place," Jason said. "I want to beat the crowd."

"It can get crowded alright."

"Let's make it 10:45. We'll meet you there."

He clicked the phone off and turned to me. "We're all set."

"Thanks, I think. Why did you make me sound like I just arrived on the last plane from the Lower 48? I've lived here all my life."

"I didn't want him to know we're working together. My presence here is supposed to stay low-key."

"Ah, I see. I have another question. Why haven't you mentioned that you're known as "Heck"?"

He laughed. "I got a kick out of Angie's nickname and everyone struggling with my name, so I just went with it. Shall we get back to work?"

Chapter Forty-six

The boss sat beside me, and we resumed reviewing photographs. He stopped abruptly, checked the stereoscope, then slid it over to me. "Here, take a look at this pair."

I checked Dad's picture first. A crumbling bunker with no sign of an antenna was centered in the shot. "This was obviously taken before they converted it to the Avian Center."

"According to your dad's log sheet, this was taken in 1985. There's not much to see. Now, take a look at the footage you took."

I rubbed my eyes before focusing through the lenses. A three-dimensional image of the current structure appeared. "Quite a change. They put a lot of work into renovating it."

Jason nodded. "Exactly. But oddly, even in these recent shots, it's hard to make out much of the antenna detail you captured from the ground. I think it was intentionally designed to be deceptive from the air."

"I actually took a better picture with my cell phone?" I asked, surprised.

"In some important respects, yes. No wonder they didn't want visitors snooping around. Since our team reports that the men you encountered have cleared out of the Research Center, our team is examining what they left behind. Unfortunately, they disassembled much of the antenna before they left."

"What do you think they were up to?"

"No good, as my grandfather used to say. The problem is figuring out what kind of no good."

"I'm glad they're gone, but it would have been better if the police had been able to arrest them."

"I'm sure they would have liked to. From what I hear, Billy was a popular resident, but with no witnesses, the police weren't able to come up with any evidence they were guilty."

"Have your Chinese language experts translated the screen shots I took?"

"No. At least I haven't received the translations yet."

Angie walked in, and he looked up to face her. "Beri and I have an early lunch appointment, but I'm not comfortable leaving you here alone. Why don't you lock up and take an early lunch, too?"

She shook her head. "I have too much to do. I'll secure the place and work from the flight instruction office. Dean can keep me company there."

"Good plan." Jason loaded the two stacks of photos into his briefcase. "I'll take these with us, and I can drop them off at the Federal Building on our way back."

My phone chirped. I glanced at a message from Charlie's PI, Wallace Killion, suggesting we meet as soon as possible. I turned to Jason. "I have an errand to run after lunch. Why don't we take separate cars?"

Spence Watkins entered the Moose's Tooth with long strides. He looked professorial, dressed in slacks, dress shirt and tie and sported an immaculately trimmed goatee and close-cropped hair.

Jason clapped him on the back. "Spence, I want you to meet Beri Quinn, the friend I mentioned to you."

He nodded, and we moved to a nearby table to our seats.

Spence gave me a smile. "So young lady, what kind of business are you starting?"

I glanced at Jason. "Mapping and photography. I've been told there's a lot of interest in photogrammetry projects in Alaska recently."

"Always has been. So much land here to study."

Jason spoke up. "Any specific geological study trends you're aware of?"

"Sure. Name a natural resource, and there's someone out there who's interested."

"You're not a lot of help here," Jason said.

I turned to Spence. "What would you say are the current top contenders?"

At that moment, the server appeared. "Are you ready to order?"

Jason looked at me. "Want to split a pizza?"

"Too early for pizza for me. I'd like a bowl of your tomato basil soup with some sourdough bread, please."

"I'm with you, Beri," Spence said. "But I'm thinking along the lines of breakfast." He turned to the waitress. "It's not on your lunch menu, but do you think the chef could make me a cheese omelet?"

"Sure," she said. "She went to culinary school, after all." She winked and looked at Jason.

"Make mine a small mushroom and olive pizza, and more coffee, please."

As the server left, Jason turned to Spence. "Getting back to business, what were you saying about trends?"

"I'm getting the impression you have an agenda here that I'm not clear about. What's going on?" He rubbed the whiskers on his chin and frowned.

"Nothing you need to worry about." Jason raised his shoulders in a shrug. "We just need some information but didn't want to drag you into anything that might get complicated."

"So you say, but somehow knowing you as well as I do, I'm not reassured." Spence turned to me. "And you, young lady, your name sounds familiar. Are you really starting a business?"

I nodded. "It's true. I'm starting a new business."

The server arrived with our food and conversation stopped for a few minutes before Spence picked up where he'd left off. "What kind of work are you doing, again?"

Jason spoke up. "She's working for me. We're involved in something that may have international implications. We're in the early stages of an investigation, but there's nothing for you to worry about, I promise."

Spence cleared his throat. "I guess it isn't a big secret anyway. Anyone with common sense could figure out what's going on. The latest buzz in the industry is rare earth metals. They're required in the manufacturing of a number of critical high-tech products. China and to some extent, Russia, have a stranglehold on supplying them. We have an urgent need to become less dependent on other countries by developing our own resources and even more critically, our own processing ability.

"Where are they located?" I asked.

"That's the question, isn't it?" Spence smiled. "The answer is everywhere. The problem isn't so much finding them, it's finding them in concentrations that are cost-effective to retrieve."

"And Alaska may be one of those locations?" Jason asked.

"It's possible. Volcanic rock is one good possibility, and Alaska has lots of volcanoes. Also, the Japanese have had some luck mining areas of the seabed, and our state has lots of coastline. All very speculative, though. The environment here can increase both exploration and retrieval costs. On the other hand, the state has invested resources in and established policies that increase the state's desirability for exploration."

"Like what?" I asked, curious. I spooned up the last of my soup.

"There are potential plans that the state may help fund a separation plant in Ketchikan. That could be key, because separating out the critical minerals is technically difficult, and we lack sufficient capability in this country."

"If a good source is located, it sounds like it could be quite a boon to our economy," I said. "Maybe even the beginning of a modern-day gold rush?"

Spence took a sip of his drink. "That's one way to look at it, but a strike would be very different from the one in the Klondike in 1896. Small-time prospectors wouldn't have a chance. This would require high-stake investors and government-level participation."

He glanced at his watch and took a last bite of his omelet. "I hope I've been of some help." He stood and tossed his napkin on the table.

"Remember, I'm not in the loop anymore. I'm probably not the best person to be asking about this."

Jason stood and thanked Spence before he left. As he returned to his seat, he pursed his lips. "What do you think, Beri? Sound like what we may be dealing with to you?"

"It could explain a number of things." I shook my head. "But it also raises a lot more questions."

As we left the restaurant, a thought struck me as we approached our cars. "Would you mind waiting to drop off the photos at the Federal Building? Something Spence said about undersea mining makes me want to take a second look at that development we noticed on the east end of the harbor."

Chapter Forty-seven

Wallace Killion was already seated when I arrived at the Anchorage Municipal Library study room he'd reserved for our meeting. "Thank you for agreeing to meet on short notice, Beri. I figured this would be as private a spot as we could find in this town, and it's a favorite hangout of mine."

"It's perfect. I love the library, but don't get here often enough."

He handed me an envelope. "I'm not sure whether Charlie will feel our business is complete with this report, but I want to give you my official notification that any agreement I've had with him is now terminated." He gave me a lopsided smile. "I didn't know how to contact him directly, so figured you were my best conduit."

I slid the envelope into my notebook. "I'll keep it on file, but I don't expect to see him again myself. Can I ask what brought you to feel it was necessary to make your break with him so official?"

"I can sum it up in one word. Deception." He shook his head, his lips pressed tightly together. He pulled out the photo of Gina that Charlie had provided. "I discovered this is a fake for starters."

"What do you mean?"

"The woman in this photo works for Northern Mapping and has since they opened their doors. Her name is Victoria Saunders. When I checked her background, there was no record of her ever living in Texas where Charlie said they worked together. I have no idea what he hoped to accomplish by sending me on a world-class goose chase."

I frowned. "It's strange alright. I don't know why he would do that, either."

"And that's not all that's strange. I followed up on the tip you gave me about Gina being a tennis player. I checked with the Alaska Club and found they had no one on their membership list by that name. When I checked for Victoria Saunders, they knew her. She's apparently quite a good tennis player. This is all in your final report." He pulled a copy of a news clipping from a folder. "They gave me this copy of a clipping of her with another member after they won a doubles match a few months ago. She does not look like the woman in the photo he gave us. Her friend looks more like the picture than Victoria AKA Gina does. The club also said they haven't seen either woman recently. Turns out there's even a missing person alert out on Gina's partner."

I studied the image of the two women. "There was a flyer posted at the entrance of the club about the missing woman last time I visited the club. Did you do a facial recognition check on the photo Charlie gave us? For either of them?"

"No," he said. "The quality of the photograph wasn't good enough to justify the expense."

Killion stuffed his paperwork back into his folder, preparing to leave. "The final insult was when the FBI came snooping around my office. As you know, I'm careful not to reveal the location of my office. I even pick up my mail at the post office rather than having it delivered, but they managed to find me."

"What did they want?"

"They asked what I knew about a man named Arthur Hennigan. When I denied knowing him, they didn't believe me and asserted he was a client of mine. I was totally confused until they showed me a photo of the man, and get this, it was Charlie. I never was that comfortable knowing only his first name, but I never bought it when he told you his last name was Greer. I couldn't find records of him under that name. Since I only talked to him on the phone, I wouldn't have recognized him if you hadn't shown me the picture of him with Gina you brought back from Nome."

He slapped his hand on the table and heaved a loud sigh. "I should've followed my instincts and required a face-to-face meeting before taking the job. Apparently, Hennigan is wanted for embezzlement, and possibly murder."

Stunned, all I could say was, "You've got to be kidding."

"No, I wish I were. They grilled me for an hour about what he'd hired me to do. They seemed very interested when I told them he wanted to find Gina. I guess she's one of the persons they suspect him of killing."

"I can't believe this. True, he was a pest, but I never suspected him of anything like that. I'm so sorry I got you mixed up with him." I winced and cleared my throat. "I wonder why he wanted me to help him turn over the records of offshore account numbers to the FBI just a few days ago? It doesn't seem like something a crook would do."

"Crook or not, I want to wash my hands of any involvement with him. I feel sick over the idea that I tried to help him find someone he wanted to kill."

"I agree, but somehow I suspect there's more to the story than what they gave you."

"It seems with this guy, there's always more. You should stay away from him."

"That was my intention even before all this came out. The problem in the past has been that Charlie finds *me*. It was almost like he was stalking me, but perhaps because he'd been a student of mine, I didn't feel threatened."

"Before all this came to light, I did have a lead I planned to follow up on. Probably a moot point now, but you may want to check it out. His house that you searched while trying to locate Gina? It now has a 'For Sale' sign out front. I'd planned to meet with the realtor to see if Charlie actually owned the place. Thought I might learn more about him and his finances."

He sighed. "Also, I talked to the kids in the neighborhood and learned that the person you met, Caroline, is the sister of the lady who lives next door. She was visiting to help get her sister's house ready to put on the market. Summer's the time to sell houses in Alaska, I guess. Anyway, I didn't mention any of this to the FBI. It's probably not important, and it didn't cross my mind at the time."

"Thanks for all your hard work. Again, I'm so sorry about this."

"Just be careful, Beri. He's dangerous."

I left the library confused. Nothing about Charlie made sense. I needed to talk to Norm to see if he could enlighten me. When I got back to the office and called, his line went straight to voice mail. It didn't say if he was still out with his injuries. Was he avoiding me? Since I didn't want to talk to anyone else at the FBI, I left a message asking him to call me ASAP.

I already knew Charlie rented and didn't own the house with the 'For Sale' sign, but more than one real estate property was on my mind. After checking in with Angie, I decided to drive out to the subdivision where I'd picked up Charlie to fly him to his remote cabin hide-out. Maybe the homeowner or a neighbor would know something about him, and I could pass it on to Norm.

The drive took a lot longer than when I'd flown there, but I had no trouble finding it. A middle-aged woman with a broad smile opened the door. "Can I help you?" she asked.

"I hope so. I'm looking for Charlie. I picked him up here a few weeks ago. I hoped I might find him here now."

"Oh yes, I remember you. Charlie loaded up your plane with supplies. He couldn't fly them out himself because there was no place near the cabin to land his float plane."

"He has a plane?"

"Yes, he keeps it on a small lake near here." She laughed. "It's his favorite toy."

"Do you think he might be there now?"

"Hmm, maybe. I haven't seen him in a few days, so I really don't know. He's probably out of town."

"Darn, can you tell me how to find the lake, just in case he's there?"

"Sure. Let me draw you a map. I don't know the name of it." She left me at the open door and disappeared inside for a few minutes. When she returned, she handed me an advertisement for a carwash with a map she'd drawn on the back.

"Thanks," I said. "You've been a big help. You wouldn't happen to remember his plane's tail number, would you?"

She took the map back and scribbled the number at the bottom. "There you go." She smiled again before she shut the door.

I returned to my SUV and headed out in the direction indicated on her sketch.

After a fifteen-minute drive, I located the lake flanked by a small airstrip. A cedar sign read "Reeve Lake" a few feet in front of me. Several single-engine planes were tied down at one end, and three float planes were docked at the near edge of the lake. The walk from the parking lot was a scenic one. I watched a couple of teens on Jet Skis zipping across the fireweed-edged lake and a pair of widgeons dip their heads, looking for aquatic plants and insects.

The plane with the tail numbers I was looking for was a Cessna 182 secured third in line. I scanned the area but didn't see Charlie or anyone else.

I walked up to the plane and opened the door to peer inside. There wasn't much to see, so I crawled in and looked under the front seats and around the floor, but still found nothing.

I squeezed into the back and was disappointed again. Charlie was a neat man. I didn't find a thing until I reached under the far seat and my fingers closed on something that felt like a shoe. I pulled it out and stared at a woman's tennis shoe.

Disappointed, I returned it under the seat and started to climb out when I heard footsteps approaching the plane.

Chapter Forty-eight

Curled into a tight ball behind the left front seat, I waited, expecting the door of the plane to open at any second. Instead, the footsteps stopped briefly before moving away again. A few minutes later, the engine of the adjacent aircraft roared to life.

As the other plane began to taxi across the lake, the wake from its floats gently rocked me. When silence resumed, I relaxed my position and continued to wait. Fifteen minutes passed before I braved exposure and crept out the door of Charlie's plane. After scanning the area and seeing no one, I climbed out. I started for my SUV but came to an abrupt stop when I saw a white SUV tucked between my vehicle and an unoccupied gray one.

This didn't look good. Unless there had been two occupants in the plane that just left, chances were good I had company and nowhere to hide. I changed course and ducked behind a couple of scraggly black spruce growing on the edge of the parking lot.

During this short diversion, I sent Norm a quick text. *I need to talk to you. I think I'm about to be apprehended at the float plane docking area of Reeve Lake. Please check on me if you don't hear back in the next few minutes.*

As I approached my SUV from behind, the two front doors of the vehicle next to mine opened simultaneously. A couple of muscle-bound men emerged, and as they came nearer, I realized the bearded one looked familiar. He was the person who'd approached Jack and me at the golf tent, but he'd driven off in a green van that night.

"Saw you trying to hide behind that poor excuse for a tree. You didn't need to bother. We tracked you from the plane, but we knew there was no place for you to go unless you tried to swim across the lake. We even had that possibility covered because the boss lady doesn't leave anything to chance. Now, give me your keys."

What could I do? He easily outweighed me by a hundred-plus pounds and his companion was bigger still. I dug the keys out of my pocket, along with the realtor's business card I'd used to jot the name of the subdivision I'd just visited on the back. He snatched the keys from my hand, and I dropped the card to the ground.

"Now your phone." He pocketed it, yanked my arms behind me and zip-tied my wrists. He tossed the keys to his companion. "Kevin," he said, "you drive her car, and bring it back to the house."

He shoved me into the passenger seat of his SUV, got in himself, and locked the doors. He sat back, cocked his head and gave me a satisfied grin. "We meet again," he said. "But this time, you're alone."

"What do you want with me anyway?"

He laughed, started the engine, and drove away from the lake. "You'll see soon enough."

A short drive later, we pulled up in front of the same house I'd visited prior to driving to the plane.

My captor jumped out of the SUV, ran to my side of the vehicle and pulled me out by my elbow. We marched inside and through the living room to what appeared to be a family room in the back of the house. Elinor Chen sat in a high-backed chair across from a television set that she snapped off when we arrived.

Kevin had followed behind us, and Chen motioned for him to seat me on a wooden stool in front of her, and for them to take a seat on the adjacent sofa.

"Well, if it isn't the neighbor who killed my prize Persian," Elinor said.

"I already told you, I didn't kill your cat. I found her lying on Rabbit Creek Road and checked to see if she was alive. She wasn't. I buried her to prevent other cars from hitting her. I also contacted the nearest vet in case he knew who the owner might be."

"Likely story. You probably sold her and her litter." She shook her head. "I knew all along you were trouble."

"Look, I'll tell you where she was buried. You are welcome to look for her yourself."

We were interrupted when the woman I'd met earlier at the door entered the room and whispered something in Elinor's ear.

"Hello, again," I said to her.

She ignored me and left.

I turned back to Elinor. "She appears to work for you. I can assume her earlier friendliness was fake. Who is she anyway?"

"Sophia? She's an actress in my employ and quite good at her job. We wanted her to direct you to the lake, and she performed admirably."

"But why?" I asked.

"I'm sure you'd like to know. But that's not important right now. I want to find Charlie. Turns out you're looking for him, too, so I'm guessing you don't have the answer."

"No, I don't." I wiggled my wrists behind my back but there was no give.

"But you must be able to get messages to him."

"No."

Elinor smiled grimly and nodded to her two henchmen. "Kevin, you're on."

Kevin rose and jerked my head back by my ponytail. He then grabbed my wrists by the zip-ties and pulled them upward until I fell forward off the stool, my arms in spasm.

"Enough," Elinor said. "For now."

I struggled to a sitting position on the floor.

"Let's try another approach," Elinor said. "Why did you steal footage from our film library? When you sold your business, the complete film library was included. The company we bought the business from swears they didn't keep or remove anything."

"I don't know what you're talking about." I rotated my shoulders, trying to loosen the muscles. "I didn't keep or steal anything."

"I'm talking about the negatives of the Aleutians that were shot for the Navy in the eighties."

"That was before my time, but if there are images missing, it's likely the Navy restricted the film and kept the only copy."

"You're lying. Why would they do that? They'd fly it themselves if it were secret."

"Military contracts are often classified. They may choose to contract a job out if they want flight lines at lower altitudes than their planes fly," I explained. "Also, I understand in those pre-digital days, they didn't always have the right planes. Their planes were too fast for some projects. According to my father, sometimes the military restricted him from developing the film on especially sensitive projects."

"That's hard to believe. I'll have to talk to him about it when he arrives."

Elinor stood over me and glared. "I want those photos. If you don't know about them, maybe your father can help me. We'll see what he says when he and your son get here."

"Keep my family out of this. My son is only twelve and knows nothing. My father retired years ago, and he's never met Charlie. Neither of them can help you."

"I don't believe you." Elinor nodded toward the two men. "Pick her up off the floor and go. Bring them here."

Chapter Forty-nine

Left alone with Sophia, I watched her straighten the room after everyone left. She picked up Elinor's empty coffee cup and ran a small battery-operated vacuum over the floor. She vacuumed under all the furniture, moving everything except my stool.

"Don't you want me to move?"

She ignored me, so I tried again. "What I want to know is why you were instructed to direct me to the lake?"

Sophia narrowed her eyes, pressed her lips together and left the room.

She didn't return, and I squirmed uncomfortably on my perch. I considered toppling to the floor but couldn't come up with a valid plan for escape after I landed. At this point, I could only hope Elinor's bruisers wouldn't find Dad and Jack at home. Dad owned firearms, but chances were good he would be overcome before he recognized the danger. He tended to believe strangers were well-intentioned unless proven otherwise.

I tried to remember what I'd told him about my previous encounters. He knew about the storage unit and the office break-in, which might help keep his guard up. And, since it was Tuesday, chances were good he'd have taken Jack to the Elmendorf course to play golf this morning. I willed them to still be there.

I sighed. Jack would be an easy target unless Dad protected him. I had to hope Elinor's threat was an empty one. My hip ached and I shifted my weight. Would Norm be able to figure out what happened and where to find me before it was too late? Was he even in town?

Sophia swept back into the room, feather duster in hand. She completed a quick run around the entertainment center and coffee table with the duster. The scent of ammonia filled the room as she spritzed the windows and wiped them clean.

"You're a woman of many talents," I said. "I'm especially impressed with your acting abilities. You convinced me that you were doing me a favor by giving me directions to the float plane."

A small smile flitted across her face. "It was easy. I told you what you wanted to hear."

"True, but you were so friendly doing it."

"You seemed like a nice lady."

"I am nice. Can't you tell me why they wanted you to send me there?"

She looked over her shoulder toward the door before answering, "The plan was for you to find something, I think. Now, I have work to do. The boss likes everything perfect."

After a few minutes of silence, I heard a vehicle pull up to the house. A door slammed, followed by two more.

"Hey Mister, don't hurt my grandpa!" The sound of Jack's voice sent shivers down my spine.

"Shut your mouth, brat, or I'll gag you both."

The door to the house opened and soon Jack and Dad came stumbling into the room, shoved forward by their captors.

The man, Kevin, dragged a couple of wooden chairs in from the dining room and pushed Dad hard into one of them, zip tying his already bound wrists to the slats of the chair. He repeated the process with Jack.

"Mom," Jack said as he pulled against his restraints, "what's going on?"

Kevin took a roll of duct tape from his jacket pocket. "Shut your yap or I'll tape it shut."

"Hey," I protested. "He's a kid. You can't treat him that way."

"I heard more than enough from him on the drive here." Kevin turned to Sophia. "Be careful with him." He rubbed his swollen jaw. "The kid clobbered me with a golf club when I grabbed the old man."

I nodded at Jack. *That's my boy.*

Sophia left for a few minutes and returned with a bag of ice for Kevin in one hand and the vacuum in the other. She gave him the ice, then switched on the vacuum and swept away the tracks in the carpet that'd been made when the men had dragged in the chairs.

"Cut out the cleaning," Kevin said. "The place looks fine."

She left again, and I could hear her cleaning in the other room.

I looked over at Dad. Physically, he looked normal, but his expression appeared otherwise. I could almost see the steam rising from his scalp.

He looked at me, his mouth set in a grim line and shook his head in disgust. He wanted to be in attack mode, but the circumstances stymied him.

Jack's expression mirrored his grandpa's. This was my fault. How could I have brought them into this disaster?

Sophia's voice, raised in protest, erupted from the entrance. She called the two thugs to help, but the door slammed against the wall before they could intervene.

"FBI, slide your weapons to me, and get down on the floor."

A few minutes later, Norm and another agent rushed in, guns held at the ready. Norm surveyed the room and lowered his gun. "What have you gotten yourself into this time, Beri?"

"These yahoos kidnapped us, that's what," Dad said. "They broke into my home."

I started to explain that I was the only one at the lake and they needed to arrest Elinor Chen O'Hara of Northern Mapping.

Norm interrupted. "This sounds complicated. I'll call for back-up to transport everyone to headquarters. We can sort things out once we're there."

"Cool," Jack said.

I rolled my eyes. I just wanted to go home; not spend more hours at the FBI office. But anything was better than being held captive.

Chapter Fifty

Norm shepherded Dad, Jack and me into a small conference room at FBI headquarters.

"Take a seat. I want to make this quick. I know you're exhausted, and I'm overwhelmed with suspects to interview. We're going to video record your statements, and let you go home. We may need to bring you back later when I know more about what's going on." He turned to me and exhaled loudly. "Okay, Beri, give me the highlights of what happened today."

I described my visit to the house where I'd previously picked up Charlie, and how Sophia had directed me to the lake where I was subsequently abducted, brought back to the house, and interrogated by Elinor.

"How did your dad and Jack get involved?" Norm asked.

"Elinor ordered her minions to grab them for leverage to force me to talk."

"What did she want you to talk about?"

"She wanted foremost to know how to contact Charlie, but she also wanted me to reveal the whereabouts of some images from Dad's old film library."

"I'm assuming you didn't cooperate?"

"No, I couldn't. I didn't keep any negatives from the library when I sold the business. And I don't know how to contact Charlie."

"Who is this Elinor Chen? We're running background on her, but I don't have anything back yet?"

"I don't know much. I understand she bought Northern Mapping and lives down the street from me. I'm now two owners removed from the business Dad founded. I'm currently employed at AIA Mapping, a competitor of hers."

"We already have at least a working knowledge of the slippery Charlie. What's Chen's interest in him?"

"I don't know. I assume there's a connection between Northern Mapping and the company where Charlie was employed in Texas, but that's only an assumption."

Norm shook his head and focused on Dad. "Your turn, Frank."

"Don't have much to tell you. Jack and I had just arrived home from playing golf when the doorbell rang. I opened the door and two hoodlums slammed past me. The bearded one had a gun. Jack was still in the garage putting our gear away. I shouted to warn him to run."

"So, Jack, what happened next?"

Jack shuffled in his chair before speaking. "I took my four iron from my bag with me and I sneaked in through the kitchen door. There were two of them, so I went for the one with the gun first. Hit him with my golf club hard enough he dropped his weapon, but the other guy pulled his gun out. I couldn't get him. He tied our hands behind our backs while the first guy picked up his gun and pointed it at us. Then, they shoved us in their SUV and drove to where they had Mom tied up."

He shrugged. "Guess it wasn't too smart to try to tackle both of them, but I did call 9-1-1 from the garage first."

"Did the police respond?" Norm asked.

"I don't know. We left too quick."

Norm sat on the edge of the table; his legs stretched out in front of him, feet on the floor. "Do any of you have anything to add?"

I piped up. "Two things. I don't know if it's important, but I had a brief encounter with one of the two men earlier."

"Tell me about it."

"He approached me in an intimidating fashion at the golf tent a couple of weeks ago. He left in a hurry when Jack and Detective Diaz came outside to meet me."

"Detective Diaz?"

"Yes. Jack and I ran into him there. He's into golf, too, apparently. We watched Jack practice his swing for a while."

"Did the detective talk to this man?"

"No. The guy faded into the parking lot and left. He must have followed us there."

"You said two things?"

"Yes, I found a woman's tennis shoe under the seat of Charlie's plane. I gathered from Sophia that her employer wanted me to find it there."

Norm pinched his eyebrows together, furrowing his forehead. "I think that's enough for now. I want to hear what the others have to say and try to figure out what's going on. You can go. I'll have someone drive you home. We'll be in contact."

"Norm," I said.

"What?"

"Thanks."

"Go. I'll be in touch."

Dad was so relieved to be home that he sank into his recliner and clicked on the television, his go-to relaxation technique.

Jack bent down and righted an overturned side table in the entry. "We were really scared, Mom."

A cracked leg skewed the table's stance. "Thanks for standing it up, Jack, but I think it's ruined. I hope Gramps can fix it. I have my doubts unless he makes a whole new leg."

"Sorry, Mom, I know you liked it."

"It was handy to drop my hat and gloves on when I came in from outside, but we're lucky if that's the only damage we suffered." I headed for the kitchen. "How about a sandwich? I'm starved."

"Can mine be grilled cheese?"

Jack sat down at the table to keep me company while I cooked. He stared into space without talking.

"Are you okay, Jack?"

"Huh?" He startled. "Yes, just thinking about things."

I left the stove and walked over to give him a squeeze. "Norm will put them in jail. It's okay."

"I know. It was scary, though."

While the sandwiches browned, I cored and sliced a couple of apples. As I lifted the first sandwich off with my spatula, Dad yelled from his recliner. "Beri, you might want to see this."

I hastily turned off the stove and slid the last sandwich on a plate before I dashed into the den.

A somber newscaster stood with a group of troopers standing near a glacier's edge. "The body of a missing tennis star, Maxine Stedwell, has been recovered after being found by hikers yesterday morning. Her grieving husband, Michael, identified the wedding band she wore as the one he'd designed for her."

"Oh, no," I said. "Sounds like Gina's friend from the Alaska Club."

Chapter Fifty-one

The doorbell rang. It was six o'clock in the evening, and I wasn't expecting anyone. A glance out the window revealed a Fed Ex truck driving off. Sure enough, a package sat outside my front door. A very large package.

Surprised, since I hadn't ordered anything, and Dad was not a shopper, I opened the door and scrutinized the box with suspicion. About two feet long and a foot and a half wide, with no Amazon "smile", it offered few clues to its contents until I read the return address on the label. I knelt to read the small print: Bridal Designs by Enzo.

Aha! Sarah had ordered my dress.

Inside, wrapped in yards of tissue paper, I found an understated cerulean blue tea-length dress in my size. I shook out the silk charmeuse skirt and took it upstairs to try on.

I loved the dress immediately and held my breath that it would work. This close to the wedding date, it would be hard to start over.

The dress fit perfectly and transformed my no-nonsense appearance. I looked almost glamorous. Sarah was proving herself to be not only a special prospective stepmother, but a talented wardrobe consultant as well. And I could use one.

Jack, home from the driving range, slammed the front door and ran upstairs toward his room. He stopped short when he saw me standing in front of the mirror. "Wow, Mom. You look pretty. Where are you going?"

I laughed. "Nowhere at the moment. Just trying this dress on for the wedding."

"Oh. Well, you look nice."

"Speaking of the wedding, you need to try on your suit to make sure it still fits." I tugged on his tee-shirt sleeve, which rested several inches above his wrist. "Do it tonight, so we'll have time to alter it or shop for a new one."

"Yeah. Okay, if you say so."

I changed back into my jeans and button-down, then hung the new dress carefully in my closet. I was relieved it didn't even need pressing.

The phone rang. As soon as I picked up, Sarah asked, "Did your dress arrive?"

"Yes, I just tried it on. It's perfect."

"Good. I loved the color so much that I've used it as the primary color to coordinate with the flowers. I would have hated to have to change everything if it didn't work."

"No need for that. I love the color and the dress."

"It's so nice to see everything finally coming together. We only have a week, you know."

"Yes, it's almost here. I'm sure it will be a beautiful wedding."

"I've done my best. If a small, simple ceremony takes so much planning, I can only imagine the work involved in one of those extravaganzas you read about in magazines."

The phone rang the next morning as I dressed for work.

"Beri, this is Detective Diaz. Norm Underwood with the FBI tells me you recently found a woman's tennis shoe in one of his suspect's planes."

"I guess word gets around. Yes, I told Norm about the shoe. He may have retrieved it."

"It may be nothing, but we recently discovered the body of a young woman wearing one shoe of the same type. Do you have any idea how it ended up in the plane?"

"None at all. I've even wondered if the shoe was planted there due to the circumstances of my finding it. I had no idea the person I was looking for even owned a plane. He was a student of mine, but he was taking glider lessons and hadn't mentioned it."

"Not the student who ran off after your emergency landing at Birchwood?"

"The very same."

"What can you tell me about him?"

"Not much more than you already know. I'm not even sure the name he gave me is his real name. Norm probably knows a lot more about him than I do."

"Speaking of Norm, he's running DNA testing on the shoe. If it comes back a match to our victim, I'll need you to come in and give a full statement about your connection to this mysterious student."

"Glad to, but I don't know much."

"Understood. Thanks, Beri."

The idea that Charlie owned a float plane nagged at me as I drove to the office. Why hadn't he mentioned it during our lesson time together? I was aware he had previous flight experience, but he'd implied he'd only been a recreational pilot while living in the Lower 48. He'd mentioned he'd enjoyed flying when he lived in Phoenix some years ago. The desert would be an unlikely location for float plane ownership, but some areas of Texas might have offered more opportunities.

I arrived at the office early and brewed some coffee. As I sat at the conference table sipping my first cup of the day, I pondered why everything about Charlie was so confusing. Was he responsible for a murder? Who was he really? And why had he chosen to connect himself to me?

My last attempt to learn more about him had been returning to the home of his friend where I'd picked him up, but that had fizzled and only added to my consternation. If the people I encountered there were friends, I'd hate to meet his enemies.

Chapter Fifty-two

Kincaid Park, a wilderness playground nestled within the boundaries of the Municipality of Anchorage, provided the ideal site for Dad and Sarah's wedding. The park's rustic chalet near the entrance would give protection from the elements if inclement weather dared present itself on the big day. If they'd only built it on a hill, on a clear day you would be able to see Mount Susitna from the parking lot. A flower garden splashed the otherwise wild growth of alders and trees with a dash of color. The chalet's loft served as a dressing room up top and a side room off the main floor provided space for the caterers to set up.

Sarah initially suggested the Aviation Museum as their wedding venue, thinking Dad would be in his element among the vintage planes, but he'd objected, saying the day should be about romance, not about business.

Ross turned down the gravel road leading to the park, and a ten-minute drive later, parked in the mostly empty lot adjacent to the chalet. We exited the jeep, with me carrying my dress on the hanger and Jack lugging the box I'd filled with miscellaneous necessities.

Ross held the door to the chalet open for us. Obviously, we weren't the first to arrive, as an arbor draped in chiffon and a podium for the minister already faced two groupings of chairs divided by a carpeted aisle. This filled the rear of a large open room surrounded by windows. I took it all in, amazed at the transformation of the formerly rustic empty space from only hours ago. Small tables decorated with tall vases filled with larkspur, white gladioli, and bells of Ireland were centered on each. The tables flanked a dance floor set up for a disc jockey. A small table with a guest book sat to the right of the entrance.

Gravel crunched in the parking lot outside. A moment later, Dad hurried inside. He was decked out in his best suit, complete with a white rose boutonniere. He greeted us and reached for the dress I was carrying.

"I'll take this upstairs for you. The gals are helping Sarah get ready up there. He turned to Ross and pointed to the restrooms. "Men can change in there if you need to primp any."

"I think I'm as pretty as I'm going to get," Ross said, "but thanks, Frank."

"Me, too." Jack turned toward the door. "Can I go out and look around while everyone's getting ready?"

"Sure thing," Dad said. "Just stay close. It's not long until showtime. Remember, you're my best man. You have an important job to do."

"How could I forget after all that practice last night?" Jack opened the door to leave as another car pulled into the parking lot. "Don't worry, I won't get my clothes dirty."

"All I can say is someone did a lot of decorating since we left. Was that you, Dad?"

"Not really. A team of Sarah's friends volunteered to help and started as soon as we finished our practice. They came back this morning to arrange the flowers, and the caterers are due any minute to get their gear in place." He led me upstairs to what amounted to the bride's dressing room.

"Beri." Sarah looked lovely in a shimmering ivory dress cut in a style that matched mine. She drew me into her arms for a hug.

"Careful. You don't want me to crush your dress." I held her at arm's length. "You look gorgeous!"

"Doesn't she, though?" A petite, doe-eyed brunette patted Sarah's hair. "I've been telling her that she's the most beautiful bride I've ever seen."

"Well, if I am, it's because you've done your magic on my hair. Beri, this is Henri, my long-suffering hair stylist."

"Pooh! I haven't suffered a bit. I always look forward to your appointments."

"Better hurry up, gals," Dad called up. "The minister's here and the guests are arriving."

Sarah zipped up my dress, then moved to a table holding my small bouquet of white roses with a sprinkling of forget-me-nots and her similar, but more elaborate bouquet next to it. As she handed me mine, the fragrance of the roses increased my sense of celebration.

"Forget-me-nots! How perfect. I'm surprised you could find a florist who could provide them."

Sarah leaned in close to me and whispered, "I cheated. They were too fragile, so I found some made of silk that looked real. The florist wove them in with the roses."

"Well, you fooled me. I love the results. You couldn't have found anything more Alaskan than the state flower, and they're certain to be hypoallergenic." I grinned.

Strains of harp music drifted up the stairs. I looked over the railing to see the rows of chairs almost completely filled.

Directly below the railing, two men appeared to be deep in conversation. I was shocked to see Spence in animated discussion with another man whose back was turned to me. I couldn't make out what was said. The words "rare earth" caught my attention. I wondered if Dad knew Spence. If he did, it wouldn't be surprising. Spence had been skeptical about Jason's story from the beginning.

"Ladies, it's time," Ross called up, and we made our way down to the bottom of the stairs.

The minister took his place at the podium and asked everyone to take their seats. Soon after, a soloist sang a beautiful love song I'd never heard before.

"It's an oldie," Sarah whispered, "but we both love it. When we go dancing, Frank requests it and usually stumps the band."

The minster read a scripture and said a few words about the couple, and before we knew it, strains of Bach began and Dad with Jack close behind him, moved up to the minister's side.

The flower girl's mom adjusted the girl's dress and did her best to reassure her daughter that all she had to do was follow me down the aisle and scatter a few petals for Sarah to walk on.

The girl looked up at me and smiled. "Okay. I'm glad you go first."

We walked slowly forward. Dad couldn't stop smiling when Sarah started her walk down the aisle.

As she approached, the harpist somehow caused the music to swell in volume, and the audience stood. Dad took Sarah's hand, and after the couple exchanged vows, the minister asked for the ring.

Jack pulled it out, held it to his mouth and gave it a huff of moist air before polishing it on his sleeve.

The guests chuckled.

Dad quickly slipped the ring on Sarah's finger and drew her into his arms for a kiss.

The minister introduced the new Mr. and Mrs. Frank Quinn. They turned toward the guests, and Dad, with his arm still around his bride, moved to the microphone and addressed the group.

"Thank you all for sharing this day with us. We'd be honored to have you join us in a celebratory brunch. Please seat yourselves at one of the nearby tables. Servers will come by to offer champagne, mimosas and coffee, and the buffet will be open shortly."

"What's to eat, Frank?" Jeb Jeter called out. "I've worked up an appetite flying in from Nome."

"Sarah will have to answer that," he said and moved to the side so she could reach the microphone.

Sarah pulled the mic down to accommodate her shorter stature. "We're serving a buffet with King Crab crepes and spinach and mushroom quiche with assorted salads and breads. And, of course we have fruit and cake for dessert. Lots of cake."

"I'll be first in line," Zeb announced.

"Shush, now," said Mary, sitting beside him.

"Since everyone is all together, and I'm already up here facing you," Sarah said, "I think I'll take care of one of my remaining tasks and toss my bouquet. Please feel free to stand to improve your chance of success." She turned her back to the guests and tossed the bouquet high in the air and directly to Ross. He reached up and grabbed it before ceremoniously handing it to me.

"You know what this means," he said with a wink.

I stood there with a bouquet in each hand while he bent down for a kiss. My face flushed with embarrassment when applause erupted.

Chapter Fifty-three

Following the bride and groom's first dance, Ross pulled me out on the dance floor. He held me close and sighed. "I've never seen Frank look so happy."

I smiled up at him. "Yes, Sarah, too. I'm so glad they found each other."

The tempo of the music changed, and our conversation ended as we moved further apart. When the number concluded, we moved back to our table.

"That was fun," Ross said as he squeezed my hand. "We should do that more often."

"I agree, but right now I have a question about that scenario with Sarah's bouquet. When did the two of you cook that trick up?"

Ross laughed. "Actually, we discussed it some time ago, and I'd forgotten all about it. Thought it was a joke at the time, and after my heart attack, I figured you'd have doubts about our getting married. I was as shocked as anyone when she pitched those flowers at me."

"You can't seriously think your heart attack would change my feelings for you?" I asked.

"Well, I did. I've hardly seen you lately." He paused and looked down at the table before continuing. "When you stop by, it's more like you're checking to make sure I'm okay."

"I'm so sorry. I've been so tied up with the challenges of the new job that I didn't realize how much I was neglecting you and our relationship." I squirmed in my chair. *Had I subconsciously been drawing away from Ross to avoid the pain of losing him?*

"Here's a suggestion to remedy the situation," he said. "Why don't you stay at my place tonight?" He reached around me and pulled me as close as our seating arrangement would allow.

"Oh Ross, I'd love to, but Jack is leaving for Arizona in the morning."

His face fell. "I understand…"

"No, you didn't let me finish. Why don't you stay at my place instead? Dad will be gone, and Jack has to go to bed early so he can get up in time for his early flight."

Ross leaned over and kissed me. "Brilliant," he said. "I've missed you."

Dad approached the table and pulled out a chair. "Mind if I join you two lovebirds for a minute?" He clapped Ross on the shoulder. "Looks like you're next. I couldn't be happier for the both of you and I know Jack is tickled about it, too."

"We're working on it," Ross said. "I've got to get my health under control first. My doctor wants me to have a procedure done to help forestall future problems. He said his own father had the same procedure over twenty years ago and went on to live to age eighty-six." Ross shrugged. "I'm scheduled to have it next month, so maybe if Beri will still have me afterwards, we'll get serious about setting a date."

"Of course, I'll have you, but why wait? If we're already married, the doctors will keep me in the loop about your progress a lot better than if I'm your girlfriend."

Ross laughed. "I like the sound of that. We'll have to talk."

Dad pushed his chair back and started to rise. "Speaking of brides, I'd best go claim mine. She's having too much fun on the dance floor without me."

"Dad, before you go, I have a question. I noticed Spencer Atkins among your guests before the ceremony. I didn't know you knew each other."

"I just met him today, actually. He's Sarah's cousin, although I don't think they're close. She invited him because he's family."

"I recently met him at work and was surprised to see him again so soon. Did you happen to notice who he was talking to before the ceremony? I overheard a snippet of their conversation from the loft that made me curious."

"Hmm, I was distracted at the time, but I think I saw him talking to Zeb for a few minutes."

He stepped away from the table. "Got to go cut in before Sarah forgets who she just married."

I looked around the room, hoping to talk to Spence, but it appeared he'd already left. "Excuse me for a minute, Ross. I need to say hello to a couple of people."

I moved over to Zeb and Mary's table. "May I sit with you for a few minutes?"

"Sure. The couple sitting here have been dancing non-stop, so we don't expect them back any time soon," Zeb said.

"It's so good to see you both. I know it means a lot to Dad that you made the trip, especially after your injury. How are you feeling?"

"A lot better, despite his stubbornness. Besides, we wouldn't have missed it," Mary said. "It was a beautiful wedding, and it's wonderful to see Frank so happy."

"He's happy now, and he may be even happier real soon," Zeb said.

"What do you mean?" I asked.

"He hasn't told you? Well, word is that we may have another kind of strike on his claim."

"I don't understand."

"A bunch of geologists have been testing our tailings for heavy REEs and it looks like they found what they were looking for."

"Back up. What the heck are heavy REEs?" I felt certain I already knew, but I hadn't expected a Nome connection.

Zeb laughed. "REE stands for rare earth element, and the heavy ones are the most valuable. They tell me former placer gold areas are a great place to look for them, because they're much easier to extract from sand and gravel than when they have to break down rock. Apparently, it's about

Alaska's government investing in separation plants and looking for more raw material within the state."

"Sounds interesting," I said.

"Yeah, there's one plant under construction near Ketchikan already, and they may try to build another one somewhere near a good port. Who knows? Alaska may give China some competition as a worldwide REE supplier someday. At least, that's what they tell me."

The couple who had been sitting at Zeb's table left the dance floor and began walking our way. I got up and returned to Ross after bidding the Nome couple good-bye.

We rounded up Jack and headed home. He'd already done most of his packing, but I helped him with the finishing touches and tucked him into bed. He was so excited he wasn't sure he could sleep. When I checked on him, he was already out a few minutes later.

The wedding had been wonderful, but alone time with Ross was even better. Circumstances and work responsibilities had caused us to temporarily lose some of our closeness. I was grateful we'd realized it in time to remedy the problem.

Chapter Fifty-four

Ross reached over and patted my knee as we drove back from the airport. "Don't worry about Jack. He'll be fine. His dad will watch out for him."

"I guess that should make me feel better, but knowing my ex, he cooked up the whole scheme in order to have Jack live closer to him."

"Maybe. Dennis can be manipulative, but I think Jack's golf bug is genuine. I had to laugh when he flipped out after the ticket-taker carelessly threw his clubs on the conveyor belt at check-in."

"It was funny, but not to Jack. He's focused like a laser beam on playing golf." I shook my head. "Unfortunately, Alaska doesn't offer many golfing opportunities. Why couldn't he have chosen cross-country skiing or hockey?"

Ross chuckled. "If he'd chosen hockey, you'd be worried he'd get hurt. I think you're wise to let him follow his passion. He'd resent you for smothering him if you didn't. Besides, you can't qualify as a helicopter mom. You don't have the right ratings."

I jabbed my elbow in his ribs.

"Hey, I'm driving." He turned his head toward me. "Want to stop for an early lunch before I take you back to work?"

"Thanks, but no. I'd better get to the office. I've fallen behind on things, what with the wedding and all. Besides, work will help me keep my mind off my absentee son."

"See you tonight. It'll be just the two of us. We'll have to think of something to entertain ourselves."

I stepped out of the jeep after Ross pulled up outside the office. A thought struck me, and I poked my head back in before closing the door. "Thanks, you were a big help getting Jack on the plane, although I think I needed you more than he did. And thanks for that crack about my ratings. It reminded me of something I need to do."

"Anytime, babe."

Once inside, I turned to the FAA website to check Charlie's ratings. Sure enough, his claim not to have a float plane rating was accurate. Unless of course, he had one under a different name. But if that were true, why register the float plane under his name? It didn't make sense. I checked the name Arthur Hennigan just in case but found no results under that name, either.

It occurred to me that I might learn more by checking the past ownership of the float plane with the FAA and brought up their website. Prior to the purchase of the plane by Charlie Greer listed two months ago, information on ownership had been blocked by the previous owner.

Interesting. Charlie hadn't been listed as owner for very long, so who was responsible for blocking the plane's earlier history?

I picked up the phone and called Norm, hoping I'd catch him.

He answered with a gruff, "Good morning."

"Can you spare the time to meet with me sometime today?" I asked.

"I have a few loose ends to clean up, but I should be free in about an hour. Why don't you stop by then? I'll alert the first floor to expect you."

I cleared my desk and headed for the door, thinking I'd have time to grab a quick lunch. Halfway to the door I stopped cold. I didn't have my car.

"What's wrong?" Angie asked.

"I have an appointment and forgot Ross dropped me off this morning. Guess I can call a taxi."

"No, take mine," Jason interjected from his desk and tossed me his keys. "I'm not going anywhere until quitting time."

"You sure?" I knew he was quite particular about his recently purchased sports car.

"I'm sure. I have a stack of reports to go through; I won't be going anywhere."

"Thanks," I said. "I should be back in a couple of hours."

Jason's car was parked a few feet outside the entrance and sparkled in the sunlight. He kept it in immaculate condition, choosing to hand wash it himself rather than trusting it to a car wash. I hadn't driven it before and was a bit nervous at the prospect. I also knew I'd feel conspicuous driving it. Cars of this type are uncommon in Alaska. Too much snow in winter and mud during break-up to be practical.

As I unlocked the driver's side door, I felt my foot slip.

Looking down, I spotted a black and white aerial photo, the colors almost identical to the mottled grays of the pavement. Surprised, I recognized it as one of Dad's Adak pictures. Jason must have dropped it.

Returning inside, I slid the photo across his desk. "Look what I found on the ground outside your car."

He gave me a startled look. "I dropped my briefcase and spilled its contents this morning. I thought I'd picked everything up. Glad you rescued it."

He carefully wiped the 9 X 9-inch photo with a white cotton glove he wore when handling them. "It was one of the chief exhibits I used for my presentation at the meeting this morning." He glanced at the clock. "I wanted to talk to you about the outcome of that meeting anyway. Can you spare a few minutes for a brief recap before you leave?"

"Sure," I said. "I was going to grab a sandwich on my way to my appointment. I can do that later."

"Good. Let's go for a quick drive." He handed me the photo I'd just given him along with a second one. "You hang on to these, and I'll drive."

We drove a short distance and parked across from the cemetery a few blocks away.

I gave him a quizzical look.

"It's the quietest place I could think of," he said with a wry smile. "Not many cities have a graveyard located in the center of downtown."

"Why so hush, hush?" I asked.

"Nothing top secret, really," he said. "Just not something I'd want to leak out. While I don't think either Angie or Mickey would intentionally leak anything, they might slip and say something to the wrong person." He pointed to the photos in my lap. "Take a close look at these two shots. What differences do you see?"

"For starters, the one I found is a shot Dad took years ago and the other we took last week."

"Yes. What else?"

"As we discussed earlier, the old bunker in Dad's shot was transformed into the Avian Center and the antenna was added."

"Anything else?"

"Several old military sites are gone in the recent one. Probably bulldozed."

"Keep going."

I glanced again between the two photos. "The only other thing I notice is some changes at the far edge of the port. Looks like some new development."

"Exactly. I didn't pay much attention at first, but the analysts I met with found that fact, coupled with the antenna, very interesting. When the translation of those computer screen shots you photographed came back, things came into better focus."

"What do you mean? Something to do with submarines?"

"Yes, and something more. Adak is strategically placed in several ways that are attractive to China. Chief among them is the proximity to a suspected motherlode of REEs on the seabed. Ever since the Japanese began successfully mining an area of the seabed near them, countries have been prospecting. China included. They've held a near monopoly on those metals for a long time and don't want that to change. They've also shown an interest in arctic exploration in general in recent years, and we think this may be one reason why."

"So, they may want control of Adak?"

"It's a possibility. Our country has essentially abandoned the place. It looks like they're already exploiting it right under our noses."

"Scary. So why the antenna?"

"Our best guess is it's a new condensed technology for communication with their submarines at depths where good reception isn't otherwise possible. It's all very speculative, but definitely worthy of further investigation. Our little mission has sparked renewed military interest in the Aleutians. Consequently, they're shutting down our operation and taking over."

He faced me. "As they say, 'no good deed goes unpunished' so we need to talk about how this will affect you and the staff."

"I think Angie and I have known all along that our set-up was temporary. I don't know about Mickey."

"He was hired only for the summer flying season. He won't be surprised. I'll give them the official word tomorrow. I hope you'll be ready to take the reins on your own. I'll schedule an appointment with Sully to help us navigate the legalities."

"Sounds good." I glanced at my watch. "I hate to cut this short, but I'm going to be late for my appointment. Any chance you can drop me off at the FBI Building? I can take a taxi back."

He gave me an appraising look. "Sure."

We drove in silence until he pulled up in front of the FBI headquarters.

"Don't know if I should ask, but are they still investigating your kidnapping? I understand they have the culprits in custody."

"Yes, they have most of them. Not the top one, though," I clarified.

"All I know is what's been on the news, and that wasn't very comprehensive."

"They don't have all the answers yet. What you should know is that the person at the top, the one they don't have is Elinor Chen, owner of Northern Mapping."

"What? Why didn't you mention this earlier?" he asked.

"I'd been advised not to talk about the incident, but I think you need to know. I haven't mentioned it to anyone else at the office."

"So, that's what this meeting today is all about?"

"Partially. There are a lot of loose ends I hope they can clear up for me."

"Good luck. Let's meet early tomorrow morning to develop a plan for our staff meeting."

"I'll be there."

Norm had contacted security to let me in as promised. Grateful, I zipped up to his office in record time and found him sitting at his desk eating a muffin.

"That looks good," I said. "Sorry I'm a little late. My boss decided I needed to meet with him before I left."

"No problem." He waved at the basket of muffins on his conference table. "My mother is in town. She thought I'd need her to take care of me after I was shot."

I grabbed a muffin. "Sounds like a wise woman. Please give her my thanks. They look delicious, and I skipped lunch."

"I assume you want information?" Norm asked.

"Yes, and I have some to give you, but first, has Elinor been arrested?"

"No. We haven't located her yet. I'm sure we will before long. Do you have any new information about her or why she kidnapped you and your family?"

"Nothing we haven't already discussed. I did have an interesting conversation with Wallace Killion recently. He told me the FBI visited him in his office and informed him that Charlie, his client, was wanted for embezzlement and murder. Something about his CFO's car accident wasn't an accident and multiple financial accounts were mishandled. I was surprised by this, especially since Charlie provided you with so much information about the accounts."

"Yes. We recently learned the Texas branch of the FBI had sent agents to Anchorage looking for him. They were unaware of the recent events regarding the accounts, and we tried to calm the waters on this. They currently have no proof the CFO was murdered, but apparently Charlie's second-in-command, the man he left in charge of the company, has been stirring the waters."

"Where is Charlie now? Has he disappeared as he'd planned?"

"I doubt it," Norm said. "The Texas office has everyone on the look out for him. He'll find it difficult to leave. I'll keep you posted. Is that all? I need to keep this short."

"Just a couple more things."

Norm sighed. "Let's have it."

"I mentioned before that I was suspicious about the tennis shoe being planted in Charlie's float plane. Now I'm suspicious that the float plane itself may be a plant."

"Why's that?"

"I checked with the FAA. He doesn't have the rating he'd need to fly a float plane, at least not under his actual name or the name he's been using. I also checked the title of the plane itself and found it was listed under Charlie Greer as purchased two months ago. I doubt he'd purchase a float plane without the rating to fly it. The whole thing looks like a set-up to me. Granted an expensive set-up, but I don't think Charlie bought it, and I know they were anxious for me to find both the plane and the shoe. One more thing. The plane's owner prior to Charlie has blocked access to their identity. Have you looked into it?"

"No, but it sounds like a good idea. I'll get the team on it. Are we finished?"

"Just one last thing, a favor really." I handed him a copy of the photo of Gina that Charlie had given me and the tennis newspaper clipping. "Could you use facial recognition technology to determine if these are the same woman?"

"Why? They don't look much alike. Who are they, and why are they important to the case?"

I explained about Gina and Vicky Saunders. "It would be very important to Charlie. He's extremely concerned about Gina's safety. That's why he hired the private investigator in the first place, and Vicky is an employee of Northern Mapping."

"Thanks for the tip, Beri. We'll look into it."

Chapter Fifty-five

I watched as the staff crowded into the reception area of the office. Jason had pushed the front desk against the wall and placed a table in the center of the room surrounded by folding chairs. Mickey, Dean, Angie, and a couple of technicians claimed seats and passed paper plates and packets of utensils around.

Jason tapped the table with his fingers to get everyone's attention. "As you know, all good things must come to an end," he said. "I'm happy to announce that our mission has been successfully completed. You've all been instrumental in making that happen." He lifted his can of soda in a toast. "Thank you. I've enjoyed working with you in this beautiful state."

"It's been interesting," Angie said, after taking a sip of her drink, "but we all knew it wouldn't last forever. Frankly, I look forward to returning to simpler times. Dividing my time between two businesses has been a bit too schizoid to continue much longer." She shifted her gaze to Mickey. "I'll miss you, though."

"I need to get back to my horses. This has been quite an adventure, and I've enjoyed working with everyone. It's been a summer to remember."

"That's for sure." Angie got up and hugged Mickey. She let him go with tears in her eyes, then turned to me. "What's the plan now?"

"Ross and I need to map out the details, but generally, the plan is to merge back to one company for now. Ross will direct flight instruction, but will leave actual air time to our new staff. Basically, flying lessons will stay the same as they are now. The new staff are working out well."

"They're doing great," Angie said. "As you know, we've worked with Richard before. He's a pro, and Kaitlin is proving to be popular with students, too, now that she's certified."

"Good, because I'll be spending more time with mapping photography, especially now that I'm acquiring the AIA equipment. I'll need to find a replacement for Mickey, though. That won't be easy, but we've faced challenges before. Overall, I see this as an opportunity for the company to grow."

Angie frowned. "Will Ross be strong enough so soon after…?"

Dean spoke up for the first time. "Ross is one strong dude. He'll be fine."

"We have a good team," I said. "We'll make this happen, and the doctors agree that Ross is doing well."

I pulled Mickey aside after we finished. "Would you be willing to train a new operator before you leave? I haven't asked him, but I think it would be good to have Ross trained as a back-up. He might find he likes it."

He nodded. "Sure, be happy to. He would pick it up in no time, and I'm not on any kind of schedule at this point."

"I'll ask him about it tonight and let you know."

"Clear the way!" Jason announced. "I took the liberty of ordering food for the occasion, and it appears to have arrived." He held the door open for a delivery man loaded with insulated bags and boxes. The mingled aromas of a variety of dishes wafted through the room.

"Hope everyone likes Chinese," Jason said. "Dig in, everybody."

I piled my plate high with crab rangoons, added an egg roll and some pork lo mein. I should have stopped there, but had to try everything else, too. Everyone seemed to enjoy the special lunch.

Afterward, although I felt like taking a nap, I forced myself to return to my desk to get some work done. Choosing the top RFP from a teetering stack, I tried to focus. Instead, my mind kept returning to questions about the Adak port. Why had it been renovated and by whom?

I checked the photos again and used the stereoscope to examine the entire area. The changes appeared to primarily involve demolition of several small structures and the addition of large rectangular buildings resembling warehouses.

Could the Chinese be using them to stockpile supplies for their submarines in the area? It would reduce the number of return trips they'd have to make to their home base. Although our military had deserted the island, they were still very much present in the state. It wouldn't make sense for the Chinese to store materials they'd mined from the seabed on U.S. soil.

A quick google search revealed that fresh water wouldn't need restocking as subs can desalinate sea water for drinking. Food and other basic supplies would be more likely to limit the duration of their missions. And, the Adak port didn't freeze in the winter. It was open year-round.

I thought back to Mickey's conversation with the grocery store owner, and his mentioning that Alaska Airlines made food deliveries including fresh product to Adak twice a week. The military was probably keeping an eye on this already, but it wouldn't hurt to contact my 99s friend, Pris, who worked in cargo for Alaska Airlines. She'd mentioned to me once that she enjoyed her job at Ted Stevens International Airport. While she didn't do any flying herself, at least she was around planes all day.

I called her on her cell phone. When she answered, I could hear what sounded like a forklift in reverse beeping in the background.

"Beri! Haven't seen you at our 99s meetings lately. What's up?"

"Life's been complicated, and I've been out of town a lot. I'm calling now to see if you could locate some information for me."

"Sure. If I can. What do you need?" Pris asked.

"I recently spent some time in Adak and learned Alaska Airlines delivers fresh produce and groceries to the store there. It made me wonder if deliveries of food and other supplies are delivered in large quantity to any other Adak businesses, and if so, which ones. Could you find out for me?"

"Sure. I don't think that's confidential. Hold on." She paused. "We don't have many Adak orders. I can check the computer for you now."

After another short pause, she returned. "Here you go. It looks like a company called "Islands North" has a standing reservation for deliveries once a month."

"Do you have a delivery address?"

"I do. It's delivered to their warehouse at the port."

I thanked Pris. My 99s friends had been such a treasure over the years.

I called Jason and asked him to meet me at my office.

A few seconds later, he pulled a chair next to my desk. "This is important?" he asked.

"I'm not sure. It could be." I filled him in on what I'd learned and my theory on why it may be a way to provide provisions to submarines.

"Interesting theory. I'll pass your idea on to the brass. They may already know all this, but maybe not. What did you say the name of the place is?"

"Islands North."

"The name is apt, anyway." He chuckled. "Speaking of apt, what did you think of my menu choice today?"

"Clever. Maybe a little too obvious, but I don't think the others made the connection. Besides, the crab rangoons were tasty."

Chapter Fifty-six

Ross picked me up after I reminded him I didn't have my car. It was pleasant driving home with him.

"We should do this more often," I said.

"I agree, although logistics could get complicated at times."

"I had a brainstorm today," I said. "Mickey plans to leave soon now that our Aleutian job is finished. I asked him if he'd be willing to train you how to use the new equipment. It would be nice to have a back-up for whoever we hire to replace him. I told Mickey I hadn't asked your opinion but would let him know. What do you think?"

"I think it's brilliant," Ross said. "At least I'd be able to get in the air again, and I always like to learn something new. When can we start?"

"We can coordinate with Mickey tomorrow. He says it doesn't take long to learn."

We were both tired. After eating a light dinner and feeding the animals, we curled up in bed together to watch the evening news. With Jack gone and Dad and Sarah enjoying their honeymoon, it was nice to have a quiet evening alone. Ross was asleep ten minutes later, but I continued to watch through another program and give Piper some attention before finally falling asleep.

Suddenly, Ross threw back the covers and sat up, waking me. "Did you hear something just now?"

"No, but Tiger is barking, so apparently he did." I sat up, yawning. "What did it sound like?"

"A thumping sound. I think it came from the garage. I'll go check."

"Hold on, let me get my gun just in case. I can hear Tiger jumping on the kitchen door to the garage. That's not like him."

When we reached the ground floor, I glanced out the living room window. "All I see out there is your car in the driveway." My new phone buzzed with a text message.

I read it out loud to Ross. "Two men just left your garage. I followed them there from your neighbor's house on Rabbit Creek Road. I've been watching the place. Beware. Remember what happened at the storage unit."

I looked at Ross. "It says, 'Name Unavailable,' but it has to be from Charlie," I said, and showed him the screen. "He told me he was leaving the state, but Norm from the FBI doesn't think he's left yet. I don't know what to think about him. He drives me crazy because his behavior often doesn't make sense."

"At least he's looking out for you this time." Ross eased open the door to the garage.

I stood, gun ready, beside him.

Tiger pushed through ahead of us. I heard a click and yelled, "HALT! Stay boy." He froze in place and stared at me with his big brown eyes. "Stay," I said again.

I turned to Ross. "Did you hear that clicking sound when Tiger stepped on that cement-colored mat? I didn't buy it, so they must have left it there on the floor."

"Yeah. You think…?"

"I don't know, but we can't take a chance." I hit 9-1-1 on my phone, explained the situation and requested the bomb squad come immediately. I'd already learned that my adversaries liked to blow things up.

During the excruciating wait for the police, we kept the door to the garage open while I sat on the kitchen floor just inside and did my best to soothe the dog. Tiger, sensing our fear, had begun quivering, but didn't otherwise move. Ross stood at the ready, not knowing what to do, but ready to jump into action if it became necessary.

"Stay," I reminded him. "Good boy, Tiger."

His tail wagged, but otherwise he remained still.

"You're doing such a good job." I leaned forward and stretched my arm out to give him a treat. Surely such a small item wouldn't set anything off, and I knew Tiger would be mollified by it.

Tiger whined as sirens approached. He turned his head toward me with a worried look in his eyes.

"Stay, stay. It's okay, boy."

He quieted, but his ears perked up again when he heard tires on the road as vehicles roared to a stop outside the house. Ross went to the front door to meet the police and fill them in on the situation.

He returned and introduced me to two officers wearing bomb gear. They could have been mistaken for astronauts dressed in black. Each carried a large bundle.

"Officers Ferguson and Daly, ma'am. Glad to see you have inside access to the garage. I was surprised the outside door was closed." His eyes scanned the perimeter of the garage with my vehicle parked on the far side before returning to look at me. "Is this your dog?"

"Yes, his name is Tiger. Fortunately, he's well-trained to follow my commands."

"That's a blessing," Ferguson said. "How long has he been standing there?"

"About fifteen minutes." I held up my arm to display my phone. "I received a warning that two men had been in my garage and may have explosives. When we opened the kitchen door to see, the dog pushed ahead of us into the garage. We heard a clicking sound, panicked, and stopped him in his tracks."

"Sounds like a wise move. Do you recognize that mat he's standing on?" Officer Daly asked.

"No, it's not mine. I think they made it the color of the floor so it would blend in. I didn't even see it until I turned on the light."

Ferguson moved by me to get a better look. "My guess is we're dealing with a pressure plate of some kind. How much do you think Tiger weighs?"

"Fifty-one pounds, according to the scale at the vet's office."

Officer Daly rushed out to one of their vehicles and returned a few minutes later with what looked like a large bag of rice or some kind of pellets.

"Okay, here's the plan. We'll wrap an old bomb protection suit around Tiger's vital organs. Once that's in place, we'll use a ballistic blanket around him to slide him off the mat while we simultaneously slide the weight on. We'll hope the mat's not too exquisitely weight-calibrated. Beri, we'll need you to stay until the last moment. Ross, you should leave now." He began rummaging in one of the bundles he'd carried in earlier.

"Wait just a minute," Ross said. "I'll stay, let her go. Tiger will respond to my commands as well as he would Beri's."

"No. This is no time for heroics. We're talking about an extremely delicate operation. Our chance of success is best with the dog's owner." He waved for Ross to leave. "Go. Now!"

"Do it, babe," I said. "I'll be fine."

Ross squeezed my arm, whispered "I love you," and left through the front door.

"Okay now, ma'am, we need you to keep the dog still while we get him protected. When we're ready, I'll ask you to give him a final command to stay before you leave. We expect to complete the transfer without triggering an explosion, but we need you to get as far away from the house as you can. Leave the front door open so you can hear me yell when it's safe for you to call the dog to you. Are you ready?"

"Yes, but let me give him a treat first." I reached out and dropped another biscuit in his mouth. "Now Tiger, let these men get you out of here. Stay, and Be Nice!"

I followed the officer's directions but felt hollow inside leaving Tiger. How could I tell Jack if this didn't work?

I'd barely joined Ross on the front lawn when the order came. "Call him, NOW."

"Tiger, come! Come!"

He bounded to me, dragging black protective gear and looking ecstatic to be free. He proceeded to cover my face with kisses while I held him against my chest. Ross grabbed my arm and pulled us both further from the house.

Relief flooded through me as both officers emerged carrying a heavy looking box. They gingerly placed it inside an armored Humvee-like vehicle. Daly entered through the driver's side door, closed it with care, and drove away at a speed much slower than when they arrived.

Tiger stretched his legs, running in circles around us before heading for the remaining police vehicle and sniffing cautiously. He hiked his leg and marked one of the back tires before returning to sit by us.

Officer Ferguson shooed us to the other side of the road while he checked Ross's Jeep parked in the driveway and cleared it rapidly. "Okay, both your vehicles and the garage door are clean. I suspect the perpetrators may have been scared off by the dog before finishing the job. We'll have a team scour the surrounding yard to make sure it's clean, too."

He turned back toward the house. "Other officers evacuated the neighbors on either side of your home. Don't be surprised if you get a few curious phone calls from them later today. For now, though, I'll need the two of you to meet me downtown to complete paperwork and explain the situation to the detective and the Feds."

"The Feds?" I asked.

"They're called in anytime we encounter explosives."

"Do we need to go right now, or can we take an hour or two to get dressed and calm down first?" Ross asked.

"Daly is taking it slow driving back, so you can take ten minutes to get dressed, but no longer." The officer got into his vehicle and drove away.

Tiger gave me an exasperated look. Sometimes, I'd swear he understood our conversations. He followed me inside, staying close to my side, his tail low.

"I'll drive," Ross said, after throwing on jeans and a shirt.

"Okay. Let me comb my hair and grab my laptop. Charlie may have sent me that e-mail by now."

"I'll be in the jeep."

"Take care getting in," I said. "I know Officer Ferguson cleared it, but watch for anything out of the normal."

"Yes, Mom. You better hurry, though. They're going to wonder what's taking us so long."

"I'll grab my watch and laptop and be right out." I hugged Tiger and moved to the kitchen to pour kibble in his bowl. I filled Piper's bowl with kitten food. "Don't want you two to miss breakfast. We'll leave you in charge while we're gone."

Ross had the passenger door open for me. "Everything's good. As you may have noticed, the engine's running already."

While Ross drove, I checked my phone for images. Sure enough, a video appeared of two men driving up in a dark SUV without headlights and parking a short walk from the house. They wore hoodies partially covering their faces. One carried a small duffel bag and the other pushed what looked like a remote device that opened the door. As they entered my garage, I noticed his gait and build looked familiar.

"How did they do that?" I asked.

Ross glanced my way. "Do what?"

"Get a garage door opener to our garage?"

"It's not that hard if you have the right equipment, especially if they've had prior access to the garage. Has anyone been inside recently? A repairman maybe?"

"Not that I know, but Dad may have let someone in." I finished scrolling through the footage. "Don't know how much use this footage will be to the police, with their faces mostly blocked, but I recognize one of them as a kidnapper from the lake. He had a distinctive build and way of walking, but I thought those guys were in jail."

"Maybe the e-mail will be more enlightening," Ross said.

Chapter Fifty-seven

After giving our statements to the police, Ross and I were asked to stay for a joint meeting with the Feds. Norm joined Detective Diaz, Officer Ferguson, Ross and me in the APD conference room. Norm sat at the far end and struggled to fit his long legs under the table.

"Glad the FBI could make it," Diaz said. He pursed his lips before continuing. "It looks like we're dealing with a failed homicide attempt involving explosives." He turned to me. "You've shared the alert you received early this morning." He flashed a copy of the text on a screen at the front of the room. "I understand you're certain it was sent by a contact of yours by the name of Charlie Greer. Who is this person, and how is he related to the case?"

"He's a former student of mine who is in fear for his life," I explained. "He's been in contact off and on since we observed the murder of our tow pilot at Birchwood Airport. Charlie went into hiding after that, convinced the killers were also after him. Norm may be able to tell you more about him."

Diaz broke in, the furrow between his eyes deepening with his frown. "Unfortunately, we've been unable to make any progress on the Birchwood murder investigation." He looked at Norm. "I can't wait to hear you connect the dots on this and tell us about this Charlie Greer."

Norm looked down at his notes. "Wish I could. We do have a lead on Charlie's true identity. We tried using our facial recognition program with a photograph Beri provided, and we came up with a possible match, but it's preliminary. As I'm sure you know, the technology isn't foolproof. We've concluded from evidence he turned over to us that he has reason to believe his enemies want to capture and kill him."

Diaz cleared his throat. "So, Charlie decided to be proactive and spy on his pursuers?"

Norm shrugged. "I don't see how he can succeed, considering the resources of the group he's dealing with. Before you ask who that is, I have to repeat that it's classified at this point. I'll keep you posted with our progress as best I can."

"Not good enough," Diaz said. "This doesn't make sense. Why are these unknown people trying to blow up Beri if they're actually after Charlie?"

"We're not sure," Norm said. "We know they've harassed her before this, trying to get her to reveal Charlie's whereabouts, but this second attempt on her life is hard to understand. Perhaps they got wind of the news, that with her help, Charlie has turned over the information they wanted."

Diaz sighed. "We're trying to investigate with one hand tied behind our back. I assume the best place for us to start our investigation is with this neighbor Charlie was spying on. Beri, can you tell us who this is?"

Norm held up a hand. "I'd appreciate your holding off on that, Diaz. We don't want to alert them to our surveillance."

Diaz ran his hands through his well-styled hair. "You realize you're blocking our chances of finding these bombers. I can't allow this unknown group to continue to try to blow people up."

Norm nodded. "I'll get back to you. It's a complicated situation with possible international implications. I'd suggest you investigate the way you would if you were not aware of Charlie's warning. Interview all the neighbors. They're bound to be curious anyway after your team evacuated several of them during the bomb scare."

"I'll handle the investigation on this end, thank you," Diaz snapped.

"Copy that," Norm said and turned to me. "I'll need to take your phone for our techs to analyze the alert you received. We need to confirm the name and location of the anonymous sender. I know you feel sure it was from Charlie, but we'll need to document that and where he was when he sent it."

"I don't want to give up my phone for long. My home security is on it, and I need my business contacts and aviation aps." I pointed to the overhead screen displaying the message at the front of the room. "The police have already downloaded it. Can't you use that?"

"Afraid not. We do need the phone," Norm said. "I'll request the phone be returned as soon as possible."

Officer Ferguson cleared his throat and we all turned to him as if we'd forgotten he was there. "This is all very interesting, but I don't think it involves me. I've written up the details of the bomb and our removal technique. In a nutshell, the pressure plate was sophisticated, but not extremely sensitive. We disarmed it without any complications." He looked at Ross and me. "You were lucky to have that alert and to have such a cooperative pooch."

"I want to thank you for saving us, our dog, and our home this morning. You and your partner did a fabulous job and risked your lives for us," I said.

The officer blushed and rose from his chair. "Our pleasure, ma'am."

The meeting broke up. Ross and I signed our statements and exited police headquarters. As we headed for the parking lot, Ross said, "I'm surprised they didn't put the contents of your e-mail on the screen along with Charlie's initial alert."

"I wondered about that, too. My guess is that Norm blocked it because it identified the neighbor. He didn't want the police to focus on Elinor Chen. They probably only evacuated the houses on either side of our house. I doubt they went as far as the houses across Rabbit Creek Road. Maybe we'll learn more when I talk to him later. I have an appointment at his office at two o'clock."

As we approached the jeep to leave, Hutch came running up to us. "Beri, I need to talk to you."

I stopped and introduced him to Ross. "What's up?" I asked.

Hutch, a big grin on his face, said, "I just heard about your hero dog! It will make a great feature story, might even make the front page. When can I bring Al and take some pictures of him? I'll need all the details about what happened, too, of course."

"Uh, I'll have to get back to you on that."

"But speed is important. I need to get going on it now before some other reporter gets a whiff of a dynamite story." He smiled. "No pun intended."

"I can't imagine how you heard about it so fast."

"Come on, Beri. You know I have contacts in the police department."

"I have a suggestion. Why don't you write a story about the heroic bomb squad while you're at it? They really put their lives on the line doing what they do."

"Good idea, I'll see what I can do, but readers love animal stories, especially feel-good ones like this. And you do owe me a favor as I recall. You needed some free advert…"

"Okay, okay, I understand," I interrupted as Ross frowned at me. "There are some sensitive issues connected with the situation that I'll need to get cleared first. I'll try to accomplish that at a meeting scheduled this afternoon and will get back to you this evening. That fast enough for you?"

"I suppose it'll have to be. We'll plan to be at your house at six tonight. Have Tiger ready to smile for the camera."

Chapter Fifty-eight

I entered Norm's office in the FBI building. I nodded my thanks as my guide opened the door and pulled out my chair at a small conference table inside.

"He'll be with you in a few minutes," she said before leaving and closing the door.

I glanced at my watch.

Norm entered a minute later and sat across from me. "Appears your day is packed with meetings, too. I promise this one will be faster than the one this morning."

"Sounds good. What would make me even happier would be getting my phone back. Have you finished with it?"

"Soon. I'll give tech a call before you leave. I can tell you this much. You received another text. I had the phone on my desk, ready to return to you when it came in. I returned the phone to the tech guys to identify who it came from. It said "Name Unavailable" and you can guess who I suspect sent it."

"Charlie."

"Yes, I'll read it to you: 'Watch your six. They're following you. I'll be in touch.'"

"I delivered it back to tech to trace," Norm said, "but I feel confident it'll come back to a burner phone as before. And, you'll be happy to know, I put a rush on it."

"Has your investigation turned up anything on him?"

Norm opened a folder on the table in front of him. "Have you heard of a company in Texas by the name of 'Precision Investment Strategies'?"

"No."

"We'd traced him to it earlier but didn't realize the extent of his involvement. Turns out Charlie has been using an alias. When we uncovered his actual identity, we learned he wasn't a low-level employee. He's the owner and CEO."

"Was he the one behind the money laundering scheme?"

"No, we don't think so." Norm paused and scratched his neck before continuing. "He was known as a behind-the-scenes type of leader. Stayed out of the limelight and let his second-in-command and his CFO be the face of the company. He had a reputation as an eccentric genius. The shit apparently hit the fan when the CFO was killed in a car crash, and the man we know as Charlie became aware of major irregularities in the company's finances."

"Is that why he disappeared?"

"No. We think he'd seen a popular television show starring the boss of a business who disguised himself and went to work in a low-level position in the company. Charlie adopted the format and filled the vacant CFO position under an alias. Only the head of the board of directors knew about the plan."

"And Gina?"

"There's a lot we don't know, but we think Gina was his downfall. He'd been a loner, almost an eccentric hermit for years. He fell for Gina, who he thought was on his side. There's still some question about her role. We know she worked in the finance department in a customer service position. He didn't have reason to suspect her of being part of the financial irregularities. When a sophisticated attempt was made on his life, he realized how vulnerable he was and ran. He took Gina and the evidence with him."

"It's a weird story, but at least parts of it fit. Charlie is smart, although I haven't noticed any anti-social tendencies. It explains why he never seemed to run out of money, but I don't understand why he'd choose to hang out in Alaska."

"That is odd, considering his resources, but I suspect Gina had a lot to do with it. I don't think he's given up on her even now."

"No, she does seem to stay foremost in his mind."

"I'm hoping you can convince him to come in and talk to us. Tell him we appreciate the evidence he provided and are anxious to crack down on the group that infiltrated his company. He may have the information we need to uncover their identities. Also, officials in Texas have uncovered evidence that the CFO's death may not have been accidental. Charlie was considered a suspect in his death for a while."

"I'll do my best, but I have little direct contact with him, as you know. Besides, I doubt he'd trust you to keep him safe."

Norm frowned and stood, indicating the meeting was over.

"You were going to check on my phone before I go, remember?"

He sniffed. "How could I forget? I'll give them a call now." After a brief conversation, he hung up the receiver. "They'll bring it right up."

"While we wait, I have a question for you. Would there be any problem with my allowing a local reporter to write a story about my dog's role in the attempted bombing? I discouraged him, but he reminded me I'm in his debt for a story I requested he write recently."

"I don't see a problem with it as long as you don't get into who's suspected to be behind the crime. Maybe he could ask the public if they have any information that would help the police arrest those responsible."

Norm answered a quick knock on the door and then handed me my phone. "The text was from another burner, as we suspected. Keep me posted on any new developments. If you can help in any way, give me a call."

Chapter Fifty-nine

The next morning, I started coffee brewing and walked outside to pick up the newspaper. Daisy Fitzgerald, who lived two houses farther down the road, slowed and stopped her car. She lowered the window, stuck her head out and shouted at me.

"Thanks a lot, Beri. Guess it's not enough you almost got us all blown up. Now, we're all under suspicion. Enough is enough."

She stomped on the gas and left me standing in the yard with my mouth open. While Daisy could be a bit of a busybody at times, she was usually good-natured and friendly.

I went inside, grabbed my coffee, and sat at the kitchen table. With a sense of foreboding, I opened the paper. Large photos showed Tiger in my garage sniffing at the door leading to the house and outside in the driveway with me. Officer Daly posed in his gear standing by his official vehicle at police headquarters for an accompanying photo. Hutch had outdone himself with a by-lined article that continued onto the next page. I relaxed a little as I read. The story was well done, and Tiger and the bomb squad officers were heralded as true heroes.

Then I turned the page and gasped.

> Sources who decline to be named report that a neighbor of the dog's owner has been identified as the chief suspect. The neighbor is also the owner's competitor in a local mapping business.

Hutch ended the piece with a plea for anyone with more information regarding the incident to contact the FBI. The damage was done. Norm would never trust me again.

What was Hutch thinking? He'd promised he wouldn't do this. It seemed out of character and not in a good way. I grabbed my phone and dialed his number.

"Rob Hutchinson here."

"Hutch! How could you?"

"How could I what?" he asked.

"Stop playing dumb." My voice quavered with anger. "You promised not to identify any potential suspects."

"I didn't give any names."

"No, but you alienated all my neighbors, and it wouldn't take much research to figure out which one is a competitor."

"Sorry. It was the best I could do after the info fell in my lap. I am a reporter, you know."

I took a deep breath. "Who *did* give it to you anyway? The FBI will be furious and assume the tip came from me."

"I told you I have a reliable source in the police department. He volunteered the tip as long as I kept his name confidential."

I tamped down my anger. "Too bad you blew it. Your scoop was great until the very end."

"Maybe I can make it up to you. I got a message to call a reader who said she had information I might be interested in hearing. She didn't want to call the FBI."

"What did she tell you?"

"Nothing yet. She sounded jumpy, so I suggested we meet right away. We're set for two hours from now." He paused. "Any chance you'd like to come along?"

"I'd love to. Where?" I grabbed a pad and pencil to jot down the address.

"Crandall's Used Cars of all places. At ten o'clock this morning." He chuckled. "She said to look for her by the bright chartreuse colored vehicle parked on the east side of the lot."

"That shouldn't be too hard to find. I don't think I've seen many chartreuse vehicles." I disconnected and walked out to my SUV to go to work, but before I got the garage door open, my phone buzzed with a text from Norm.

What the hell! Have you seen today's paper? Call me.

I sighed. The last thing I wanted to do was call Norm at that moment. If I did, I'd have to tell him about Hutch's meeting, and the place would soon be crawling with FBI agents. I sat for a moment before backing out of the garage, then called Angie and told her I had an engagement that would tie me up for the morning. If Norm called, she should tell him I'd get back to him after lunch. I cut the call short before she could ask more about my plans.

I felt disloyal to Norm, but I did have some research to do at the library. I could fill him in on everything later.

At a quarter till ten, I left the library and headed for the rendezvous spot with Hutch and his source. It was only a five-minute drive to the car lot, and I easily found it. Hutch, always prompt, stood beside the sunflower yellow car.

"Right on time, I see," he said.

"Wouldn't miss it. Have you heard from her?"

"No, not yet."

We'd waited fifteen minutes when Hutch's phone rang. He put it on speaker.

"Who's the chick with you? I told you I wanted to speak with you alone," the woman's voice said.

"Sorry. She's the owner of the dog. She has an interest in the story and doesn't want the cops involved. You can trust her."

"What I have is for your ears only. We'll reschedule for another time. I'll call you, and next time, no party crashers." The connection went dead.

"Damn," Hutch said. "Keep your eyes open on your way out. She must be nearby since she could see you were with me."

"Will do. Let me know if you hear from her again." I turned to leave and gave the car one last look. "I still can't imagine why anyone would paint a car this color."

"Someone safety conscious, maybe?" Hutch said.

We walked together back to the office where Hutch had parked. He gave me a sheepish grin and got in his car. "I'll let you know if I hear from her," he said before starting his engine and leaving.

I continued walking back to where I'd parked on the street. As I started to open the door to my car, a young woman with short blonde hair and dark roots approached me. She looked familiar, but I couldn't quite place her.

"Beri Quinn?"

"Yes?"

"I'm Gina Figgins. I was surprised to see you with the reporter and thought it would be better if I met with you alone first. Can we talk in your car for a few minutes?"

"Yes, the door is unlocked, you can get in." I slid in under the steering wheel, and Gina settled in the passenger seat beside me. I turned to face her. "I've been hoping to talk to you as well. Someone I know is very anxious to see you."

Her eyes lit up with her smile. "Charlie?"

"Yes, he's been on a mission to find you."

"Please let him know I'm alright. I evaded the attackers, but my tennis friend, Maxie, must have been mistaken for me and was murdered."

"I'm so sorry. Do you know who did it? Was it the same person who tried to kill me by blowing up my garage?"

"I'm not sure. All I can say is that it wasn't your neighbor, Elinor Chen, as the newspaper story implied. She has many faults, but she's innocent of that. She asked me to set the reporter straight."

I interrupted. "How do you know Chen?"

"She's my boss. I've been working at Northern Mapping for some time, but I think you know that."

"What makes you think she didn't orchestrate it."

"That's a stretch, don't you think. Why would she?"

"I never understood why she kidnapped me and my family in the first place."

"She had her reasons." She smiled. "You don't recognize me, do you?"

"Should I?" I scrutinized her face at close range but still couldn't place her. "You look familiar and I'm wondering how you know so much about Elinor."

"I thought you might remember me, but I have changed my appearance. I called myself Sophia at Elinor's place when I vacuumed around you. As I mentioned before, I've always been a good actress."

"You were convincing, but I don't understand. What is your actual job for Elinor? You're not her housekeeper."

"No," Gina said. "I've been in Elinor's employ all along. I reported to her even when I worked with Charlie in Texas. After I grew close to him, I tried to extricate myself from her clutches, but it wasn't possible. She forced me to keep tabs on him for her. Please tell him I'm sorry I deceived him."

"I still don't understand. Why did Elinor kidnap me? And who murdered Maxine and Skip?"

Gina chewed her lip before answering. "You ask a lot of questions. Let me ask one. Who's Skip?"

"My tow pilot at Birchwood. He was shot while Charlie and I were in the air during a glider lesson."

"That must be when Charlie tried to call me. He sounded panicked, but I didn't know anyone died." Her head whipped around when a car drove past with a male driver inside who appeared to be scrutinizing us. Gina looked over her shoulder as he passed, her eyes following the car. "I've got to go."

"Wait." I grabbed her arm. "How can I contact you?"

"You can't. You'd get me killed."

Chapter Sixty

Norm didn't waste any time calling me. "I need to see you. Now!" he said in the voice mail he left for me.

Sensing his mood was not good, I arrived at his office as soon as I could get there. How could I explain?

Once I was ushered through the door, Norm pointed to a chair by the conference table. "Sit."

He glowered as he pulled up a chair opposite me.

"I apologize. I had no idea the reporter would go back on his promise." I shook my head. "He claims he's exonerated by the fact he didn't give the suspect's name in the article."

"Not in so many words, but it wouldn't take a genius to figure it out from the description he gave."

"True," I agreed.

"Did Chen order the bombing?" Norm opened a folder on the table beside him and pulled out a stack of photos. He fanned them out in an arc facing me. "Do you recognize any of these men?"

I scanned the group before answering. "Yes. The second one on the left. I've seen him several times. He accosted me at the golf tent and again at Reeve Lake. The third man I briefly saw only once, again at Reeve Lake."

"How about the man who forced his way into your house?"

"No, I don't see him here. That guy was accompanied by a woman."

Norm gave me a squinty-eyed look and shoved the photos back into the folder. He crossed his arms over his chest and leaned back in his chair. "So, when are you going to tell me what you were up to this morning?"

I gave him a look. Guess it was time to share. "The reporter who wrote the article about Tiger and the attempted bombing invited me to join him when he met with a reader who'd called him. She said she had related information."

"Why didn't he urge her to contact the authorities?"

"First, he's a reporter with a source. Second, she said she was leery of the FBI."

Norm rolled his eyes. "What did she have to say?"

"Nothing, as it turned out. When she saw I was with him, she scrammed."

"An opportunity lost because neither of you notified us."

"Maybe. Hutch is hoping to reschedule without me. We'll see how that goes."

"Meanwhile, I'll inform him that he was out of line dropping hints about the suspect's identity. I'd hate to have to charge him with obstructing an investigation." He gave me a puzzled look. "How did he come up with the identity of the suspect anyway?"

"He mentioned he had a source in the APD."

"So, not you?"

"No, definitely not me." I paused to give myself a moment to think. Should I reveal my private meeting with Gina?

Before I could decide, Norm's phone chimed. He answered, rose from his chair and headed for the door. "Sorry, I've got to go," he said. "I'll be back in touch soon."

"I hoped you could update me on the facial recognition check on the photograph I gave you."

"Later. I'll send someone to see you out."

After being escorted from the building, I sat in my car to think. While relieved that the confrontation about the article was over, I hadn't learned a thing about Norm's progress. I checked my watch. The afternoon was half gone. No time to return to the library since I knew it closed early on Fridays. I decided it was time to call Maxine Stedwell's husband. I'd been wanting to talk to him, but hesitated to call so soon after his wife's body had been found. He answered on the second ring.

"Todd Stedwell, here."

"Mr. Stedwell, my name is Beri Quinn. While we've never met, I'm a member of the Alaska Club, and your wife and I had mutual acquaintances. First, I wanted to extend my condolences on your loss. I was so sorry to hear about Maxine's death."

"That's very kind of you."

"The other reason I called is to ask if we could meet for coffee. I'd like to ask you some questions about the days before she went missing. It may help give some insight into what happened to her and about another situation I'm investigating."

"I'd be glad to help if I can. Not knowing can drive a person crazy, and the authorities don't seem to be doing much." He cleared his throat. "Tell you what, I missed lunch and was just leaving to get a sandwich when you called. Could you meet me in fifteen minutes at the sub shop on Tudor Road?"

"That sounds good. I'll be the person with the ponytail and a burgundy-colored backpack."

He laughed. "And I'll be the overly-dressed business man."

It was a short drive to the restaurant. I arrived and walked through the door in less than fifteen minutes. I entered the small establishment and immediately spotted the attractive middle-aged man wearing a suit that helped disguise his small paunch. He stood at the counter. "Beri?"

"Yes. Glad to meet you, Mr. Stedwell." I extended my hand.

He shook my hand with a firm grip. "Call me Todd, please. Hey, I just finished ordering. Can I get something for you?"

"No, thanks, I'll get a coffee and join you at one of the tables."

Todd chose a table at the far end of the row across from the counter. I pulled out a chair and settled opposite him. "This place was a good choice for a quiet conversation."

"Usually, it's fairly emptied by this time of afternoon. Afraid I've been a regular lately, but I need to cut back on fast-food soon." He patted his stomach. "I've relied too heavily on it since I lost Maxie. She was a vegan and a good cook. Marriage to her kept my diet honest. And I enjoyed every mouthful." He picked up his twelve-inch sub sandwich packed with a variety of meats and cheeses and took a bite. After he swallowed, he raised his eyebrows. "So, what can I help you with?"

"First, can you tell me a little about Maxie?"

"I'm sure you already know she was an athlete. She loved tennis. Other sports, too, but especially tennis. She was very good at it."

"Yes, I followed her success at the club. Is that how you met, playing tennis?"

"No. We were opposites that way. I was a good spectator, but that was the extent of my involvement." He looked down at his food. "She was very dear to me, but we didn't share that part of her life. I was glad when she found a partner at the club who played at her level."

"Was that Victoria Saunders?"

"Yes, the two of them were evenly matched when they played singles. Their specialty, though, was doubles. They complemented each other in a fantastic way, but then I imagine you already know that."

I shrugged a shoulder. "Yes. Did Maxie mention a tennis player named Gina?"

"No, although I did hear Vickie answer her phone that way one time. I figured Gina might be a nickname of some kind."

"Did Maxie mention whether either of them had felt threatened or frightened by anyone?"

"Maxie did say Vickie was under a lot of stress, but I don't know why. She mentioned Vickie thought someone had been following her. Why? Is Vickie okay? Has anything happened to her?"

"No, just something someone said about wondering if Maxie's killer had mistaken her identity. It seemed a strange thing to say."

"They did resemble each other. They were similar in height and weight and usually had the same hair color."

"Usually?" I asked.

"Maxie would tease Vickie about that. She was always changing it. She even colored it black once. It made a dramatic difference in her appearance."

"Were they planning on playing doubles in the upcoming tournament?"

"I'm not sure. Maxie hoped to play, but she and Vickie were going through a rough patch. I'm not sure what they'd decided."

"What kind of rough patch?"

"Some kind of misunderstanding. I wasn't privy to the details, but I'm certain it wouldn't have lasted long. I feel sure they would have figured it out before the tournament. They were like that."

"Have the police shared any theories about who they think killed her or why she was targeted?"

He glanced out the window. "Nothing. I keep asking, but they either haven't made any progress or if they have, they're not sharing it with me."

"The police can be very close-mouthed when they haven't solved a case."

Todd stared down at his hands and blinked back tears. He looked so dejected; I placed a hand on his arm. "Unfortunately, it does take time."

I slid my business card across to him. "Please call me if you come across anything new, and I'll do the same for you. Who knows, we might manage to assist the police."

He glanced at my card. "Something about your name rings a bell, but I don't know why. I've probably heard it mentioned at the club."

Chapter Sixty-one

The next morning, I awoke early to bright clear skies. Somehow, the weather always seemed best for photography on the weekends. I called Mickey, rousing him out of bed, judging from the grogginess of his voice.

"These early morning callouts are the only thing I won't miss about working in Alaska," he said.

"I know I'll miss you when you leave at the end of next week," I said. "You've been a big help this summer. See you in about twenty minutes." I ended the call and headed for my garage.

We met at the office, loaded the equipment in the plane, flew a small job covering the Kenai gas fields at Sterling and had time to complete another job for the Department of Transportation flying a stretch of the Seward Highway for an avalanche study. Combined, the jobs took less than two hours to complete.

We returned to Merrill Field by nine A.M. It felt good to actually accomplish some work after so many distractions.

Mickey left to enjoy the rest of the nice weekend after helping me unload our gear and hauling it into the office. I stayed long enough to clear the clutter that had accumulated on my desk before leaving to finish up my work at the library. I needed to find out with certainty who was behind the attacks we'd been experiencing and whether Spence was involved in any way.

Dad and Sarah were due to return from their honeymoon tomorrow. I'd started doing a background check on Spencer Atkins, Sarah's cousin, but I felt disloyal to her for doing so. Best I finish the job while she was still out of town.

I hoped I wouldn't find anything questionable but overhearing his conversation at the wedding had raised a few questions in my mind. I'd already reviewed his career working with the state. His reputation appeared first-rate, but I also needed to check into his business dealings since he'd retired.

As the librarian that I spoke to suggested, I searched state real estate records for land acquisitions. She also assisted me in checking media reports mentioning him. There weren't many, but one caught my attention. A photograph of Atkins taken shortly after his retirement while meeting with a visiting Chinese delegation promoting joint economic opportunity between their country and the state of Alaska. It warranted looking into. The group pictured included several Chinese officials and both Elinor Chen, identified as an Alaskan business owner and Victoria Saunders, translator. My eye froze on Victoria. She could have been Gina Figgins' sister or possibly Gina herself.

I photocopied the article and photograph, thanked the librarian and left. As I approached my car, I heard someone shout my name.

I turned to the sound of the voice. Spencer Atkins loped toward me.

"Slow down," Spence said. "I want to talk to you." He smiled as he drew near. "I'm sure I'm the last person you expected to run into here."

He stood so close I could smell his coffee breath. I stepped back and scrutinized him before answering. "True enough. What can I do for you?"

"Not here. How about we go someplace for a quiet conversation?" He reached for the door handle on the passenger side of my vehicle.

"It's locked," I said. "And it's going to stay that way. We can talk here." I smiled. "Let's just say I'm not comfortable driving passengers."

"Have it your way," he said. "I wanted to ask you why you've been snooping around in my affairs."

"I'm researching everyone associated with some jobs I've acquired."

"What are you looking for?"

"I've been attacked recently, and I want to know the reason why?"

"And you think this involves me?" he asked, showing surprise.

"Not you specifically, but everyone associated with my recent projects."

"You can take me off your list. I haven't been involved in your projects and I certainly haven't attacked you."

"Just how did you know where to find me now?" I tilted my head to the side and narrowed my eyes at him.

"I have a friend who works here as an assistant librarian. She called me and said you were nosing around, looking for information about me and my affairs. I suspected something was off about you since that morning we met at the restaurant. I could tell you weren't the naïve young woman breaking into business like Heck suggested."

"I'm sorry about that. I didn't understand why he took that approach, but the truth is I was starting a new business. For some reason, he played down my experience. Maybe he thought you'd be more helpful that way."

"Maybe so. Heck can have his quirks." He smiled. "In the future, if you have questions about me, just ask."

"Okay. I have one now." I showed him the newspaper clipping I'd copied. "What is your relationship to these two women?"

"Funny you should ask. I felt there was something off about them, too. I was asked to participate in a symposium with the Chinese contingent to provide a geological perspective. It seemed their primary interest was minerals. I didn't have good vibes about this younger woman. She was an American but seemed more interested in China's interests than ours. She posed as a translator but wasn't a very good one. She usually deferred to the older lady when translation was necessary."

"Are you aware the police are looking for Ms. Chen?"

"No. I haven't seen or heard about her since the day that picture was taken months ago."

"You might want to mention your experience to the police or the FBI. I know she's under investigation."

"For what?" he asked.

"A number of things. One of them is for kidnapping me."

I arrived home earlier than usual and took a grateful Tiger for a run. A little of the tension I'd been holding melted away with each step. *I should do this more often.* Then I called to check in with Jack. He missed Tiger and Piper, but otherwise seemed to be enjoying himself.

Knowing Jack was okay, I focused on the troubles at hand. The photograph I'd copied remained in my mind. Who was Victoria Saunders? I hoped to see Gina again soon. I'd ask her about her probable alias after I asked what she knew about the attempted bombing. If she contacted me. I'd expected to hear from her again by now.

I showered and changed before I called Hutch to ask him if he'd heard from his reader.

"Not a word," he said. "How about you?"

"Yes and no," I said.

"What is that supposed to mean?"

"I did talk to her for a few minutes after she cancelled our three-way meeting. She followed me to where I'd parked on the street. She got in my car and we had a short conversation, but she bolted when she thought another car drove by too slowly. She appeared to be terrified but paused long enough to say she'd call me. So far, she hasn't."

"What else did she say?"

"The only thing I learned was her name."

"That's more than I know. What is it?"

"She said her name was Gina Figgins, and she works with my competitor, Elinor Chen."

"Interesting…"

"Actually, she did say one other thing. She claimed Elinor didn't have anything to do with the bombing attempt because she was out of town."

"Elinor may be gone, but she still could have given orders to her associates," Hutch said. "And it's not consistent with what she told me earlier. I wonder what she's up to?"

"Yeah, I don't understand why she wouldn't meet the two of us yesterday, either."

"Call me if you hear from her again. She doesn't seem anxious to get back in touch with me," Hutch said.

Chapter Sixty-two

A call woke me at five o'clock the next morning. Gina wanted to meet. *Now.*

Happy Ross hadn't spent the night, I arrived at the meeting location and saw a solitary car parked outside the office of the ski jumping school on the outskirts of town. This time of year, and this time of day, it wasn't surprising the place was deserted. It seemed like an extreme choice of location, even if you were looking for privacy.

I reached under my seat, withdrew my Glock I put there as a back-up and tucked it into my jacket pocket. Probably an unnecessary precaution, but it eased my nerves.

I trudged uphill from the parking area to the first jump. Gina stood near the stairs to the summit. She waved as I approached.

"Good morning," I said. "Could you have chosen a more deserted meeting place?"

Gina smiled. "It's true not much happens here during summer months. A few classes and the occasional hiker."

"Do you ski?"

"I have fun trying. I prefer downhill to cross-country or jumping," she said.

"You've piqued my curiosity. Why here when you could answer my questions with a phone call, and why not invite Hutch, too?"

Gina pulled a revolver from beneath her windbreaker. "This is why. You've been nothing but trouble. Boss gave me orders." Gina shoved her gun into my ribs, barely missing my own gun tucked below. "Head for the back of the jump. Move."

"Sounds like your boss added 'assassin' to your job duties."

"That's nothing new. My job has always included everything she asks me to do."

"Is that why you killed Maxine?"

"I'll admit that one was hard. We played a mean game of doubles together, but she overheard something she shouldn't have."

With Gina behind me, I couldn't react to her gun. I'd taken about a dozen steps when a masculine voice called out. "Stop!"

Charlie emerged from the tree line ahead of us. "Drop your gun, Gina!"

I glanced behind me.

"Sorry." She aimed her gun at him and fired. "I wish you hadn't made me do that."

She poked me again. "Over there," Gina said, and shoved me closer to where Charlie had fallen on the grass.

I whirled, grabbed her arm, causing her shot to bury itself in the ground between my feet. I reached for my Glock, but Gina was faster. Now I was staring down the barrel of her gun. Jack's face flashed through my mind. I couldn't leave him like this, but what could I do?

A shot rang out. Gina crumpled to the ground.

Charlie, on his knees, dropped his weapon and lunged toward Gina's lifeless body. He pulled her into his arms and stroked her face. "I'm so sorry, baby, but you didn't give me a choice."

He looked up at me. Tears streamed down his cheeks. "I tried to shoot her gun arm, but I've never been that good a shot."

I called 9-1-1 for the seventh time this month and knelt by Gina to feel for a pulse. Nothing. "She's gone."

I checked Charlie's wounded shoulder and cautiously drew him close, putting pressure on the wound. "You saved my life. Thank you."

"I owed you that." He shuddered and sank further down in my arms.

"You need a doctor," I said as Charlie lost consciousness.

The police and paramedics arrived a few minutes after my call. I watched as they loaded Charlie into an ambulance and whisked him away.

An officer asked me questions as other officers cordoned off the area and collected all three of the weapons involved. The medical examiner arrived to attend to Gina.

At the police station, I was ushered into an interview room where I waited for the grilling that was sure to ensue. Detective Diaz burst through the door. "What in the hell are you involved in now? A double shooting? A homicide?"

I stared at him. "I'm beginning to think you're the only detective in Anchorage. We certainly seem to run into each other in awkward situations."

"No one else wants to get near you with your reputation. Now, tell me what happened. These notes don't make much sense."

"I'm not surprised. Because it's a long story, I won't start at the beginning. Today's events began with a phone call from Gina Figgins asking me to meet her at the ski area. I thought it was strange, but she had done something similar in the past. After I arrived, she pulled a gun and indicated she planned to kill me. Charlie Greer showed up and tried to save me. She shot him in the shoulder. He fell to the ground and tried to shoot her gun arm. He missed and killed her accidently trying to defend me."

"Quite a story. How do you know he tried to shoot her arm?"

"He told me before you arrived. Besides, he loved her."

"You seem to know a lot about this man."

"True. How is he doing?"

"He's alive, as far as I know. Haven't received an update from the hospital yet. You better hope he makes it."

"As annoying as he has been at times, I'm praying he does. He saved my life."

I stood by Charlie's bedside. He lay there, his shoulder wrapped in bandages, his face as white as the sheets around him, but he had a smile on his face.

"Good morning. I had to tell the nurse I was your sister before they'd let me in. I hear your surgery took most of the night but went well. They say you should recover full use of your arm."

"Don't feel so good," he said. "I'm groggy and sore, but the groggy part may be a good thing. I don't want clarity right now. It's hard for me to come to grips with the fact that I killed Gina."

"She didn't give you a choice, Charlie. She was going to kill both of us."

"That's what I told the police. I don't know how I could have been so wrong about her."

"Gina was a chameleon and made herself into what she thought you wanted her to be. Apparently, she was working for Elinor even while being employed with your company in Texas. Gina was a dangerous woman."

"I don't want to think about it right now. Maybe we can talk more tomorrow?"

"It's a date." I smiled and patted his uninjured shoulder. "See you then."

Chapter Sixty-three

Hospital visiting hours began at seven in the morning. I walked into Charlie's room five minutes after and found Norm already there.

"Good morning. You're looking much better," I said. "Hope I'm not interrupting anything."

"No." Norm stood to leave. "We just finished." He dropped his notebook and bent to pick it up. "Now, don't leave town, Charlie." He gave him an exaggerated wink.

"I hope you've ordered security to watch his room. I wouldn't put it past these goons to come after him, especially if they're all out on bail now."

"Good idea. I'll get on it," he said with a smirk. He moved to stand near me. "Beri, I need to talk to you when you finish here. How about we meet in the lobby when you're done."

I nodded, and he walked out into the hallway.

"Good riddance," Charlie said after Norm left. He lifted his head from the bed. "Pull your chair a little closer so I can see you. I've already noticed you came empty-handed. Couldn't you at least have brought flowers or a cheeseburger?"

"Afraid I've been too busy being interviewed by the police to go shopping, but I'll get right on it."

"Just joking." His head dropped back on the pillow.

"How bad is it?" I asked. "The nurse said you had another surgery last night."

"I'm lucky. The bullet went through my shoulder at an angle and just missed my spine. They repaired some muscles in my neck. It's hard to hold my head up for long, but they say I'll be good as new soon."

"When do you think you'll be discharged?"

"Not until next week. The doctor started me on IV antibiotic therapy, but I plan to convince him to give me pills instead. I want to leave."

"Don't rush it. You don't want to relapse and be forced to come back to the hospital."

"Yeah. If only Gina had fared as well." Charlie's voice broke. "Can we talk more later? I need to rest. Agent Underwood gave me quite a grilling."

"Sure." I said good-bye and walked to the elevator. I had so many questions for Charlie. I wondered if he'd ever give me the answers.

Norm sat in the lobby near the elevator bank waiting for me. "That was quick."

"Charlie said he was exhausted and wanted to rest. Guess you wore him out. What time did you get here anyway?"

"About an hour before you did. The FBI has ways around visitor's hours, but I did have to wait while a doctor came in and checked his wound."

"What do you need from me that I haven't already told the police?" I asked.

"We have quite a lot to discuss, Beri. How about I drive you to my office with a stop at Starbucks drive-through on the way?"

"Why don't I drive myself, so I won't need a ride back to my car?"

"That's a better idea. I need to do this by the book. I've been getting comments from the higher-ups suggesting I'm too friendly with you."

Uh oh. Could this mean trouble ahead? I gave him my most innocent look and shrugged. "I'm guessing you didn't mention that I regularly beat you on the racquetball court?"

"Regularly? Very occasionally, you mean." He shook his head. "No, I didn't mention that."

"Are you taking me into custody?"

"Officially? No, but I'd appreciate your cooperation."

"I want to talk to you anyway, and coffee sounds good. I'll meet you at your office, and I'd like a skinny latte, please."

Seated at the small conference table in Norm's office, I reviewed the events of yesterday morning with him. I could tell he already knew the details, but he listened with rapt attention and asked a question now and then.

Afterward, I signed my statement. "Okay, now that we have that out of the way, please fill me in on your investigation of Gina and Northern Mapping. Was Charlie in cahoots with them?"

"No, I don't think so. It appears Gina was a plant in Charlie's investment business, which was being used to launder Chinese money coming into this country. From the records Charlie turned over to us, we believe he was unaware of this activity until after his CFO was killed. Charlie had been a loner all his life, and when he went undercover, he was highly susceptible to Gina's charms. After Charlie discovered what had been going on, Gina played along to keep tabs on his activities. Charlie probably wasn't suspicious that she was involved because her customer relations job didn't appear related."

"And the Chinese millions?"

"Charlie took control of the money when he changed the offshore account numbers. Elinor and her superiors in China were not happy when they discovered this and attempted to capture him. He had to stay alive until they could force him to talk."

"But why did he decide to hide out here?"

"Charlie realized land in Alaska was involved in some way. He may have heard about the rare earth element separation plant scheduled to be constructed. China has a near world-wide lock on separating these minerals and wanted to keep it that way. If Alaska proved to be a good source of the minerals, and even more importantly, also developed the ability to process them, the Chinese wanted control."

Norm looked down at his notebook and frowned. "We think Elinor was attempting to get the inside scoop on critical locations in order to obtain ownership or control of them. Photogrammetry proposals can provide an inside look into potential geological activity. I suspect that's why Elinor and her sponsors purchased your former business so soon after the new owner purchased it and at an inflated price.

"I wondered about that." My work with Jason had given me insight on that angle.

Norm's phone rang. "He what? When? Keep me posted." He slammed the phone down.

"What was that about? Anything to do with the case?"

"Charlie left the hospital. Against medical advice. They discovered him missing a few minutes ago."

"But how did he get past security?"

"The agent I'd stationed there left for a few minutes to use the restroom, and Charlie was gone when he returned."

Chapter Sixty-four

Phone in hand, I ran with Norm to his car parked in the FBI lot. Halfway there, my phone began vibrating but I didn't recognize the number.

I stopped running and accepted the call. Before I could say hello, Charlie's voice came over the line. Norm stopped a few steps ahead of me, a questioning look on his face. I held up a hand and mouthed the name "Charlie."

"Please come get me. I'm in danger." His words came out in staccato bursts. I could barely understand him.

"Where are you?" I asked.

"Still at the hospital, but I had to leave my room. When I got out of bed to look for my clothes, I opened the door and found my guard was gone. Down the hall, I spotted a man I recognized as one of Elinor's goons checking rooms and I knew I needed to get out of there before he got to mine. I ran, well not exactly, but I managed to escape before he got any closer. It's going to be hard for me to blend in though, because I have no clothes."

"Where exactly are you?"

"One floor down by the stairway. I didn't have the strength to go up the stairs. I'm now hiding in an unused patient room, but I'm sure I'll be found soon." He sighed. "I'm too weak to run, and I'd be too conspicuous in this backless hospital gown anyway."

"Hold on. I'm with Norm at the FBI Building now. We'll make sure you're safe and bring you some clothes."

"Just make sure you bring some pants."

Norm ran the rest of the way to his car and started the engine. I followed and got in. I'd barely closed my door before the car was moving. I clicked my phone off, fastened my seatbelt and filled him in on Charlie's dilemma.

Norm grabbed his phone and called for back-up to meet us at the hospital. As soon as he disconnected, he hit the gas pedal even harder. As we drove, Charlie texted me the room number where he was hiding.

"We can't stop long enough to get him some pants, can we?"

Norm shook his head. "I have a change of clothes in my racquetball bag. Should work. It's in the trunk."

I eyed his lanky frame. "You're a good six inches taller than Charlie."

"Doesn't matter. All I have in my bag is a pair of shorts and a tee-shirt. Besides, I don't think we'll be trying to sneak him out."

"Which room?" Norm asked as we entered the elevator.

"Third floor," I said. "Room 347."

"We'll find Charlie and alert the staff to be on the lookout for a suspicious visitor. Can you stay with Charlie while I find our man, William? He hasn't answered my calls."

"Sure, no problem."

"I'll send an agent to join you as soon as back-up arrives. Ask to see his credentials."

We got off on the third floor and located Charlie's room. As we opened the door, a sheepish Charlie emerged from behind it and lowered the jug of disinfectant he held in his good hand.

"I knew this wouldn't save me, but I was desperate. I swiped it from the housekeeper's cart she'd parked in the hall outside. Almost got caught doing it, too."

Norm's mouth twitched from the effort he needed to keep a straight face. He handed the bag with his exercise clothes to him.

Charlie held up the pair of shorts. "This was the best you could do? I'll still be a spectacle if I try to walk out."

I looked at the size of them. Both Charlie's legs could easily fit in one hole. It was my turn to suppress a smile.

"There's a drawstring if you need it to keep them up. We'll retrieve your clothes after we catch your stalker," Norm said.

"No, we won't. They cut them off me when I came in. Besides, they were covered in blood from my gunshot wound."

Norm, impatient to leave, turned to me. "Beri, stay with him. If you sense danger, Charlie can lock himself in the restroom and you can pretend to be a patient. I assume you're armed?"

"You think?" I pulled my jacket aside to show him the gun I'd retrieved from my nightstand since my Glock was still in the evidence room and pulled back the covers on the bed. "This does look inviting. Should I ask for a gown?"

Norm shook his head and left.

Charlie grabbed the sports bag. "Guess I'd better get dressed in case we have to dash out of here."

I climbed into the bed. "Bring me your gown when you're finished with it."

"Uh, okay."

I'd no sooner pulled the sheets up to my chin when the door to the room opened. A stout man wearing a sports jacket over a long-sleeved shirt and tie walked into the room. He had a stethoscope curled around his neck.

"I'm Dr. Morgan," he said. "What's your name? It isn't posted outside your door."

I instantly knew this was no doctor. "Morris, I said. Ann Morris. I was just admitted."

As he turned toward the bathroom, I could make out the bulge of a weapon under his jacket. I pulled my gun and jumped out of bed. "Stop or I'll shoot!"

His hand moved to the small of his back.

"Don't try it. I *will* shoot you." I moved behind him and took his gun.

"Come on out, Charlie," I said. "My phone's on the table. Call Norm and let him know we have your stalker in custody."

Charlie spoke rapidly into the phone before he turned back to me. "He'll be here in a few minutes."

"Are you alone *Dr. Morgan* or are there others with you?"

"Wouldn't you like to know?" the man said.

"Charlie, get that tee-shirt you had. I need something to use to tie his hands."

He walked over to the counter by a small handwashing sink and looked through the supplies there. "Here's a roll of tape that would work better than the shirt."

I taped the pseudo-doctor's wrists together behind his back using a copious amount of paper tape and hoped it was strong enough to do the job. I pulled a visitor's chair over to him. "Sit down and don't try anything."

Norm returned with another agent a few minutes later. He took one look at our captive and smiled. "Good work, you two. Agent Griffin here will take him into custody. Grif, you'd better put him in cuffs. Not sure I trust that tape job."

Norm turned to me. "We need to get Charlie back to headquarters. I'll clear his release from the hospital later."

"I wouldn't be surprised if this guy isn't the only one who is searching the hospital for Charlie," I said.

"Another reason to get him out of here. The rest of the team will stay until they finish the search."

"And William?"

"We found him in a locked public restroom upstairs. He was bound and gagged. Embarrassed, but okay," Norm said.

"That's a relief." I grabbed Charlie's hand. "Let's go."

"Like this?" He looked down at his bare chest and baggy shorts. "I think I want my gown back. I couldn't get the tee-shirt over my bandaged arm and shoulder."

Norm clapped him on his good shoulder. "I'll see if I can rustle up a wheelchair and a blanket to cover you."

Chapter Sixty-five

Two hours later, Charlie dozed in a leather recliner Norm had managed to move into his office for him. He slept comfortably as a small group gathered. Detective Diaz, three Texas-based FBI agents, Jason Heckenlively and I took our seats around Norm's conference table.

"I'm afraid Charlie's pain meds may have kicked in. Let's get through the preliminaries before we wake him," Norm said.

"First, we have confirmation through facial recognition and testimony from Dr. Spencer Atkins that Gina Figgins and Victoria Saunders are the same person. She was employed by Elinor Chen O'Hara before being sent to Texas where she met Charlie. I called this meeting to inform all of you that Elinor and her sidekicks involved in the bombing and kidnapping events have been arrested and charged with murder, attempted murder, kidnapping, and money laundering. It's likely that more charges will follow related to questionable activities involving Northern Mapping."

Charlie opened his eyes in time to see Norm address the Texas FBI agents present. "As you know, Charlie Greer AKA Arthur Hennigan has been under investigation in Texas. We think subsequent information supplied by our Anchorage office will resolve those issues. Information he's provided has proven invaluable in retrieving money illegally stashed in offshore accounts. The person suspected guilty of the CFO's murder has since been identified and arrested in Texas. This has been a complicated case, and our investigation will continue into criminal international activities."

Norm looked around the table. "So far, other murders committed in Alaska and linked to this crime spree have not been completely resolved. We feel certain both Maxine Stedwell and Skip Lewis, the tow pilot shot at Birchwood, were victims of Elinor and her crew. I feel sure these crimes will eventually be added to the long list of charges against them."

A hand shot up. A Texas agent pointed at me. "What makes you think she wasn't involved? She hired the pilot in the first place."

Charlie spoke up. "Don't be ridiculous!"

Norm interrupted the Texas agent's attempted response. "If you have questions, I'll be happy to review the evidence we've collected on these murders in detail with you, but now is not the time."

The Texas agent smirked and gave his cohorts a knowing look. "We'll be sure to take you up on your offer."

Norm's posture stiffened. "That's all for now, but I want to thank everyone in the room for your invaluable assistance." He picked up his phone and called another agent to assist Charlie into a wheelchair and take him to the rehab center where he'd been registered.

Chairs pushed back from the table as everyone else stood to leave. "Beri, could you stay for a few minutes? I have an update for you," Norm said.

I sat back down as the room emptied. Norm joined me at the table. He smiled. "I mentioned that Elinor is under arrest, but I didn't say where that took place."

"No. Is it important?"

"You might think so. She was arrested along with her husband at a warehouse in Adak. They'd flown there a few days ago on Alaska Airlines as Mr. and Mrs. Thomas O'Hara. Indications were that they planned to leave from there for China, possibly via submarine. Unfortunately for them, a raid at the port took place early this morning, and they were arrested along with several other suspects. Another point of possible interest for you is that Mr. O'Hara has an extensive background with illegal explosives."

"I appreciate all you've done."

"And there is one more thing. Our ownership record request to the FAA came back for the float plane. It was previously owned by Thomas O'Hara. He's kept a low profile, but it appears he's been an active participant in his wife's activities. They have been trying to frame Charlie for Maxine Stedwell's murder, something I wasn't ready to share yet with our Texas contingent."

"Thanks, Norm. That explains a lot. I'm so glad they're both in custody. It couldn't have happened to a more deserving couple." I pushed my hair back from my face. "Now, if there was only some way to arrest Billy Ivanoff's killers."

"That's a tough one. There's always the possibility that the men from the Avian Research Center may be among those arrested at the warehouse while awaiting transport to China, but proving they killed Ivanoff may not be possible. Other espionage charges could put them away for a long time, though."

Charlie (I couldn't bring myself to call him Arthur) was scheduled to be released from the rehab facility he'd been moved to after he was referred by the hospital. He'd called and asked if we could meet before he made his final plans to return to Texas.

I waited in the lobby for him.

He walked out dressed in a new set of clothes and even managed to have his arms through both sleeves of his shirt.

"Beri, thanks for coming. I couldn't resist asking you for one last favor."

"Why am I not surprised. What can I do for you?" I asked.

"First, I want to thank you for all you've already done. I especially enjoyed our glider lessons before all the trouble started, but I do need the favor."

"What's that?"

"I don't like leaving things half-finished," Charlie said. "I'm hoping you'll give me one final glider lesson. I want to get my certification before I leave, and I want to get the bad taste out of my mouth about my behavior during my last lesson. I don't want to end my gliding experience with the memory of my cowardice that day."

"Cowardice?"

"When we had to land on the beach with so little altitude, you stayed calm and got us down safely. I panicked. I don't want that to be how it ends."

"To be fair to yourself, we'd never practiced making an emergency landing, and it's unlikely you'll ever have to make one again with gunmen waiting below."

"True, but I shouldn't have panicked."

"I think a lesson is a great idea. I'll be happy to sign your certification, assuming you can pass muster, of course." I grinned.

"That I can do. I promise."

"The weather looks good. This afternoon would work if you like."

"I like. I'll see you there about two o'clock," he said.

I grabbed my phone and made a hurried call to enlist a tow pilot. Fortunately, one was available.

Ross and I drove Charlie to the airport departure area two days after he passed his certification flight. He'd sent his luggage ahead as he said it was too much bother with his injured shoulder. He bid us farewell and left for security and his gate.

Ross turned to me. "Seems like we've been spending a lot of time here watching other people leave. Next time, we should be the ones leaving. For our honeymoon."

"I like the sound of that." I gave him a kiss of approval. "Business slows down in winter, how about a Christmas wedding on the beach in Hawaii?

It could be just the two of us or we could invite Sarah, Dad and Jack for the ceremony."

"Mmm, mai tais and sunsets on the water. And you. A winning combination if I ever heard one."

"We'll need to schedule reservations far in advance for that time of year."

"That's doable. Did I tell you that Richard made me an offer to buy our flight instruction business? It would simplify things if we sell. He wants to sit down with both of us to discuss the possibility. My guess is that he'll probably want to keep Kaitlyn on."

"It will be hard to let it go, but he would be the perfect person to take over."

Ross nodded. "Yes, and Mickey helped open my eyes to the opportunities working with LIDAR technology. Thank you for suggesting he talk to me about it." He gave my hand a squeeze. "Rather than my backing up a new hire for his position, however, I'd like to take it over full-time. I also plan to work on creds to become a commercial drone pilot. I checked, and a medical certification isn't required to be licensed. Since more and more mapping photography is flown with drones these days, it's a way I can be involved in our new business and stay in aviation. I'll also fly real planes with you as pilot-in-command, of course."

"Oh, Ross, that sounds great!" I said, grinning.

"Let's go home." He grabbed me around the waist and pulled me to the door.

Acknowledgements

To Anthony Follett, Warren Penny, and David Vaughn for their technical photogrammetry and LIDAR assistance.

To Warren Niesen and Bob Seiler for their critical aviation expertise.

To Scottsdale Scribes Patricia Curren, Jackie Sereno and Jay Kinney for their suggestions and support. I also appreciated the input of former members, Liz Marshall and Wyn Yocum.

To Brittiany Koren for her editing and professional assistance in making *Eye in the Sky* a better story.

Author's Note

While drones have become commonplace in aerial data collection for mapping, there are both pros and cons to their use. Airplanes, while more expensive, offer several advantages in many projects.

About the Author

Toni Niesen lived in Anchorage, Alaska for twenty-four years. She spent much of that time in a plane's right seat during flights with her pilot husband. She also reveled in tales of flying adventures from their many Alaskan pilot friends. She is the author of *Parts Unknown: An Alaskan Mystery* and four short stories in the *Desert Sleuth's So West* anthology series. She currently lives in Scottsdale, Arizona with her grandson and Boston Terrier, Moose.

www.ingramcontent.com/pod-product-compliance
Lightning Source LLC
Chambersburg PA
CBHW030511080526
44586CB00011B/147